THE
BERMUDA
CONNECTION

ROBERT RAPOZA

THE BERMUDA CONNECTION
by
Robert Rapoza
Copyright © Robert Rapoza 2017

Robert Rapoza
Rancho Palos Verdes, CA 90275
http://www.robertrapoza.com
Email: bob@robertrapoza.com

First Printing September 2017
Second Printing June 2018

Printed in the United States of America

Printed in the United States of America

ISBN-13: 978-1-7323912-4-6
ISBN-10: 1-7323912-4-6

Thank you Jim, Jill and Laurie for being early supporters of my work and for your thoughtful input and edits, which transformed a rough draft into a polished work of fiction.

Chapter One

August 17, 3:02 A.M.
Hamilton, Bermuda

Jamie Edmunds knew something wasn't right. The sensation of a million microscopic feet traversing her skin was an omen of something terrible about to happen.

She lay in her bed, staring at the ceiling of her second story apartment. The sound of her heart beating in her chest echoed through her mind like a jackhammer. The darkness of her room interrupted only by the bright glow from her bedside alarm clock. She stole a glance. 3:02 a.m. The coming day would be hell.

She brushed her long brown hair behind her ears and rolled onto her side, hoping a new sleeping position would help. It didn't. Everyone she knew was asleep at this late hour. Except her. She was completely alone. Isolated in her bedroom away from the rest of the world.

She forced her eyes closed, and laid there in her nightshirt, willing herself to sleep. Her body shivered, and she pulled the flower-patterned sheets and blanket up to her chin. But it wasn't the cold causing her body to tremble. It was fear. Memories came flooding back of past nights when she couldn't sleep, and she remembered what happened next. Dread washed over Jamie like a wave smothering her in darkness.

The trembling grew worse. Her breathing fast and shallow.

There's something in my room.

The words popped into Jamie's mind. She tried to dismiss the thought as an overactive imagination.

I'm alone in my bedroom, I'm alone in my bedroom.

No matter how many times she repeated it, the words rang empty. The sense that someone, or something, was nearby overwhelmed her. She didn't want to look but had to know. She tilted her head to the side and saw … nothing. Her eyes drooped shut and she breathed a sigh of relief.

A soft clicking noise rose from the corner. Jamie's eyes popped open. Her muscles tensed as terror ripped through her. Sheets of perspiration trickled down her face and chest, her nightshirt clinging to her wet body. She slowly turned her head toward the sound. A figure lurked by her dresser, masked by the darkness that enveloped the room. It moved slowly, as if studying her from a distance. She sobbed.

No, please. Not again!

More movement, this time steady, calculated. The being moved from the shadows until it stood over her, its translucent skin gleaming in the moonlight. It peered at her with cold, dead eyes. She tried to scream but couldn't. The being controlled her now, her body under its influence. It moved closer, its bald, mouthless head tilted to one side as it examined her.

It drew back the sheets in a slow, mechanical fashion, exposing her nightshirt-clad body. It reached for her with long, slender, fingers. She wanted to cry, but tears wouldn't come. The creature wouldn't allow them. The fingers inched menacingly closer to her.

෮෩

Nick Randall sat upright in his bed, torrents of sweat cascaded down his body. Disoriented, he grabbed the bat he kept propped against the wall. His trembling hands bumped the nightstand. The bedside light nearly crashed to the ground, wobbling before settling again. He gripped the bat tightly, and scanned the room, ready to strike the creature.

He looked toward the corner where he had first seen it. Nothing there. His eyes darted around, adrenaline coursing through his body. He twitched at every sound. Slowly, sanity returned, and he realized it had only been a nightmare. He set the bat across his lap.

Why do I keep having this dream and why am I always the same woman?

His pulse quickened at the thought of being alone in the apartment with the creature. In the dream, he had felt completely powerless and isolated, unable to keep the being at bay. He shivered at the thought of being violated by it. A mixture of despair and anger welled inside of him as he balled his fists.

He glanced at the clock: 3:05 a.m. He fell backward onto his bed, gulping large breaths. His heart pounded so hard it felt like it would rip free of him. There would be no more sleeping tonight. Fear would keep him from returning to the land of dreams.

Randall thought back to when these episodes had begun. The nightmares had started a couple of weeks after his trip to the jungles of Peru, searching for the lost city of Vilcabamba. The odd physical attributes of the tribe that led him to the ruins—enlarged heads with bulging eyes—was a minor footnote compared to the discovery of Vilcabamba … and its otherworldly inhabitants.

The discovery of the lost city had changed the way he viewed archaeology. Sadly, the eruption of El Misti, the volcano that powered Vilcabamba, had destroyed any proof of his discovery, and brought the entire episode to an end. Or so he had thought. The experience was now influencing his dreams.

Can this really be happening?

Randall shook his head. They were only nightmares. He sat on the edge of his king-size bed and glanced at the side where his wife Ann used to sleep. He wished she was with him, by his side, her warmth comforting him. His fear was suddenly replaced with deep sadness and longing. He turned to face the window and dropped his head into his hands.

What the hell is happening to me? Am I losing it?

He forced himself to his feet, feeling the hard wood floor beneath him. Shivering, he slid on his lamb-wool slippers and reached for his robe. He didn't dare look at the thermometer; he knew that it wasn't the temperature causing him to tremble.

He stumbled over to his desk, plopped down in his black leather chair, and flicked on his desk lamp. The sudden brightness caused him to wince. He sat motionless while his eyes adjusted, unsure of what to do next. Pressing the power button of his computer, he heard the hard drive whine to life. Research. That was the solution to his problem. He needed to learn why he was having these terrible dreams and needed coffee. Lots of it.

4

Chapter Two

August 17, 3:32 A.M.
Arlington, Virginia

Dr. Jacob Taylor swiped the hijacked keycard through the reader. The red denied button glowed.

Just relax and do it again. Slowly this time.

He wiped the sweat from his temple using the back of his hand and took a deep breath. This time the green access button lit, and the electronic lock popped open, allowing him access to his company's restricted archives. He grimaced at the sound of the lock disengaging. It might as well have been a gunshot. He glanced over his shoulder. No one there.

He didn't have clearance to be in this section of the archives. If he was caught here, he'd never see the light day again, but he needed to know what his company was planning to do with his research. He and his research partner, John Randall, had worked too hard and for too long to be shut out now.

The problems had started months ago. First, there were unannounced visits by military personnel to their lab at Alpha Genetics. They had questioned Jacob and John about the memory blocking serum they were creating. Then came the unexplained removal of clearance to certain areas within the lab. Finally, they lost oversight of their research, the supervising scientist, Dr. Monroe, assuming full control over the project.

It had become clear to Jacob that the company had plans for their serum, but those plans didn't include him. He couldn't let that happen. He had to find out why he had been blackballed and what role the military had played in these developments.

The company had spent hundreds of thousands of dollars to maintain secrecy, installing multiple layers of security to protect this information. As a result, Jacob had been forced to liberate Dr. Monroe's security badge to access the archives.

He had chosen the evening shift, hoping that whoever monitored the security cameras was either dozing off, or simply didn't realize who was allowed there. From his brief encounters with the muscle-headed security guards, they considered each scientist to be just another lab coat. If he didn't look directly into the cameras, there was an excellent chance, no one would be able to identify him. He hoped.

He skulked over to the main workstation, taking a seat in front of the monitor. He slid Dr. Monroe's badge into the computer's card reader. The monitor blinked to life, a single green box on the screen asking for a password.

A creaking sound came from the door. Jacob popped up from the seat, and dove behind the desk, which partially shielded him from view. He held his breath, pressing his body against the metal file drawers to minimize his exposed profile.

He waited. Nothing.

Slowly, he slid along the side of the desk and peeked around the corner toward the door. No one was there. His body fell slack, his head pounding with each heartbeat.

He returned to the monitor and typed Dr. Monroe's password into the system. He had attained it from Julie, one of the technicians, telling her he was in hot water with Monroe. He had lied, saying he couldn't find a file on his computer and needed to pull it from the lead researcher's system. At first, she had been hesitant, so Jacob had turned on the charm. The rumor had been that Julie had a thing for Jacob. The rumor had been true. A combination of Monroe's legendary temper and Jacob's good looks had done the trick.

She had even told Jacob about Monroe's secondary password, explaining that the security system employed a dual layer of encryption.

Jacob hit enter and a message blinked on the screen.

Password does not match profile. Security protocol engaged.

To his horror, a timer appeared on the monitor. It was counting down from fifteen seconds.

What did I do?

His mind went blank.

The timer counted down, *14, 13, 12…*

Jacob pulled a strip of paper from his pocket, re-reading the password. It matched what he had entered.

10, 9, 8…

He stared at the paper, then the screen.

It's case sensitive!

Jacob re-typed the password, one button at a time.

5, 4, 3…

He hit enter. The timer froze at 2.

He nearly cried when the screen blinked, granting him access to the archives.

He scanned the folders on the hard drive, finally finding the encrypted file for his research.

He clicked on it.

Another password request.

He carefully typed Monroe's secondary password, this time making certain he made no errors.

I hope this is right.

He said a silent prayer and hit enter.

The system went quiet, a string of repeating dots filling the center of the screen.

Oh crap, what now?

The file popped open, revealing multiple documents.

Jacob searched the list of files, carefully choosing which to open and read. After twenty panic filled minutes of reviewing documents — his heart stopped each time he heard a sound — he found what he was looking for.

Jacob pulled a flash drive from his coat pocket and inserted it into the USB port, copying the files he wanted. Finished, he unplugged the drive and stashed it back into his pocket. Next, he removed Monroe's card from the computer.

I've got to get the hell out of here!

He crept toward the door. His footsteps sounded like thunderclaps.

Jesus, someone's going to hear me!

He pressed his ear to the door, straining to hear if there was noise on the other side. The only sound was his deep and shallow breathing. He cracked open the door and looked through.

All clear.

He pushed it open, wincing as it creaked on its hinges. Finally satisfied that no one was in the hallway, he slid out of the archives.

Both terrified and exhilarated, Jacob allowed his imagination to run wild knowing that what he had done here today was worthy of a Robert Ludlum novel. But he wasn't home free yet. He still needed to escape the building and get somewhere safe to read the contents of the flash drive. He took the stairs down to the parking level, occasionally glancing upward to make sure he wasn't being followed.

Finally reaching level P4, he paused, placing his hand on the metal handle. It was icy in his grip, his fear amplifying every sensation. He pushed the door open and strode into the garage, trying his best to appear natural.

Jacob walked briskly through the gray concrete parking structure, the sound of his footfalls the only thing to keep him company.

Just a little farther and I'm home free.

He reached into his pocket and fumbled his keys, nearly dropping them. His hands shook violently, his legs like jelly. It was hard to walk, but he willed himself forward.

"Working late today, Dr. Taylor?"

Jacob froze a moment, then spun on his heel to face the voice that had addressed him. Three men in suits stood several feet from him. The one in the middle wore a sickening grin. He was flanked by two larger men. They were all armed.

"Um, yes … just wrapping up a project," Jacob's voice cracked.

"I believe you have something that doesn't belong to you."

"What do you mean?"

"We can do this the easy way or the hard way. Either way, you're not leaving with that drive."

"Wait, I can explain…"

Chapter Three

August 17, 1:04 P.M.
Georgetown, Washington D.C.

Randall walked along M Street in Georgetown, past the small shops that resembled small cottages more than businesses. Crowds strolled by him, enjoying a quick bite to eat or a sweet treat at one of the many small food shops that lined the popular avenue. Lost in thought, he barely noticed them. Having just played twenty questions with his old friend Peter over lunch, he shook his head and sighed. His friend, noting the bags under his eyes, had tried to pry an explanation for his ragged condition. Randall had simply shrugged it off, saying it was just a bad night's sleep and nothing more. He shuffled slowly down the street like an old man one step removed from using a walker. Normally full of energy, Randall felt exceptionally old, the lack of sleep sapping him of his strength.

His phone rang. It was Peter.

"Yeah Pete."

"Nick, you gotta tell me what's wrong."

"Like I said, just a couple bad nights' sleep."

"Save that shit for someone else."

"Pete, I'm telling you, I'm fine. Just insomnia."

"Look, if you won't tell me, then I'll just have to call John."

Randall frowned. The last thing he wanted was his son worrying about him. "That's not necessary."

"Then tell me what's going on!"

His mind in a fog, Randall didn't notice the sound of an engine roaring to full power. He continued walking, then heard a commotion on the sidewalk behind him. He spun around. A black Cadillac Escalade had hopped the curb and was bearing down on him. Pedestrians jumped off the sidewalk to avoid being crushed. The driver steered the vehicle directly at Randall.

Shit! "Pete, I have to go." He clicked his phone off and started running, straining to stay ahead of the charging SUV. The vehicle ran over vendor signs, sending shards of metal, and wood raining down on the sidewalk. Randall looked ahead for any sort of shelter. He saw entryways into shops. No good. If he went into one, whoever was trying to kill him would get out of the car and follow him in. There was only one option. Run.

The Cadillac continued to plow over everything in its way. It was gaining on him. Randall's mind raced. He glanced over his shoulder, the huge vehicle loomed ever closer. Its grille and headlights looked like the evil grin of some maniacal beast, smirking at Randall's impending doom. Randall cursed at the sight, barely able to make a sound as he raced along breathlessly, slowing as his oxygen-depleted body could no longer maintain a dead sprint.

He could feel the heat of the engine now, the vehicle mere feet away. Ahead he spotted his salvation. An alley. He gritted his teeth and pushed forward. He rounded the corner just as the Escalade flew by, scraping the brick façade, sending a shower of sparks skyward.

Randall doubled over, feeling like his lunch was about to join him in the alley. He tried desperately to catch his breath. The gunning of the engine grew louder again. In an exhausted stupor, Randall looked to the far end of the alley. The dark SUV rounded the corner. Once again it bore down on him, its driver hell-bent on making Randall a bloody hood ornament. His eyes darted around the alley, desperately searching for an escape.

The Cadillac hurtled toward him. There wasn't much time. Randall spotted a fire escape. He sprinted toward the metal ladder, glancing between it and the evil grin of the SUV. He jumped onto the bottom rung. Climbing frantically, he reached the first platform just as the Escalade sheared off the bottom of the ladder. He continued to climb, afraid to look down. He heard the sickening sound of screeching tires as the driver slammed on the brakes.

Who the hell is this?

It was a race. Randall tried to put as much distance as possible between himself and his would-be assassin. His sweaty hands grasped clumsily at the rungs above and his feet struggled to find footing. He nearly slipped off the ladder, his left foot missing the rung entirely, his sweaty hand ripping free. He hung dizzily, twenty feet above the alley, looking down at the street as two men in dark suits emerged from the Escalade holding guns.

Randall regained his composure and continued climbing as shots rang out from below. Bullets ricocheted past him. He glanced down for a moment and saw the SUV back up, under the now damaged ladder. The two men, using the Cadillac as a step ladder, were now making their way onto the fire escape.

Dammit, they're fast!

The younger, fitter men made short work of the climb, while Randall struggled onto the rooftop, his hands and legs aching. He glanced around and saw a doorway. He sprinted toward it.

Please be unlocked!

It wasn't.

He could hear the two men drawing near the top of the fire escape. Randall raced around to the edge of the building. Looking down from the dizzying height, he realized, to his horror, there was no other way down. He heard the panting of the men who had now cleared the fire escape and were making their way onto the roof. Desperately searching for a way out, he recognized that he only had one option. He had to jump or face the merchants of death.

He judged the neighboring building to be about six to eight feet away and several feet below him. He backed up several feet, then sprinted to the ledge of the building, jumping with his toes planted on the concrete edge. The jump felt like slow motion as he arced through the air, floating in space for what seemed like minutes.

For a moment, Randall thought he had misjudged the distance between the buildings and wouldn't make it, but he cleared the gap and tumbled onto the sandpapery surface. His body flopped across the roof until he came to a skidding halt, face down. There was no time to assess damage, he had to get moving.

He stood on wobbly legs, then steadied himself as he glanced back to the other building. The two men appeared angered by his attempt to elude them. Turning, he spotted an exit. Half limping, he made his way to the door, once again praying for it to be unlocked. The knob spun in his hand and he pulled the door open. Ducking into the stairwell, Randall heard the unmistakable thudding sound of the two men landing on the rooftop. He slammed the door shut behind himself, then slid the deadbolt into position.

He hobbled down the stairwell, bracing himself as he went. His leg throbbed with pain, making it difficult to run, but he had no choice. He had to keep moving. He worked his way down the spiral staircase. The sound of heavy pounding on the metal door above reverberated down the enclosed stairway like a drum.

Gunshots. They were shooting out the deadbolt.

Randall reached the ground floor and sprinted across the street, dodging oncoming traffic. He entered the narrow doorway of a restaurant, working his way past evenly spaced tables as surprised guests looked up from their afternoon lunch. He stepped into the kitchen where he was met with shouts of protest from the kitchen staff. Pausing briefly, he spotted the exit, went into the alley and turned right. The street ended in a wall of buildings.

Not good!

Randall turned, running back toward the restaurant. He covered half the distance when the door burst open and the gunmen stepped out. Skidding to a stop, he searched frantically for a way out. There was none. The taller assassin reached into his jacket and slowly withdrew his weapon, while his associate looked on in amusement. Randall closed his eyes, awaiting death. His ears were greeted by a surprising sound: the heavy bass of a large engine followed by skidding tires.

Randall opened his eyes and spotted a dark sedan with tinted windows materialize from the adjacent street. His would-be assassins, caught off guard, turned to look at the source of the noise. A single figure emerged from the driver's-side door, wielding an assault rifle.

"Drop the guns, before I make you see-through," the rifleman said with a heavy Australian accent.

The taller assassin, as if testing the veracity of the rifleman's pledge, shifted his aim from Randall. The rifleman fired a volley at the tall man, causing his body to dance in midair as he was peppered with gunfire. Randall watched in horror as the man's lifeless body slumped to the pavement, a torrent of crimson running freely from his wounds.

"You son of a bitch!" The shorter assassin's hand disappeared into his coat as he watched his partner complete his death dance. The rifleman responded by swinging his weapon until it pointed directly at his chest.

"I don't think that's a good idea fella. Slowly, put your hands over your head and drop to your knees."

The shorter assassin complied, but not without some argument. "I don't know who you think you are, but you just made the biggest mistake of your life."

"Yeah, can't you tell I'm worried sick? I'm practically shaking in my boots." The rifleman walked over to the assassin and dropped the butt of his rifle onto the back of his head. The assassin fell to the ground like a sack of rocks, lying unconscious on the pavement next to his associate.

In shock, all Randall could manage was a muffled grunt as the rifleman walked toward him. Randall pegged him at over six and a half feet tall. His broad shoulders blocked out the sun like a giant Sequoia.

"You alright, mate?"

Randall didn't answer, his eyes shifting from the man with the rifle to the dead body on the ground.

"Dr. Randall, right?"

Randall looked up. "What just happened?"

"Well I'd say you must have pissed off someone pretty good now."

"Who are you?"

"Let's just say someone asked me to keep an eye on you and it's a good thing she did. These two blokes seemed intent on making you into Swiss cheese."

"Who are they?"

"Well now, I think we both have a pretty good idea who sent them." The rifleman was smiling now.

"Francis Dumond," Randall responded.

"Right you are, mate! I'd say you better keep an eye out from now on, maybe both eyes for that matter."

"What should I do?"

"Can't answer that one for you, but I suggest you stay away from the places you normally go. My guess is that once they find out these fellows didn't take care of you, Mr. Dumond will send someone else to finish the job."

"I can't go home?"

"Not unless you want to be on the front page of tomorrow's newspaper like our friend here." The rifleman gestured toward the blood-soaked assassin lying on the ground nearby. "I suggest you come up with another plan."

With that, the rifleman walked back to his car.

"Wait! You still didn't tell me who you are."

"The name's Michael Thompson."

"What are you doing here? Who do you work for?"

"Let's just say that my employer has an interest in your research and leave it at that."

"So, you've been following me?"

Thompson smiled broadly. "Take care of yourself Randall."

Randall blinked, unsure of what to do next. "Thanks."

"Don't mention it." Thompson slid his tall frame behind the wheel of his still idling car, closed the driver's side door, and slowly backed out the way he had come in.

16

Chapter Four

August 17, 1:37 P.M.
Arlington, Virginia

John Randall sat at his desk mulling over his options. To say that this had been a bad morning would be the understatement of the year. First, he had learned that his research partner, Jacob Taylor, had disappeared. John had tried calling and texting Jacob's cell phone all morning without luck. He had even called Jacob's fiancée Margaret and his parents. No one knew where he was.

Then there had been a break-in at the lab and someone had stolen all of John and Jacob's research. Now John's supervisor, Dr. Monroe, had just informed him that the National Institutes of Health was pulling their funding. Apparently, they no longer felt that developing a drug to erase traumatic memories was a worthwhile venture. It was a trifecta of bad news, one that was sure to make an otherwise beautiful summer day as gloomy as the first rainy Monday in September.

The sound of his phone ringing pulled John from his reverie and caused him to jump in surprise.

Now what?

He picked up the phone. "John Randall."

"Hi John, its Peter. Sorry to bother you at work, but do you have a few minutes to talk?"

"Actually, now's not the best time."

"I'm worried about your dad. I had lunch with him today and he looked like hell. He says he's not sleeping well, and he had the black circles under the eyes to prove it. He mentioned something about having strange dreams since he got back from Peru. Has he mentioned anything to you?"

John shook his head. This was the last thing he needed. "No, he hasn't said anything to me, but I haven't talked to him for a week. I've called and left messages, but he hasn't called me back. I figured he was just busy with work. You know how absorbed he can get with his research." John reclined in his chair, frowning at the thought that his father was keeping secrets again—a habit he had developed prior to his last excursion to Peru. In fact, John still didn't know what had happened there.

"Well, he didn't look good, and I thought you should know. I didn't want to bother your sister Sam with this since she and Nick just patched things up. I know you're busy, but it might be a good idea to check in with him. He can be a stubborn old codger and he might not want to bother you with this, but he just isn't himself."

John rubbed the back of his neck. "Okay, I'll stop by and see how he's doing. Thanks for the call."

"Take care and let me know if there's anything I can do."

"Will do, speak to you soon."

John hung up and shook his head. "This day just can't get any worse."

An audible alarm from his phone reminded him that he was scheduled to take his final flight exam for his helicopter pilot's license in a couple of hours. John frowned, realizing that, given the circumstances, making it to his flight test was at the bottom of his priority list. He made a mental note to call and reschedule the exam.

His thoughts returning to the conversation with Peter, John considered calling Sam. He dismissed the notion almost immediately. She and their dad had just gotten back to a good place and he wasn't sure how she would take the news. Besides, it was entirely possible that Peter was just overreacting. John checked his watch: 3:27 p.m. There wasn't anything else he could do at work, so he might as well visit his dad. Picking up the phone, he dialed his dad's cell number. It immediately went to voicemail.

"Dammit, why aren't you picking up?" John clicked the phone off and left his office, heading over to his father's house.

Chapter Five

John pulled his SUV to the curb in front of his dad's house and immediately knew that something was wrong. The front door was smashed open and hanging at an odd angle. Clicking off his seatbelt, John hopped out and sprinted to the door. His stopped at the entryway, calling out to his father. There was no reply. He reached for his cell phone, ready to dial 911, but realized he had left it in the car. He gingerly pushed the door open and stepped across the threshold. Books and papers were strewn throughout the living room and chairs were overturned.

He turned to run back to his car and call the police but heard a noise from the back of the house.

"Dad, are you okay?" He called out.

There was no reply. Concern for his father overrode worries for his own safety and John stepped deeper into the house.

He crept into the kitchen and found a cold pot of coffee still on the cradle. Glancing down the hallway, he strained to see into the back office where his dad normally worked. The room appeared to be empty.

Realizing he had no way to defend himself, he grabbed the largest kitchen knife he could find and moved slowly down the hallway, the stillness oddly menacing. The only sounds were his footfalls ... and his labored breathing.

He reached the back of the house and peered around the doorjamb. Someone had upturned the bedroom. Drawers were open, and clothes littered the floor, but still no sign of his father. Full-blown panic gripped him. He wanted to run, but he needed to know if his father was hurt...or worse.

The sudden sound of breaking glass drew John's attention. He jerked his head up, looking toward his father's study. He hugged the wall as he crept down the hallway, his left arm in front of him and the knife drawn back in his right. He heard the unmistakable sound of rustling.

John gripped the knife tightly as he approached the door. It was half closed. He eased the door open revealing... an empty room. John examined the study and found the cause of the sound. A broken coffee mug had apparently fallen from the desk. It lay smashed on the floor, directly in front of the window above his dad's workspace. The window was wide open, a strong breeze ruffling the curtains.

John let out a prolonged breath. His hands were shaking, adrenaline coursing through him. The house was empty.

He walked back to the front door and heard his phone ringing in his truck. He sprinted out and answered it. His dad was calling.

"Hello?"

"John, its Dad, where are you?"

"I'm at your house and it's torn apart. I thought something happened to you!"

"I'm okay, but I want you to get out of there."

"What? Someone ransacked your house. We need to call the police."

"You're in danger! Get the hell out of there!"

"In danger from what? What's going on?"

"I can't explain right now, just listen to me!"

"I just got off the phone with Peter and he's worried about you, he said he had lunch with you yesterday and you looked terrible..."

"Get out of the house! NOW!"

"I'm not in the goddamn house, I'm at the curb! What in the hell have you gotten yourself into! You don't return my calls, you show up for lunch with Peter and have some big secret you won't tell him, and now you're screaming at me to get out of your house! Does this have something to do with your trip to Peru? What in the hell happened there?"

"I don't care about any of that, I just want to make sure you're safe!"

"Stop yelling at me! Goddammit dad, since you got back from that trip, you've acted weird. You don't return my calls and you're not around when I come to see you!"

John pressed the phone to his ear. It might not have been a fair time to hit his father with this, but he was angry and confused. His father must have gotten the message as there was only silence on the other end of the phone.

"Are you still there?" John asked.

"Yes, son, I'm here."

John took a deep breath, sitting down behind his steering wheel. "I'm not sure what's going on, but we need to talk."

"I know you're frustrated, but you're going to have to trust me. I want you to get as far from my house as you can. Do you understand?"

"I'm in my car now."

"Good, I'll call you in a little while."

John heard the phone click. He set it down on the armrest and shook his head.

Can this day get any weirder?

Chapter Six

August 17, 8:12 P.M.
Cooper Island, Bermuda

Colonel Shaw reclined in his chair, taking a long pull from his cigarette. He slowly exhaled the smoke from his lungs, his eyes closed as he enjoyed the moment. Spread out on the desk were the files his men had retrieved from Alpha Genetics the previous day. He had seen the contents of some of the files before, but recent events had accelerated the need to fully assess the situation and determine a course of action.

The first file he reviewed was labeled "Project MKUltra." Inside was a black and white photo of a man in uniform holding pieces of a weather balloon. The photo made Shaw smile. He was one of the few people alive who knew the true story of the staged picture and the cover-up it concealed. He flipped to the next page. There was a brief synopsis of the program, which explained that the covert government

24

program had been initiated by the CIA and involved the testing of mind control techniques on unsuspecting American and Canadian citizens. He scanned the report to refresh his memory and then picked up a more current folder labeled "Randall / Taylor Study - NIH." He opened it and began to read.

He reflexively picked up the cigarette again and took another long drag. Breathing out a chain of gray smoke, he closed the folder and dropped the cigarette in the ash tray. They had dodged a bullet. If that son of a bitch Taylor had gotten away with the information he had taken, there would have been a lot of explaining to do. Probably even a Congressional hearing like the Church Committee. But with the good doctor stored away safely, that wasn't a concern anymore. Now he just had to tie up one more loose end.

Shaw grabbed his cigarette again. It had nearly burned all the way down, but he knew he could get one more puff. He enjoyed the last pull immensely, then snuffed the cigarette out in the tray. It was a dirty habit, but everyone had their vices and he was no different. Besides, it was a reminder of the good old days, before people gave a crap about everything they put into their bodies. People were so weak these days and easy to control. They needed strong men—like him—to lead them now more than ever, and that's what he intended to do. Whether they liked it or not.

He picked up his phone, punched in a series of numbers, then waited. Someone on the other end picked up on the third ring.

"Get the prisoner ready. I'm coming over to interrogate him."

"Yes, sir."

Hanging up the phone, he picked up his hat and placed it on his head. Looking into a mirror on his desk, he adjusted it to a rakish angle and decided that a cigarette in his mouth would add just the right dash to the reflection staring back at him. He fished one out of the pack, lit it with a match, then shook it out with his cupped right hand. He tossed the spent match into an ash tray and walked out of his office.

The night air was invigorating. He thoroughly enjoyed his walk to the holding area. Shaw didn't anticipate any problems getting the information he wanted out of his guest. Again, the men of today didn't hold a candle to the tough guys of his era. *Hell, we helped make the world a free place, so these young idiots could text smiley faces to each other all day.*

He arrived at the cell a moment later. "Is the prisoner ready?"

"Yes, sir, he's waiting for you."

"Carry on, soldier."

"Thank you, sir!"

Shaw punched his code into the electronic lock and was rewarded with a faint hissing noise that announced the opening of the cell door. As he entered, he found the prisoner seated on the steel bench inside, hands bound behind his back and handcuffed to a metal rail. The holding area was a sterile gray color, with bare and windowless concrete walls. White fluorescent light fixtures hung from the ceiling and a single security camera was tucked away in the far corner. The floor was also painted gray, adding to the coldness of the room. Shaw removed his hat and brushed his short, neatly trimmed gray hair back with his free hand. He strode purposefully to the prisoner and stood towering over him.

"Have you decided to talk to us today Dr. Taylor, or do we need to provide you with more convincing?"

Taylor looked up at Shaw. Dark circles under his sunken hazel eyes attested to his fatigue. His clothes were rumpled, and his face sported recently acquired bruises to go with two days of untrimmed stubble. His rumpled appearance resembled a vagrant who had consumed too much cheap booze and fallen asleep in the first convenient spot he could find.

"Go to hell, you asshole!"

"Tsk, tsk, tsk doctor, that's no way to speak to your host." The colonel struck Taylor across the chin with his left hand, the ring on his finger leaving a small dimple where it connected with the man's face. A small trickle of blood ran down his chin. Taylor moaned in pain.

"Care to try again? We have all your research, except for one critical piece. Oddly enough, it's not on the network or the electronic archive. Where is it?"

"I already told you, I don't know where it is. Most of our records were digitized, but some weren't. I didn't even know they were missing."

"Wish I could believe you, but unfortunately I don't." The colonel unleashed another backhand, leaving a matching dimple just above the other. More blood trickled down Taylor's chin and onto his wrinkled white shirt.

"I can do this all day." The colonel smiled, almost hoping that his prisoner wouldn't talk. He derived great pleasure from these episodes.

Spitting blood now, Taylor said, "Look, the only people who had access to the files were my partner Dr. John Randall and me. I don't have it and protocol over the handling of files is very strict, so the only other place it could be is in John's office."

"We checked. It's not there."

"Then I don't know where it could be. I'm telling you the truth! Please, my fiancée and parents are probably worried sick. You have to let me go!"

"Go? Oh no, doctor, we can't have that. You're going to be staying as our guest for a while."

The colonel placed his hat on his head and walked toward the door.

"Wait, please, I just want to go home. You can't keep me here. I'm an American citizen. I have rights! I want to see an attorney!"

Turning, the colonel looked at Taylor with mock concern. "I'll see if I can find one for you as soon as I can. In the meantime, do try to get some rest, you look terribly tired."

He smiled, turned toward the door and walked out.

Chapter Seven

August 18, 5:58 A.M.
Baltimore, Maryland

Randall sat in the motel lobby staring out the window. Using what cash he had left in his wallet, he had rented a room under a false name. One of the few advantages of staying in a run-down motel in a shady part of town was the anonymity provided by innkeepers, when a guest paid in cash. Randall strummed his fingers as he waited for the ancient computer to come to life. A relic from a bygone age, the computer was part of what the motel owner referred to as its business center.

The lighter shade of gray sky announced the approaching day as Randall wondered which would arrive first, the morning sun or the computer log-in screen. After what seemed an hour, Randall opened the web browser. Feeling a bit sheepish, he began searching for reports of abductions, hoping to find something that might match his nightmares. As strange as it seemed, he had a hunch that his dreams were more than just nocturnal recaps of his recent adventures. His first searches turned up entries of individuals claiming to have been probed, poked, sliced, and diced by an assortment of otherworldly creatures who had snatched them from their slumber.

Some accounts appeared to have been written by rational, normal people, while others seemed liked the ravings of lunatics. Unfortunately, none of them matched his recurring dreams. After nearly an hour of searching the web, he was no closer to an answer. Frustrated, Randall closed the browser, rubbed his eyes, and decided he needed a break.

Pushing himself up from the desk, Randall stepped to the front counter where an old coffee machine sat with black liquid resting in its well-worn pot. He thought for a moment and decided to give it a try. No sugar or cream, just black. Much to his surprise, the flavor of the coffee wasn't bad. Taking the cup, Randall walked around the small lobby, examining the décor. It was decorated in an eclectic, seventies motif, complete with faded faux wooden paneling, shag rug, and avocado-green furniture. The proprietor was either a genius decorator who loved the retro look or was just plain cheap. Randall decided it was the latter.

He returned to the computer, reopened the web browser, and started his search again. This time he landed on a site called MUFON, the Mutual UFO Network. MUFON had a search engine that allowed users to enter criteria and search for incidents.

What have I got to lose?

Once again, he searched and once again, no luck. After more browsing, he still hadn't found anything remotely like his nightmares. He removed his glasses and rubbed his eyes, which ached from staring at the computer for so long.

Doubt crept into his mind. If he couldn't find an episode that matched his dreams, what would he do? Randall took another sip from his coffee, which had grown considerably colder since his last drink. He contemplated giving up but realized that he didn't have other options, so he dove back into his research.

After another thirty minutes of searching, he found something that sparked his interest. A young woman named Jamie — she didn't provide a last name — had several entries describing recurring abductions. According to the information, Jamie was in late twenties and lived in a small town called Hamilton near the ocean. She didn't specify where the town was located, but the description of her experiences caught Randall's attention. She described, in painstaking detail, her most recent encounter. It had transpired in her second-story apartment. The open window overlooking the water, the feeling of dread, and the late hour of the occurrence all matched Randall's latest nightmare. But the thing that sent cold shivers down his spine was the date of her latest abduction. It had happened two nights ago, the same night as his latest dream.

Randall stared at the computer, unsure of what to make of this revelation. Finally, he realized what he had to do.

Minimizing the MUFON window, Randall searched the web for English speaking cities named Hamilton near a major body of water. It didn't take long to find his target. Several listings down on the first search page was the result *Bermuda's City of Hamilton*. Randall searched real estate listings for apartments in the area and scoured pictures posted by agents, hoping to find one that matched the room in his nightmares. Without finding an exact match, he discovered several views that were very similar to those he had experienced in his visions. There was a very strong chance that this was where Jamie lived.

He opened an airline site and checked flights to Bermuda. He found one leaving in a couple of hours.

Chapter Eight

August 18, 7:43 A.M.
Arlington, Virginia

John drove his truck toward the underground parking structure of his research facility at Alpha Genetics. He was tired, having not slept well the previous night. Too many thoughts had fought for attention in his foggy mind as he tossed and turned throughout the evening.

A guard stopped him as he approached the parking booth. John noted that there were now four guards at the entrance instead of the two that had been assigned prior to the break-in. He also noticed that they were heavily armed unlike the previous day. The company was taking yesterday's incident seriously.

Good. I lost two years' worth of research in the blink of an eye.

John glanced down at his clenched knuckles, which gripped the steering wheel. They were white and trembling with anger.

He breathed in deeply and exhaled, relaxing his grip. As he pulled up to the concrete booth, the guard gripped his gun more tightly with one hand while pressing his earpiece with the other. The man's body language conveyed a seriousness that made John shudder. Another guard approached the driver's side door of his car and motioned for John to open the window.

"Name?"

"Dr. John Randall, I work in Building D."

The guard placed his right hand on John's open window. His left hand went to his earpiece where he depressed a small button, which activated the microphone in front of his mouth. His eyes never broke contact with John, who suddenly felt very exposed.

"Randall, John, Building D." After an excruciating several seconds, the guard spoke again. "Go ahead."

The guard waved to another man in the booth, signaling him to raise the barrier. As the large wooden arm slowly lifted, an eight-foot strand of large metal bollards, spanning the length of the entryway, disappeared into the ground. The guard looked back at John, motioning for him to enter, his gaze boring into John's face. John coaxed his truck through the narrow entryway as a shiver traveled down his spine.

The facility's protection by armed guards had initially seemed an appropriate response to yesterday's events, but now he wasn't sure. As John wound his way down the concrete tunnel into the underground parking structure, a strange thought played in the deep recesses of his mind: *Are they trying to keep someone out or someone in?* He wasn't sure why the thought occurred to him, but something gnawed at the pit of his stomach. He quickly dismissed it as paranoia.

John parked his Toyota FJ Cruiser in his assigned parking spot, turned off the ignition, and sat with his hands folded in his lap for several minutes. Not one to give in to worry, he couldn't help but feel that he was missing something important. In a little more than a twenty-four-hour span, Jacob had disappeared, someone had stolen two years of his research, and his father's house had been ransacked. Worse still, the last time he had spoken to his father, he had freaked out over John's safety. In fact, his dad had been downright paranoid about him being inside his home.

Suddenly, a thought occurred to John. His father had never told him where he was when John had called him. In fact, his dad hadn't called him back. John picked up his cell phone and dialed his father's number. The phone rang and went to voicemail. He tried again with the same result. John smashed his phone onto the gray, leather console of his truck. He heard a snap. Lifting it, he saw that the glass was cracked.

Dammit!

He exited the vehicle, slamming the door in the process. Taking long strides, John chose to use the stairs instead of the elevator. He made short work of the steps. Reaching his floor, he grasped the door handle and swiped his ID card through the card reader. A red light indicated that his card hadn't worked. John gritted his teeth. He tried his card again with the same result. Sighing, he turned and trudged down the four flights of stairs back into the parking garage. He reflected that, if this was any indication, today would be no better than yesterday.

Instead of trying the elevator, John decided to enter through the main lobby of Building D. As he exited the parking garage, a cool breeze washed over his face. He closed his eyes, breathing in the fresh air. He felt better almost immediately.

The parking structure fed into the main courtyard of the facility, which was laid out in a circular pattern with Building A resting squarely in the center. The other buildings encircled

Building A with passenger breezeways spaced out on various levels connecting them. The result was a pattern, which, if viewed from directly above, looked like a bicycle wheel with the breezeways serving as the spokes connecting the outer five buildings to the central hub.

John strode through the double glass doors of the lobby and approached the front entrance, which now had additional security as well. He didn't recognize any of the new guards but caught a glimpse of a familiar face moving through the lobby. Jeff Stinson was medium height, medium build with strawberry red hair and a beard. In other words, he was hard to miss. John noticed that he was practically jogging toward the newly reinforced security detachment. He figured that Jeff must be late for a meeting. John matched his pace and caught up with him.

"Jeff, what's going on here?"

"Hey, John. After the break-in yesterday, I guess they decided to increase security around here."

"Yeah, I tried to access my floor through the stairwell in the parking garage, but my security card wouldn't work."

Jeff flashed a knowing smile. "Me, too. They must have restricted access to the main lobby. I guess they don't want our new friends here to get lonely." Jeff gestured at the hulking, unsmiling faces now positioned between the front entrance and the elevator banks.

The two stopped as they reached the line feeding into the checkpoint.

"Sorry to hear about Jacob and your research, that's a real shame," Jeff said.

"It gets worse. Sounds like they're pulling my funding, too."

Jeff shook his head. "When it rains, it pours."

As they spoke, the line inched forward until they finally reached the front. Jeff answered questions from the security detachment and walked through. He waited on the other side as John stepped up to the guards.

"Name?"

"Dr. John Randall, my offices are on the fourth floor."

The guard glanced down at John's identification badge and then looked directly into John's face without saying a word. He glared at John as if trying to memorize every feature.

"Is there a problem?" John asked.

"You'll have to come with me."

"Why? What's going on here?" John glanced at Jeff, who shrugged.

A second guard joined the first, gripping John's elbow in his meaty right hand.

Surprised, John turned to look at him. "What are you doing? Let go of my arm." John jerked his elbow free, frowning at the man.

The two guards, scowling at John now, were joined by another man who was older and slighter of build.

"Dr. Randall?" he said. John turned to face him. "My name is Rodrigo Alonzo. I'm in charge of security now, and my men and I are here to escort you to your office."

"I've watched other people who were just checked by your men and let through. Why am I being singled out?"

"You're being singled out because of the circumstances surrounding your partner and your research. Yours is the only research taken from the archives and your partner has disappeared … yet nothing has happened to you," Alonzo replied.

"Are you accusing me of having something to do with Jacob's disappearance?"

"That's not for me to say, but someone is waiting to speak with you in your office."

"Who?"

"I cannot disclose that information."

"If you think I'm coming with you, you're crazy."

"Fine, we can simply call the authorities, and have you arrested."

"For what!"

"Your fingerprints were found on your partner's door handle, and you were the last person to speak with him in his office the day he disappeared. We confirmed this with video footage taken from the hallway outside his door."

"Of course I spoke with Jacob! He's my research partner!"

"Nevertheless, this makes you a person of interest in the eyes of the company. Now, you can come with us to your office or I can call the authorities, which will it be?"

John looked up to see Jeff still standing on the other side of the barrier, his face ashen.

"Fine, I'll go up to my office, but tell your pit bulls that I won't be man-handled."

"Very well, Dr. Randall." Alonzo gave his men a withering look and they grudgingly backed away from John. The four walked over to the nearest elevator bank, where one of the guards pushed the round elevator call button. A single *ping* announced its arrival. As the door slid open, John felt a hand grasp the back of his arm. He instinctively swatted it away.

He turned and stared at the guard. "I told you to keep your hands off me."

The guard replied with a condescending smirk and gestured for John to enter the elevator. The four men made the rest of the trip in silence. As he exited the elevator, John realized that something was wrong. The normal bustle of personnel going about their daily business was absent from the fourth floor. Only he and his escorts were present today. He immediately felt the hairs on the back of his neck rise.

38

As they walked through the hallway, the everyday sight of the facility took on an otherworldly sensation. It was as if he were seeing it for the first time. Offices were ghostly quiet, the walls stark and sterile despite familiar pictures he had seen for years. Just before they entered his office, the group passed an empty stainless steel medical cart; its clean metallic surface gleamed in the cold fluorescent light. The strong smell of disinfectant, mixed with cigarette smoke, hung in the air. It wasn't immediately clear where the smoke was coming from. The lab, being a clean environment, was a smoke-free zone.

As they walked into his office, John discovered the source of the foul odor. An older man was sitting in his chair with his feet on the desk. Next to his feet was a stack of file folders from John's locked file drawer. John's eyes shifted to the man, who held a red folder in his hand. He was reviewing the contents with rapt attention. Once again, a wave of anger swept over John as he balled his hands into fists.

"Who the hell are you and what are you doing with my files?" John asked.

The older man didn't immediately reply. He finished reading the document, set it down on the desk, and crossed his hands on his lap. Without looking up at John, the man retrieved a pack of cigarettes from his coat pocket. With great care, he removed a single cigarette and held it between two fingers. He then fished a lighter out of the same pocket with his other hand. Placing the cigarette between his lips, he lit it carefully. Taking a deep breath, he sucked in the smoke, seeming to enjoy the flavor. He then exhaled in a long, slow fashion. The smoke blew directly into John's face, causing him to cough.

"*Your* files, Dr. Randall? I think you're mistaken. These files are the property of Alpha Genetics."

Brushing away the smoke in front of him, John scanned his office. One of his escorts was standing in the corner watching him. The other was standing in the doorway, blocking his exit route. The third man was nowhere to be seen. Files were stacked on the rolling chairs in front of his desk and the contents of his drawers were scattered about. Clearly these men had turned his office inside out looking for something, but what? John turned his attention back to the man sitting at the desk with his head cocked to one side. He looked at John wistfully, sucking his cigarette. John noticed a file that he didn't recognize near the man's feet.

"Mind me asking what's in that file?" John asked.

The man's eyes narrowed as he continued puffing. Finally, he gestured theatrically with his hands and said, "This file? Nothing you should concern yourself with, John. You don't mind if I call you John, do you? I know that bothers some professorial types. After all, I'm sure you spent a lot of time and effort earning your title ... Doctor."

He's trying to goad me.

John choked back his anger and said calmly, "John's fine." He smiled.

"Very good. As I'm sure you've already deduced, my associates and I are looking for something. Something I thought we would find in your office, but it appears that it's not here." He paused to take another drag of his cigarette. "I was hoping you might be able to help me find it."

"What are you looking for?"

"A file from one of your patients. A man named Timothy Cobb."

John flinched at the mention of the name.

"Ah, so you know him," the older man said.

John blinked, unsure of what to say. His research on Timothy was classified. Aside from Jacob, only a handful of

40

people knew about him. Suddenly, recent events assumed an even darker undertone and John realized that he was in danger.

"How do you know about Timothy?"

The cigarette man stared directly into John's eyes, "Dr. Randall, I've been more than patient with you, but I don't believe you understand the gravity of the situation. You're not in a position to ask questions. I want that file and I want it now. Where is it?" His eyes turned to the guard in the corner whose hand disappeared under his coat.

"It's in the third office down the hall on the left. In a locked steel case file," John said, his eyes fixed on the guard. "Would you like me to get it for you?"

"I don't believe that will be necessary." The man nodded to the guard behind John, who disappeared down the hall. He then shifted his gaze back to other guard, who slowly withdrew a gun from under his coat. John realized that he had only seconds.

He kicked the rolling chair in front of his desk directly at the guard with the gun. Stunned, the man buckled over as the chair struck him in the legs. John grabbed the unfamiliar folder from the desk, spun, and sprinted down the hallway, grasping the empty metal tray from the surgical cart in the hall as he passed by.

He raised it back as he approached the third office. As if on cue, the second guard emerged from the office, gun drawn. John brought the tray down on his outstretched arm, knocking the gun loose as a shot ricocheted down the corridor. The tray bounced upward, and John swung it directly into the guard's unprotected face. The sound of metal crushing the man's nose was sickening. He careened wildly backward into the wall.

John dropped the tray and grabbed the fire alarm as he ran by. The dizzying sound of sirens and the flash of strobe lights flooded the hallway as John raced to the stairwell. He could hear shouting and footsteps down the hall by his office. He punched the emergency lever releasing the door lock to the stairs. He burst through the door and slammed it shut as gunfire ripped into the metal on the other side. The reinforced steel door held.

John leapt down several stairs at a time, never turning to look over his shoulder. He reached the third-floor landing just as the stairwell door on the fourth floor burst open. He heard footsteps ringing from the stairs above. John's heart pounded as he continued down to the parking garage. Gunshots echoed through the stairwell, ricocheting off the metal railing. John flinched, his foot missing a step. He nearly tumbled out of control but caught himself by grabbing the rail with his left hand, but not before he twisted his ankle.

The injury burned like fire with every step. John reached the second floor, the heavy footfalls of his pursuers getting closer. He pushed on, knowing that delay meant death. He made the last turn onto the first-floor landing, turning wide and striking the wall with his back. He saw the first guard, who raised his gun and fired a short burst of rounds. They struck the wall where John had been just moments before.

John reached the exit door and flung it open. Another man stood in the doorway. John froze momentarily, then recognized him as an employee from another building, John pushed past him, causing the man to stagger backward.

"Watch where you're going!"

John sprinted for his parking space, hearing the man yelling again as the door to the parking garage opened once more. The shouting stopped suddenly as gunfire raked the parking garage. John turned a corner, looking back to see the man lying dead as the gunmen sprinted past him.

John tried desperately to remove his keys from his pocket while not breaking stride. He fumbled his keys, nearly dropping them, but managed to catch them in mid-air on the run. His FJ Cruiser came into view and he hit the fob, causing the taillights to blink, letting him know the doors were unlocked.

He glanced over his shoulder and saw the first man rounding the corner, his gun raised. John ducked reflexively as gunfire erupted around him. He reached his car and flung the door open. Bullets tore into the side panel as he jumped into his truck. Shoving the key into the ignition, John started the engine and threw the truck into reverse. Gunfire shattered his rear window as he sped backward toward the first gunman. He could see the man's eyes go wide as his car smashed into him. John hit the brakes, threw the truck into drive, then peeled away just as the second gunman turned the corner and unleashed another barrage of gunfire.

John sped forward, his driver's side door slamming shut. As he wound up the concrete ramp, the guard shack came into view. John saw several armed security men taking careful aim at his truck. More gunshots tore through his FJ. He ducked as he approached the guard shack, nearly crushing one of them as he roared by. Sitting upright, his body tensed as he watched metal pylons slowly emerging from the ground in the driveway ahead of him.

John punched the accelerator. The truck charged forward, striking the barriers as they were several inches above the asphalt. His FJ bounced wildly as the bottom scraped against the rising bollards. John struggled to keep the vehicle under control as he was knocked around the cabin. The back of the truck finally cleared the barrier and John steered the FJ onto the access road. He glanced over his shoulder to see two pursuit cars stuck behind the fully extended pylons. The first driver was hanging out the window, screaming at a man in the guard booth to lower the barrier.

John grinned, but his elation was brief. As he turned forward, he saw several cars arranged in a neat line ten yards ahead. He looked past them to see a red stoplight and realized that he was going too fast to stop in time. He swerved to the left into oncoming traffic as his FJ shot into the intersection. A large box truck bore down on him, the driver screaming obscenities as he leaned on his horn. John steered hard to the right as his truck fishtailed out of control. The box truck clipped the back of the FJ, sending John spinning in the other direction. He banged his head into the window frame. His truck came to rest in the middle of the intersection, facing oncoming traffic.

His head throbbed with pain as he sat dumbfounded in the FJ. The sound of cars honking, and tires screeching was dizzying. John shook his head to clear the foggy veil. Cars zigzagged around him as he brushed his hand against the side of his temple, feeling a warm slick of blood trickling down his forehead. He reached down and buckled his seatbelt.

Glancing to his right, he realized that his pursuers had gotten the barriers down and were now barreling after him. John threw his FJ into reverse and gunned the engine. The truck shot out of the intersection.

He had little choice but to drive backward as the black sedans gained on him. In less than a minute, the first sedan caught him. The car's passenger window opened, and a man leaned out holding a handgun and took careful aim. John tapped his brakes, causing the FJ to dip. He then throttled the engine and pulled away just as the driver of the black sedan braked his own car. The suddenness of the stop caused the man with the gun to tumble from the sedan and roll into traffic. John heard the sickening sound of bones crunching as another car drove over the would-be shooter.

The first sedan settled behind and to his left as another took a position to the right and in front of John's truck, the three vehicles forming a wedge with John's FJ in the middle. The first sedan accelerated and swerved at John's rear tire while the second sedan aimed for his front tire. They were trying to spin his car. John mashed down on the accelerator. The truck lurched backward. The first sedan swung by, scraping the bumper of John's car.

The driver, anticipating the impact with the FJ, over-steered the car, ramming into another vehicle in traffic. The impact of the collision slowed the sedan, which was rammed in the rear by an oncoming commuter bus traveling at high speed. The car crumpled like paper as metal, plastic, and rubber debris showered the road. The second sedan, now squarely to the left of the FJ, bounced into John's driver's side door, sending the truck several feet into the fast lane. John fought the steering wheel, forcing his FJ back into its lane, narrowly avoiding a red BMW.

John glanced in his rearview, trying to gauge the distance between his truck and the next car in front of him. He was greeted with solid red brake lights a hundred yards ahead. Traffic was slowing. He shot a look at his remaining pursuer. The driver looked at him and grinned broadly, realizing that traffic was stopping.

The sedan was pacing John now, blocking him in and preventing him from exiting the expressway. John slowed his FJ, but the sedan slowed as well. He tried accelerating, but the sedan kept pace, adjusting to his every move. The two vehicles were in lockstep. John searched the horizon, desperately looking for a way out. He noticed a construction zone on the median. It wasn't much but it would have to do. He waited and timed a lane change, squeezing his FJ between a silver Audi and a blue Honda. With traffic slowing even more, John wasn't sure he could reach the construction area. He estimated it was less than a quarter mile away. He looked over at his pursuer who now understood his plan and was trying to change lanes as well.

Come on, just a little farther.

As his FJ slowed, he could now see an opening in the construction barricades for work trucks to access the site. Traffic slowed to a crawl; then stopped. He wasn't going to make it to the opening. John turned back to his pursuer but couldn't find the sedan. He heard honking cars and screaming drivers. His eyes darted back and forth, finally finding the sedan stopped in the road behind him. He searched for the driver and heard pounding on the passenger side door of the FJ.

"Open this fucking door!"

John's head spun around to see the angry face of the sedan driver, pounding on his door, his handgun in plain view.

"Open it now!"

The driver pointed the weapon directly at John's face. He was trapped. He held up his hands and nodded his surrender. The gunman held his aim as John reached across the cab of the FJ. At the last possible moment, he ducked and gunned the truck in reverse, striking the silver Audi directly behind him. He rose just in time to see the gunman lurch toward the door. John flipped open the door, striking the gunman.

He shifted the FJ into drive and slammed the car in front of him. Shifting into reverse again, he turned his steering wheel and gunned the engine. Clipping the rear corner of the Audi, John's FJ scraped by the car and through the opening in the construction barricades, his passenger door shearing off in the process.

He slammed the brakes. His knuckles ached from gripping the steering wheel so tightly. Sweat streamed down his face, stinging his eyes. He wiped his forehead with the back of his hand and glanced out through the barricade, searching for the gunman. His front windshield exploded inward, sending shards of glass raining onto the seat and floorboards. The sedan driver was running directly at him, firing round after round into the front of his FJ.

John ducked, shifted into drive, and sped directly at his assailant until he heard the thud of metal hitting the man. The sedan driver's upper body flew over the hood of the truck, but quickly bounced back onto the ground in front of the FJ. John hit the brakes but couldn't stop before running over his assailant.

He sat in the driver's seat, blinking uncontrollably, his fingers digging into the steering wheel. His survival instincts finally overpowered the state of shock, and John drove again, skimming the inside of the construction barriers. The wind bathed his face as it rushed in through the smashed windshield and missing door. Eventually, he found another opening in the barricade and merged back into freeway traffic. The other drivers cut a wide berth for the damaged FJ and its bewildered driver.

John took the first off-ramp, making a series of turns to become lost in the maze of suburbia. He pulled onto a quiet side street, checking to see if anyone was following him. All clear. He pulled his broken truck to the curb, then slumped over the steering wheel trying to gather his thoughts. It was clear now that what had happened at his office was more than a simple theft. Someone was after his research and must have taken Jacob as well. But what were they looking for? With sudden clarity, John realized that he might have the answer.

47

He popped off his seatbelt and unzipped his jacket. His hands fumbled beneath his coat, searching for the file he had taken. It was there. John breathed a sigh of relief. The answers were inside, but he didn't dare stop here to read. He had to get somewhere safe. Somewhere no one would know to look for him. He thought for a moment and knew where he could go.

Before driving away, he reached under the front console, searching for something he had placed there recently. He located it and removed it from its hiding place. He stared down at the small container, no larger than an eyeglass case. It was a vial of his serum. Grasping it tightly, he realized that it was the only tangible part of his research he possessed.

I might need this.

He tucked it safely into his pocket.

In the distance, John heard the wailing of police sirens. If the authorities caught him, he would go to prison for taking the lives of two men. The thought of killing his assailants suddenly overwhelmed him. John leaned out the door and vomited onto the street. The convulsions came in waves until only clear bile ran from his mouth. John wiped his lips with the back of his shaking hand and sank back into the driver's seat.

He started his FJ and sped away, heading for the one place he knew he'd be safe.

Chapter Nine

August 18, 1:21 P.M.
Nassau, Bahamas

The FBI Sub-Office Nassau's area of responsibility includes the Bahamas and the United Kingdom Overseas Territories (Anguilla, Bermuda, the Cayman Islands, Montserrat, and the Turks and Caicos Islands). In other words, for a young, single agent, being assigned to this office was like winning the lottery. Beautiful people in minimal clothing enjoying the balmy climate was the picture of paradise. Unfortunately, yesterday had shattered those illusions.

A break-in at the field office, culminating with the murder of a field agent, had left the remaining team in shock. Things like that simply didn't happen here. Except it had happened, and Agent Rafael Hernandez had paid with his life. The reason for the break-in was unclear, but the murderer had accessed the Agency's restricted database. As if this weren't bad enough, it now appeared that the culprit was going to walk free.

Field Agent Gabriella Gutierrez paced the floor, shaking her head in disbelief as she listened to Agent-in-Charge Richard Spence give orders.

"Let me see if I understand this correctly," she said when he had finished. "We catch this scumbag who broke into the Sub-Office, accessed classified information — the nature of which we still don't know — and murdered a field agent, and we're just going to let him walk? We're the FBI for God's sake! We don't just let felons kill agents and then stroll off into the sunset!"

Fellow agent Charlie Waters sat quietly watching the situation unfold.

Spence sat upright in his seat. "That's enough, Agent Gutierrez. We are not just letting him walk out on his own. I already explained to you that the Secretary of Defense personally authorized the transfer of the subject to Mr. Shaw here. There will be no further discussion on the matter."

Gutierrez turned to Shaw, who listened while Spence reprimanded her. The bastard was smirking the entire time. She would have loved nothing more than to remove that smirk with the heel of her boot.

Gabby, as her friends called her, was small, standing just five-two, but she was as tough as they came. She had earned a reputation as a fighter by consistently demonstrating how physically punishing she could be. Whether it be fellow agents or criminals who had decided to test her mettle, she had never lost a fight.

Gabby sized up Shaw. Though he was tall — better than six feet by her estimate — he was thin and clearly on the wrong side of fifty. She knew she could snap him in two if she were given the chance. "What did you say your affiliation is with the Department of Defense, Mr. Shaw?"

"I didn't. That's need to know information. And you don't need to know," Shaw replied.

"I would just love to wipe that silly grin off your stupid face," Gabby said.

"Enough! One more word from you Gutierrez and I'll suspend you!" Spence shouted.

Gabby shot a look at Shaw, grabbed her coat, and stormed out of Spence's office.

Waters got up from his chair and followed her out the door. "Gabby, hold up," he said in his Southern drawl, jogging to catch up with his friend.

"Look, Charlie, if you have some words of wisdom for me, just save them. I'm not in the mood."

"Raffi was my friend, too, Gabby. Hell, he just had me over for dinner with his family last weekend," Waters said softly.

His words froze Gabby. In her anger about Agent Hernandez's murder and the subsequent events with Shaw, she had completely forgotten about her slain colleague's family. What would his wife Margaret and two daughters do without their husband and father?

"Sorry, you're right. My God, I can't imagine what Margaret and the girls are going through right now."

"Me either but getting suspended isn't going to help them. The best thing we can do is stay on duty and see if we can find more information about our pal back there," Waters said, jabbing his thumb in the direction of Spence's office.

Gabby looked up at Waters. He was tall and lean with a tussle of sandy brown hair on top of his head. He wore a crooked smile that always made Gabby giggle when she looked at him. If not for the suit he wore on duty, Waters was the quintessential good old boy from Texas. He was ruggedly handsome, and Gabby had, on more than one occasion, wondered what he was like between the sheets. A feeling she had never revealed to anyone.

"You're right, Charlie."

"Damn straight."

"What do you suggest, cowboy?"

"Let me check with a buddy of mine that works for DOD and see if I can get more information on Mr. Shaw back there. I get a feeling there's more to the story than we know."

Chapter Ten

August 18, 1:28 P.M.
Hamilton, Bermuda

Randall took advantage of the flight time to Bermuda to determine where he could find Jamie Edmunds, the woman from the MUFON case. It turned out that finding her hadn't been difficult. She worked for HAL Group, a local reinsurance company that occupied one of the many buildings overlooking Hamilton Harbor. What troubled Randall was how to approach her. Despite the long plane ride, he still hadn't decided. Now sitting in the waiting room of her office, he squirmed uncomfortably in his chair.

"Mr. Randall, Ms. Edmunds will see you now."

"Thank you."

Randall followed the secretary down the hallway to a nondescript office with an incredible view of the harbor.

"Ms. Edmunds?"

"Thank you, Jan." Jamie stood and walked around her desk with an outstretched hand. "Mr. Randall, pleasure to meet you. You said you needed assistance with a reinsurance issue with your company?"

Randall shook Jamie's hand. "Do you mind if I sit down?"

"Go right ahead." Jamie leaned back on her desk in a half sitting, half standing position; her dark brown eyes were quizzical.

"Ms. Edmunds, thank you for agreeing to see me. I wasn't exactly truthful when I called, but it was the only way I could get in to see you," Randall said, noting a change in her expression. "I'm not sure how to approach this, in fact, I've been struggling with what I would say to you the whole time I was on the flight." Randall looked to the floor, rubbing the back of his neck with his hand. He could feel her heavy gaze on him.

"My name is Nick Randall and I'm an archaeology professor from the United States and, well, this is going to sound kind of crazy, but I think I know what you're going through." Randall glanced up at Jamie, who was now looking at him very seriously.

"What's this about?"

Randall swallowed hard. "Ms. Edmunds, you live in a second-story apartment building with a bedroom window overlooking the ocean. If I'm not mistaken, you have blue, flower-patterned sheets and a Sony clock radio on the nightstand by your bed. You also have a small wooden desk in the corner of your room, with pictures of your family hanging on the wall. Your mom, dad, and sister, I believe."

"Is this some kind of joke? Are you stalking me?" Jamie strode behind her desk and picked up her phone. "I'm calling security."

"You were visited three nights ago, weren't you? It's come before. When it does, you're paralyzed. You can't move, scream, or make a sound."

Jamie froze in place, the phone stuck to her ear.

"Yes, Ms. Edmunds?" the receptionist asked.

"Never mind, Jan," Jamie hung up the phone. "Who are you and how do you know these things about me?" She was shaking now, tears forming in the corners of her eyes.

"Ms. Edmunds, I know this is difficult to understand, but I think we're connected psychically. I began having dreams a couple of months ago after I returned from a research trip to Peru. At first, I thought I was just having nightmares, but they seemed too real to be just bad dreams. The details were so vivid that I felt like I was actually experiencing them."

"The abductions?"

"Yes, it felt like I was looking through your eyes and living the experience with you. I think I can help you. I'm not sure how or why, but I believe I'm supposed to be here for you. Do you believe me?"

Jamie shook her head, tears streaming down her face now. "I don't know who you are, but if this is some kind of sick joke…"

"It's not. I promise."

Jaime grabbed a tissue and wiped her eyes.

"I just want to help you," Randall said, getting another tissue for Jamie.

"I don't even know you. Why should I trust you?"

"My research in Peru. I met similar creatures. I know they're real. You're not imagining them and you're not going crazy."

"But why are you here and why do you want to help me?"

"Because if I don't, the nightmares will never stop for me either. I'll have to experience your abductions every time, just like you do."

Jamie turned and looked out the window.

"Please, you can trust me."

"It's been so hard. At first, I thought I was just having nightmares, too, but they just wouldn't stop. The experiences were too real to be dreams. There was no one I could tell. I thought I was losing my mind," Jamie said, turning to face Randall.

"It's okay, Jamie, I understand. When did this all begin?"

"It started when I was in graduate school. I remember it like it was yesterday. I was living in an apartment by myself and was coming home late from the campus library. My group was working on a project. I was exhausted and just wanted to collapse with a glass of wine and maybe watch a little TV."

Randall nodded, maintaining eye contact.

"I remember dropping my purse and briefcase on the kitchen table, pouring the wine, and sitting on the couch. When I tried to turn on the television, all I could get was static. I thought the satellite service was down. All of a sudden, I got a bad headache and decided to turn in and get some rest. I changed, took some aspirin, and climbed into bed. I don't know if it was the headache or what, but I just couldn't sleep. I just lay there, tossing and turning..." Jamie paused, closing her eyes as if reliving the moment. She sighed and shook her head.

"It's okay Jamie, they're not here. Please, there might be something in the experience that could help us."

"I was just lying there. All of a sudden, I got the worst chill and this horrible feeling that I wasn't alone. There was this heavy feeling in my chest, like someone had placed a lead weight on me. I realized I couldn't move. I tried to yell, but my mouth wouldn't work. The only thing I could do was move my eyes. I looked toward the corner of my room, and that's when I saw it."

"What did you see?"

"Its face was completely smooth, and it had no mouth. Its eyes were cold and black, and its fingers were long and thin. I felt so helpless. After it touched me, I must have fallen asleep because when I woke up, I wasn't in my room anymore. I felt like I had been drugged—everything was foggy. It was like I was looking through smoke. I could see the outline of shapes and hear muffled noises but couldn't make out anything specific. There were several creatures hovering over me. I felt like a science experiment. The things they did to me…" Jamie's voice trailed off.

Randall stood and walked over to Jamie, who was now covering her mouth and shaking her head. Tears rained down her cheeks. He put his arm around her shoulder.

"It's all right. I'm here now, and nothing is going to hurt you again, I promise. Look at me. We're going to figure this out together. Okay?"

Jamie nodded, but kept sobbing.

"The first thing we need to do is figure out why they chose you and where they are. Do you have any ideas about that?"

"No."

"Well, I think I know someone who might be able to help us get some answers. I'm going to pay a visit to a friend of mine. Are you going to be okay?"

"I think so."

"Good, I'll be back later, and we'll go have dinner and figure out our next steps. What time do you get off from work?"

"I'll be off at six."

"Perfect. That will give me time to do some research. I'll see you here at six."

Jamie nodded. "Okay, Nick."

Chapter Eleven

Extending out into the sea like the end of an index finger on the far western side of the island of Bermuda sits the Bermuda Maritime Museum. Its location at the old Royal Naval Dockyard makes it easily accessible by ferry from Hamilton.

As the boat pulled in, Randall took in the beautiful, historic view. Featuring exhibits on the history of the island of Bermuda and its importance as a trade route between Europe and the new world, the museum was also home to an exhibit on shipwrecks of the area. In fact, it was precisely the number and condition of local wrecks that made it an ideal location for training young students on the fine art of systematic archaeological surveys of the reef systems. The area was also ideal to teach "would-be" archaeologists how to document, map, and test-excavate English shipwrecks from the late 18th and early 19th centuries.

Since it was summer, Randall knew that a fresh crop of students from the University of Rhode Island would make the museum their home for a session. He also knew that he would find his old friend Rob leading the course. What he didn't know was how he would be received once Rob learned the reason for his visit.

Randall walked briskly from the dock toward the museum. The architecture was a mixture of beautiful colonial-style buildings with large stone archways and a more modern structure that housed the museum itself. The entire campus was ensconced in the Fortress Keep of the old Royal Naval Dockyards. Stepping onto the property was akin to stepping back in time, something Randall appreciated. He quickly crossed the grounds and entered the museum proper. Then he approached the front desk, where a young man with jet black hair was stationed.

"Hello, I'm looking for Dr. Hoffman."

"Yes sir, and do you have an appointment with him?"

"No, I'm just an old friend and happened to be in the area. Is he leading the shipwreck program again this year?"

"Yes, he is. As a matter of fact, I believe he's out with the students right now. They should be by the lagoon prepping their gear for the next dive. Would you like me to have someone show you where they are?"

"That's okay, I know my way around. Thanks for the help."

Randall exited the building and was immediately greeted with the smell of the ocean. A warm trade wind caressed his face and for a moment he forgot why he was in Bermuda. It was good to escape, even for just a moment. He made his way down the sandy beach to the lagoon, the afternoon sun warm on his face. Just as the young man at the front desk had explained, Randall could see a group of fresh-faced college students by the water. SCUBA tanks, regulators, masks, fins, and wetsuits dotted the sand as the young archaeologists-in-training rigorously checked and double-checked everything to make sure all their gear was working properly. Off to one side of the group, Randall saw the familiar face of his old friend.

Rob was short and squat, his face like a round moon. His dark hair was cropped short and his legs and arms were tan from time spent in the sun and water. The scars on his hands conveyed the fact that this was a man used to working in rough conditions, but the smile on his face as he went about his work revealed a simple truth: Dr. Rob Hoffman loved what he did for a living. In fact, if you asked him, he would never call it work. Professor Hoffman was one of those rare individuals who had found his calling in life and spent each day doing what he was most passionate about. The paycheck was just a bonus.

"Making the kids do all of the work, I see."

Hoffman turned, recognizing the voice immediately. "Nick? How are you! What in the hell are you doing here, you old dog? Shouldn't you be in some dusty old library somewhere?" Hoffman's smile stretched across his broad face and his hand shot out to his old friend.

Randall couldn't help but smile back. "Someone's got to do the real archaeology work while guys like you splash around in the water."

Hoffman laughed out loud at the good-natured ribbing.

"It's great to see you, Nick, what brings you to Bermuda? Is this business or just a social call? If it's a social call, I have a special bottle of rum stashed away for just such an occasion."

"Same old Rob. I'm doing well, but evidently not as good as you. Hey, I was wondering if you have a few minutes to talk … but not around the kiddos here." Randall gestured to the students working behind him. His response drew a strange look from his friend.

"Sure, my guys can handle this. Let's head up to my place. Hey Sara and Roger, I'm heading up to the barracks for a minute with my friend here. Make sure the group finishes inventorying the dive equipment and stores it on the boat for the dive. I'll be back in about twenty minutes."

"Sounds good, professor."

"Come on, let's go."

The two men walked up the beach side by side making small talk, exchanging the usual questions about family and work. When they reached the barracks, Rob opened the door to the lower level corner unit, which served as his home.

"I have a feeling this isn't just a friendly visit."

"You're right, it's not. I don't know if you heard anything about my recent trip to Peru, but it's related to that ... and something that's come up since."

"I heard bits and pieces from Francisco, but he was pretty tight-lipped about the details. Sounds like things got a bit dicey. Sorry to hear about Mike, that's a real shame. He was a nice kid."

"Thanks, Rob. I spoke with his mom and it's been tough, I won't lie about that. I never in a million years would have imagined something like that happening during field research," Randall said, sadly recalling the day his graduate assistant Mike had died.

"I'm guessing maybe the official line about what happened wasn't the whole story."

"You're right again." Randall sighed and took a deep breath. For the second time today, he wasn't exactly sure what to say.

Sensing the uneasiness, Hoffman tried to break the tension. "Nick, we've known each other a long time. If there's something you need or something you have to tell me, just come right out and say it. We're both too old to be dicking around like undergrads here."

Randall smiled at his friend's candor. "Rob, how long have you been coming out here and teaching this summer class?"

"Seventeen years. Why?"

"In all those years, have you ever seen anything out of the ordinary? You know, something that looked out of place or some strange event that you couldn't explain?"

Rob's eyes narrowed. "Are you referring to something specific?"

"You tell me."

Hoffman sat back in his chair and looked around his small quarters. His glance fell to his desk and then returned to his old friend.

"Nick, I'm not exactly sure what you're referring to, but if you're talking about the lore of the Triangle, well, let's just say that after spending enough time here, some of the funny business you read about in the papers and see on television turns out not to be so funny. This area is known for some pretty funky weather and ocean patterns." Now it was Hoffman's turn to squirm uncomfortably.

Randall nodded and smiled.

"I can also tell you that I've seen a beautiful, sunny day turn to shit in a matter of hours. We've been caught in some pretty good soup a couple of times. One time was particularly hairy, and we needed to re-evaluate our program to keep from putting the students in harm's way. Is that what you were looking for?"

"Not exactly."

"Well, Nick, what exactly are you asking me?"

"Have you ever seen things out there that you just couldn't explain?"

"Such as?"

"Craft that you couldn't identify."

"You mean ships?"

"I mean ships, aircraft, underwater crafts, you name it."

"Are you referring to...?"

"UFOs. Rob. I'm asking if you've seen UFOs, or USOs I guess. I've read about unidentified craft under the water doing things that shouldn't be possible. At least doing things that are beyond the capability of any water craft we're aware of. Same thing with aircraft."

Hoffman sat back again and turned his gaze away from Randall. The genie was out of the bottle now, and Randall realized that there was no way to put it back in.

After several long moments of silence, Hoffman spoke again. "Nick, that's a really loaded question. We're supposed to be people of science and we both know how this kind of thing is viewed in professional circles. Hell, you almost didn't get tenure because of it. If it hadn't been for Francisco—"

"I don't need you to lecture me about the field, or who I do and don't owe my career to. We also both know that the science stuff is sometimes a load of crap and that many of our peers use it as a weapon to bludgeon people who don't agree with them. The scientific method tells us that the best way to prove a theory is by doing your best to disprove it. What's happening in this case is that our peers are simply shouting down researchers they don't agree with. How the hell is that being a scientist? So, with all due respect, save the sanctimonious bullshit about science."

Now it was Hoffman's turn to smile. "Why don't you tell me how you really feel?"

Randall laughed.

Hoffman scratched his head. "Okay, I see your point and you're right about the scientific community. Now, back to your question. But before I give you an answer, I need you to tell me two things. First, I want to hear what really happened down in Peru. Second, everything I say is off the record and, I swear buddy, if you ever tell anyone about our little conversation, I will publicly deny ever talking about this. Agreed?"

"Works for me. I was in Peru examining ruins near Arequipa. I had learned about the site from a local tribe in the area. Let's just say that the tribe's appearance was a little ... odd. We made multiple trips there to study them and I was finally able to convince them that I didn't want to desecrate their ancestral home. As it turned out, the guy who funded the trips was also interested in the ruins, or more specifically, he was interested in what was in them."

"Treasure hunter?"

"Not really. The ancient civilization that had inhabited the ruins was far too advanced for the time period and region. To put it bluntly, they had electricity and a power source to run it."

"Whoa, whoa, whoa. You're telling me descendants of an Iron Age civilization in the middle of the jungle had an electrical power plant and no one knew about it prior to your arrival? That's impossible."

"It gets better. Turns out that the inhabitants of this underground city were not indigenous people. In fact, I don't believe they were human."

"You actually met these ... creatures that inhabited this lost city?"

Randall pursed his lips and thought for a minute. "I believe I met them, but I'm not sure. It's a long story."

"So, you're not sure if you met them and you're also not sure if the city was actually occupied. Sounds like you're dealing with a bit of speculation."

"I know what you're thinking, Rob, but I believe the experience happened. Even if I don't have proof. One thing I know for sure is that I did see the city and it was real. Sam saw it, too."

"Okay, let's assume for the moment that you found the city and its inhabitants. What makes you think that they weren't indigenous to the area? They could have just been isolated geographically and evolved apart from other native tribes," Hoffman offered.

"I communicated with them, Rob."

"You spoke to these creatures?"

"No, I communicated with them telepathically."

"I see, and what about the guy who funded your trip?"

"His name was Frances Dumond and he was after their power source. He wanted to use it to power a satellite-based weapon system he was building to—"

"Take over the world?"

"Look, I know it sounds like a bad sci-fi movie, but it's the truth!"

"What happened to him?"

"He got away. And there's more to the story. The part about the volcano erupting was true, you probably read about that. But here's the thing. This civilization had learned how to harness the power of the volcano to create the energy they used for their city. They were really advanced, and they told me something else that I have only shared with Francisco."

"What was that?"

"They weren't the only ones visiting us."

"Come again."

"The creatures that I met and communicated with are not the only group to visit our planet. There are others."

"And you know this how?"

"The creatures told me about them. In fact, they warned me about them."

Rob turned away from Randall, nodding his head. A smirk formed on his face. "Let me get this straight ... you went down to Peru, met with some non-native tribe members who had electricity and an advanced power generating system. They talked to you—no wait, they communicated with you telepathically—and told you that they weren't the only alien creatures visiting Earth. There are others here who are up to something sinister. Then you stopped some psychopath who was trying to steal their technology, so he could take over the world and you decided to come and speak to your old buddy Rob about it. Does that about cover things?"

"Yes, except I haven't explained why I'm here yet."

"Right! Go ahead."

"I believe that these other creatures are somewhere nearby and have been abducting someone who lives here."

"Of course they have."

"Listen, you can give me as much crap as you like. But everything I've said is true, and you know what?"

"What?"

"I'm going to help this woman that these creatures have been taking and I'm going to stop them."

Randall sat back in his chair and folded his arms defiantly. Hoffman dropped his hands into his lap, shaking his head. The smirk had grown into a broad grin spreading across his entire face.

"Yes?" Randall asked.

"Nick, if anyone else in the world came in here and laid this story on me, I would have called the looney bin and asked them to send a couple of guys with butterfly nets to take them away. Funny thing is, I believe you. At least I think that *you* believe what you're saying is true. Let's assume that your story is accurate and there is some group of nefarious creatures lurking near Bermuda. What do you want me to do about it?"

"I need your help to find them. Their base must be nearby, and I figure if anyone knows this area and where they might be hiding, it would be you. I need your help to find these creatures, so I can help this poor kid who's being abducted. Besides, I want to know what they're up to."

"Geez Nick, is that all? I thought you were going to ask for something really big."

Randall ignored his friend's jab. "Will you do it, Rob? Will you help me?"

Randall watched as his old friend pondered the situation, a serious look on his face. He could only imagine what was going through his mind. After a few minutes, Randall pushed the issue.

"How about it, Rob?"

Hoffman stared into space, then looked his friend in the eyes. "I just don't know if I can. If I were to help you and word got out, I would probably lose my job."

"Look, I know I'm asking you to put your career on the line, but I'm telling you, I don't have any other options. Besides, Jamie is in trouble and if we don't help her no one will. Please Rob, I need your help."

Hoffman closed his eyes and sighed. "Can you give me some time to think about it?"

"Imagine for a minute that you're a young woman," Randall said, causing a raised eyebrow from Hoffman. "You're a thousand miles away from your family, living by yourself on an island. You're just getting started in your career, when one night, you can't sleep."

"Lots of people get insomnia," Hoffman said.

"I'm not finished. You're lying awake for hours when something terrible happens. You realize that someone or something is in your room. You try to escape or defend yourself, but you can't move. It's like you're paralyzed. Then this creature takes you and…"

"I get it I get it."

"That's what this poor kid is going through," Randall said, staring at Hoffman. "It's also what I'm going through."

Hoffman shot Randall a confused glance.

"For some reason, every time this woman goes through one of these episodes, I experience it with her. It's absolutely the most terrifying thing I've ever lived through."

Hoffman stared at the ground.

"Will you help me?"

"Do I have a choice?" Hoffman asked.

Randall smiled at his old friend. "Not really."

"Well then, I guess I'll help you. I'm not exactly sure how, but I'll do whatever I can. Where do we start?"

"I was hoping you might have some ideas. I know there's a lot of great big wide-open spaces out there, but I figure you've probably covered as much of it as anyone I know."

Hoffman sat back in his chair, his eyes darting up to the sky and back down, his arms now crossed on his chest. *He's accessing his memory files,* Randall thought.

After a few moments, Hoffman began nodding. "Yeah, I know where we can start. We can take the dive boat. When do you want to go?"

"Can we go tonight?"

"Boy, you really don't want to waste any time, do you? Can't see why not. Let me check the weather forecast to make sure we're not driving into the middle of a storm. Where can I reach you?"

"That's a really good question. Since I got here, I've been running around meeting people and haven't checked into a hotel or anything. Let me take your cell number and I'll give you a call in a couple of hours."

"You can bunk with me if you like. I have lots of space here."

"Sounds good, buddy."

"Anything else I can do?"

"Nope, I think that covers it. By the way, thanks. I know this is a lot to ask and my story probably sounds pretty crazy, but this is something I really need to do."

"Like I said, if it was anybody else, I'd give them the old stink eye, but we go way back, and if you need help, I'm here for you."

The two men stood and shook hands.

"By the way Rob, don't share this with anyone else."

"You mean I can't go out and tell my students and staff that I'm going alien hunting with an old chum? I don't think you need to worry about that," Hoffman said, grinning.

"Good enough. Talk to you in a couple of hours."

Chapter Twelve

August 18, 2:39 P.M.
Arlington, Virginia

John sat on the living room floor of Jacob's empty apartment, his back pressed against the wall and the open folder between his legs. His heart was still racing from the car chase, so he breathed deeply, trying to calm his nerves. He had ditched his truck several blocks away on a small side street, away from the main areas used by commuters. After hearing the sirens, he decided it was safer to walk to get to the apartment instead of parking his truck in front of the building.

God, they're looking for me! I'm wanted for murder!

The thought nearly caused him to wretch again, but John fought the urge to panic. He realized he couldn't go down that rabbit hole if wanted to get out of this mess. He had to focus on the information in the folder and was certain that the answers lay before him.

The apartment was devoid of anything but the blinds he had drawn after letting himself in. It was the apartment he had shared with Jacob while the two were students at Georgetown. After they started working and could afford it, John moved to his own place closer to work. Jacob, however, had stayed at the apartment with his fiancée Beth while they planned their wedding. They had just purchased a three-bedroom home, closer to Alpha Genetics, and had moved all their furniture. John was thankful he still had the key, knowing it would be a safe place to hide. Whoever was chasing him wouldn't know about his connection to the apartment since it was in Jacob and Beth's names now.

John closed his eyes, finally quieting the torrent of thoughts streaming through his mind. He opened the folder and began to read. It contained information about the patients he and Jacob had been working with at the lab. It also contained their research notes and, more troubling, a great deal of their personal information: checking accounts, addresses, names of friends and family members, and even restaurants they liked to frequent. It was information that only a few close people should have known. Whoever compiled this had clearly been studying Jacob and John for some time. But why?

Flipping deeper into the folder, John discovered a synopsis of a plan known as Project MK Ultra. A 1950s U.S. government covert operation, it involved experimenting with the behavioral engineering of humans through the CIA's Scientific Intelligence Division. What John read seemed like the plot from a thriller movie. Apparently, the program involved government scientists conducting experiments on unwitting American and Canadian citizens. The program utilized multiple methodologies to alter the subject's mental state including the use of LSD, sensory deprivation, hypnosis and, in some extreme cases, physical and mental abuse.

The scope of the project was breathtaking. Research occurred at 80 institutions, including 44 colleges and universities, hospitals, prisons, and pharmaceutical companies. The crux of Project MK Ultra, as outlined by the Supreme Court prior to the justices shutting it down, was "the research and development of chemical, biological, and radiological materials capable of employment in clandestine operations to control human behavior."

Suddenly the clouds parted, and John realized, with horror, that the government had been secretly funding his work. Still, he questioned how his father was involved.

Could this have something to do with what happened in Peru?

John pondered the situation further. His father had been very secretive about his research in Peru and what transpired on the expedition. He and Sam returned much closer than when they had left, resolving several years of conflict that had begun with the death of their mother. Sam had clearly forgiven their father during the trip, and it now appeared that the two of them were closer than John and his father.

A twinge of jealousy ran through John's mind as he sat on the floor of the empty apartment, his face contorted in a frown. He had served as the only link between Sam and his father for a couple of years, struggling to get them to reconcile. Now, they had repaired their relationship and it seemed like John was the odd man out. He set the file down and rubbed his eyes.

John finished reading the file and realized that he didn't have much time. He had to meet with his sister Samantha and find out what had really happened in Peru. He was hoping that the explanation would provide clues to explain his father's connection to recent events and help him find a way out. Meeting Sam would mean leaving the relative safety of the apartment and risking an encounter with his pursuers again, and with the authorities. But he had no choice. If he wanted answers he had to go, and hope that his face wasn't plastered on every news broadcast in town.

Forty-five minutes later, John arrived by taxi near his sister's home. For most of the ride, the news station broadcast a story about the murder of a man near a construction zone on the freeway. Police were still searching for clues, but eyewitnesses had reported a blue FJ Cruiser leaving the scene.

John paid the driver in cash and hopped out. He decided to enter through the yard of the neighbor whose house backed up to Sam's. That would prevent anyone staked out in front of her place from seeing him. John made his way down the quiet suburban street until he reached the fourth house from the corner. It was a brick colonial with white siding, black shutters, and a white wooden gate that provided access to the back yard. He decided that quick and confident was the best way to approach the situation. He strode quickly through the yard, grabbing the gate handle. It opened on the first try. John darted through and into the side of the yard.

He followed the long, straight concrete path into the back yard, which opened into a large green lawn. The landscaping was immaculate, with the grass abutting a large wooden porch with deep, brown rattan furniture, and a wrought-iron fire pit. John sprinted toward the wooden fence that separated the yard from Sam's. As he reached it, he heard clinking metal and then barking. John turned and looked just in time to see an enormous, black Doberman charging him.

John grabbed the top of the fence, pulled with all his strength, and jumped, catapulting his body up the fence until his belt came to rest on the top of the cedar planks. John teetered over the top of the railing, his torso in his sister's yard and his bottom half in the other yard. Suddenly, he felt a jerking pull on one pant leg—the dog had caught him. He struggled to pull his leg free, but the Doberman was too strong. John managed to wriggle his left leg over the fence, leaving only his right leg on the wrong side. The mass of the hound pulled his right leg down like a lead weight. John kicked at the dog, trying desperately to free himself.

When the dog opened its mouth to get a better grip, John yanked his leg hard. Hearing ripping cloth, his leg came free and he fell into Sam's backyard. He lay on the ground for a moment, the breath knocked out of him. Still winded, he scrambled to his feet, clambered over to a hedge, and collapsed on the ground behind it. Sweat poured down his face, as he lay there, hyperventilating. He was certain anyone watching Sam's house had heard the ruckus and would be coming to check at any moment.

After waiting for what seemed an eternity, he decided that no one was coming. He was safe and just had to wait for Sam to get home. About an hour later, Sam came through the front door and walked over to the slider overlooking the backyard. Prior to knocking, he checked to make sure that she was alone. She was.

The look on her face, was one of bemused wonder. Sam slid the door open. "John, what in the world are you doing in my backyard?"

"I know this looks weird, but I have to talk to you. Are you alone? Did you notice any strange cars parked out on the street?"

"Calm down. Yes, I'm alone, and no, I didn't see anything strange out front. What's going on and what happened to your pants?"

"Oh, that. Your neighbor's dog ripped them when I was climbing over your fence."

"Cupcake did that to you? Why were you climbing over my fence? Why didn't you just call and meet me when I got home?"

John steadied his nerves. "I need to know what happened to you and Dad in Peru. I know you left out a lot of details. Something happened, and Dad is in trouble and so am I."

"Dad's in trouble? What happened? We were supposed to meet for lunch today and I called him, but he didn't answer. His phone went straight to voicemail. Is he okay?"

"Slow down. Let's sit and talk."

John explained finding their father's house ransacked and the panicked call asking John to leave. He also told Sam about Jacob's disappearance and the incident at his work. Sam's eyes went wide, and she hung on every detail, her fingers nervously twirling her long brown hair.

"My God, John, you could have been killed! What are you going to do?"

"I don't know, but I think there's a connection between my research and Dad's trouble. I need to know what really happened in Peru. You and Dad weren't completely honest with me and I don't know why. Maybe you were trying to protect me, but now I can't afford to be in the dark."

Sam shifted uncomfortably. John could tell that she was struggling to decide whether to fill him in on all the details.

"Look, Sam. For a long time, I was your only connection to Dad and I always did my best to try and fix your relationship. Now that the two of you are close again, I feel like I'm being shut out."

Sam winced, letting John know he'd gotten his point across. Seeing the pain in his sister's eyes softened him.

"If not for me, then for Dad. We've just recently been able to put the past behind us and be a family again, and I don't want to lose that."

"Okay, you're right. So, you already know about Dad's research of the Capanhuaco tribe in the Amazon. He had finally convinced the tribe to take him to their ancestral home, and that's where he was last spring. Well, he and his team disappeared. Francisco called and asked me to lead a search party to find him and we did, but not before I was kidnapped."

"What? Who in the hell kidnapped you?"

"A man named Francis Dumond. He was the guy who funded Dad's trips, but Dad didn't know it was him. Dumond wanted something that Dad was looking for in Peru."

"What did he want?"

Sam took a deep breath. "A power source unlike anything known to man."

A look of confusion spread across John's face. "A power source in the middle of the Amazon? That doesn't make any sense."

"This is why Dad and I decided not to tell you. Dad was looking for an ancient civilization that lived underground in the Amazon, and he found it. But it turns out that this civilization was more technologically advanced than any other group in the region. Dad even thought they might not be human, but had interbred with some of the local tribes and taken on human traits. I was really skeptical about the whole thing, but after I met the tribe that led Dad to their ruins, I wasn't sure what to believe."

"Hang on. You met with this tribe? What was it about them that was so unbelievable?"

"The way they looked was … strange. And then there was the way they communicated with dad."

"Dad had a conversation with this tribe?"

"Not exactly. Dad said they communicated through telepathy. He believed that they were so advanced that they had moved beyond the need for speaking. They were the ones who told him that I was in trouble and what Dumond was doing."

John's eyebrow lifted at this revelation, but he wanted to know the rest of the story.

"So how did you and Dad get away?"

"Dumond had a partner who turned on him, and we escaped during a gun fight. We got out just before the volcano erupted."

"Are you talking about the eruption of El Misti in Arequipa?"

"Yep. We were there and so were these creatures, along with Dumond and his men."

"Geez, Sam! How could you guys have kept this from me?" John shook his head in disbelief, looking away from his sister.

"Sorry, Johnny, we thought we were doing the right thing. We thought the less you knew, the safer you'd be in case this Dumond character popped up again. We didn't mean to keep you in the dark. We were just trying to protect you."

John paced around the room, shaking his head, muttering under his breath. He finally cooled and walked back to Sam.

"I can't believe you guys didn't tell me about this."

Sam stared at the ground.

"I understand what you and Dad were trying to do, but if we're going to be a family again, you have to be honest with me," John said.

"You're right."

John walked over to a chair and sat down, contemplating what his sister had told him. Sam followed, taking a seat next to him.

"This may explain what's been happening to Dad and me."

"How?"

John removed the folder from his jacket and tossed it on the coffee table.

Sam wrinkled her nose. "What's that?"

"It's the reason Jacob disappeared and why these guys are chasing me. This folder contains information about a secret government program called Project MK Ultra. The CIA was experimenting on people without their knowledge, trying to see if mind control was possible. They had limited success but kept pursuing it. This is some serious stuff, and it was all illegal. The courts shut it down and the program ended in the 1970s. At least that's the public story."

"What do you mean?"

"I think the government continued the program in a different form. Do you know what Jacob and I were working on?"

"I know you were conducting psychological research on some new treatments for people with depression."

"Right, and the key to that therapy was the ability to target and erase specific, traumatic memories. We theorized that doing this would help people move past their grief, letting them live a normal, happy life. We began research to create a new drug that would interfere with the neurotransmitters that the brain uses to recall memories in the hippocampus and the frontal cortex."

"Remember, I'm not a neurobiologist," Sam said.

"Sorry. Newer memories are stored mostly in an area of the brain known as the hippocampus, while older memories are stored mostly in the frontal cortex. But recalling a memory involves both areas of the brain. Since a traumatic experience could have happened at any time in the past, we had to find a drug that would interfere with memory recall..."

"...in both parts of the brain at the same time," Sam commented.

"Right. We had a breakthrough about ten months ago in our lab. We developed a new compound that isolated the process in lab animals, but there was a side effect."

"What was it?"

"The drug caused temporary paralysis, but after a few hours, the paralysis subsided. Functional MRI showed that brain activity returned to normal.

"So, there was no damage?" Sam asked.

John shook his head. "And since there was no damage, we decided it was time to try the compound on a volunteer — Timothy Cobb — to gather data for a full clinical trial. He was suffering from severe depression brought on by a traumatic event he'd suffered years ago. We explained how we believed the drug worked and the possible side effects, and he was willing to try it."

"How did it go?"

"We discovered that the memory was only temporarily erased. But that's not what was interesting about the trial."

"What do you mean?"

"When the drug was administered, we discovered an unexpected side effect, one that we couldn't have detected in a non-human subject."

"Which is?"

"Mr. Cobb became very susceptible to suggestion."

"What exactly do you mean?"

"We could control his behavior."

"How did you find that out?"

"Mr. Cobb became non-communicative when we administered the drug and we were worried that he'd suffered some sort of synaptic damage. We told him to blink his eyes twice if he could hear us and he did. Then to check if other extremities were still working, we told him to wiggle the toes on his right foot and he did that too. It took us a while, but after several sessions, we realized that there was no paralysis involved with the use of the drug. He was simply waiting for external direction before taking action."

"You mean anyone under the effects of the drug was like a robot, waiting to be told what to do?"

"Yes. We had misinterpreted the results with the lab animals. They appeared to be paralyzed because they were waiting for someone to tell them what to do. Since we couldn't communicate with them, they just sat there."

Sam wrinkled her face. "That's creepy, John."

"I know. Jacob and I realized the potential ramifications of this. Basically, we had created a mind control substance and, if it fell into the wrong hands, who knows what they would do."

"What did you do?"

"We kept it under wraps, while we tried to develop a drug to block the mind control properties. We stonewalled Dr. Monroe, the senior partner who reviewed our work, but eventually he called a meeting with us because we weren't providing progress reports. He asked to arrange a meeting with one of our subjects and wanted to sit in on a session. He was ready to pull us off the project and hand it over to other researchers if we didn't. We had no choice but to let him know what was going on. That's when strange things started happening."

"Like what?"

"We started seeing unfamiliar faces at the lab and in our offices. Including military officials. They denied us access to parts of the lab and even some of our own research files. Jacob became worried about the military getting their hands on our research and tried to convince me to steal the files from the company."

"What did you tell him?"

"I told him I wanted to finish the project. We had just synthesized a compound to block the mind control effects of our new drug and I thought we would have a better chance of controlling the situation if we stayed directly involved. That's when Jacob became withdrawn. He only talked to me when he had to and stopped returning my calls. Now he's disappeared, and I feel guilty as hell." John put his head down.

Sam spoke quietly. "John, there's no way you could have known what was going to happen. You can't blame yourself."

"Maybe, but I think it's pretty clear that Jacob was right."

"What you're telling me explains what happened to you, but it still doesn't explain how Dad is involved."

"That's because I left one thing out, something I found in this file. According to official government records, Project MK Ultra started in the early 1950s, but it was preceded by a well-known event that might explain Dad's involvement."

"What are you talking about?"

"Roswell."

"You mean the city in New Mexico where the UFO supposedly crashed?"

"Yes, the alleged alien crash in Roswell in 1947. Project MK Ultra is a result of that incident."

"How? I thought the government said the Roswell incident was just a weather balloon experiment that went wrong."

"That was their cover story, but, according to this file, there was an alien vessel that crashed into that farm. The government moved in, took the debris and the crew of the vessel, and started conducting experiments. One of the soldiers who encountered a surviving crew member exhibited a temporary state of paralysis when the creature touched him. It was only temporary, but the incident scared the hell out of the military, so they started conducting experiments on the creature. They discovered that the alien secreted a clear, gel-like substance from its fingertips that caused the soldier's temporary paralysis."

"But it wasn't paralysis."

"Right. The substance produced a hypnotic state, under which the soldier became susceptible to influence. The military collected as much of the gel as possible before the creature died and tried to recreate it in the lab but failed. That was the start of Project MK Ultra, and I believe that the government has been trying to recreate that chemical. I think Jacob and I were unknowing participants in the project. When they discovered that we had been able to replicate the effects of the alien secretions, they stepped in to take it."

"But why go after Dad?"

"If the military knew that Dad had been in contact with similar creatures in Peru, they probably wanted to see what he knew. He could also lead them to the creatures, so they could collect more of the mind control gel from them. By snatching Dad, they would have a backup plan for the drug we created. And if they came after Dad, then they'll probably come after you."

"Great."

"Sorry, Sam, but I thought it would be better if you heard it from me."

Sam paced the floor, nervously strumming her fingers on her leg. She made a lap around her living room and returned to John's side.

"Do you know where Dad is now?"

"I was hoping you might know."

"I haven't heard from him for a few days."

"I don't think it's safe here. If the government is looking for us, we need to get out of here as soon as we can."

"Where should we go?"

"We need to find Dad. And I think I know where we can start looking."

Chapter Thirteen

August 18, 3:02 P.M.
Tagomago, Balearic Islands

Francis Dumond's estate sat perched on a hilltop, spilling down into a v-shaped canyon overlooking the Mediterranean Sea. Set on the northwest tip of the small, private island, the property sprawled over several lush acres of prime real estate — land that would have fetched a small fortune on the open market. The exquisitely manicured grounds — featuring three pools, a fountain, an English rose garden, and a hedge maze — displayed the enormous wealth of its owner.

Dumond stood on the veranda outside his office, basking in the balminess of the summer sun. He closed his eyes and exhaled deeply, releasing the tension that weighed upon his sculpted shoulders. While not an overly muscular man, Francis Dumond was strong and wiry, a by-product of his penchant for martial arts training. He had discovered long ago that physical strength and discipline resulted in a strong mind, which he needed as the owner of a multinational energy consortium. His industry was filled with captains of industry, ruthless men who forged empires based on the strength of their iron wills. Competing with such men required mental fortitude and the ability to smile in the face of danger.

Dumond fit the profile. He relished matching wits with the brightest business men in the world and rarely lost. Which only made his dilemma with Nick Randall even more difficult to comprehend. Having been on the brink of obtaining a power source unlike anything known to man, only to have it snatched away by Randall and his brood was more than he could take.

His watch alarm quietly alerted him that he had a meeting in five minutes. Dumond took one more deep breath, opened his eyes, and smiled at the turquoise waters lapping at the rocks below. Walking back to his desk, he took a seat in his high-backed executive chair and pressed the intercom button on his phone.

"Is he here?" Dumond asked his secretary.

"Yes, Mr. Dumond. He arrived several minutes ago. Would you like me to send him in?"

"Please."

Dumond sat back in his chair, folded his hands across his lap, and trained his steely gaze on the door to the office. A moment later, it opened and a short man, who wore pants with torn knees, entered the room. Dumond studied him as he took a seat opposite his desk. His clothes were rumpled, and his face was smudged with dirt. The man reeked of sweat and had a large lump on head. His eyes darted back and forth between Dumond and his own lap as he nervously rubbed his hands on his legs.

"You and your associate failed to eradicate my problem," Dumond said.

"It wasn't our fault … someone showed up right when we caught him and…"

Dumond leaned forward. "I don't tolerate excuses."

"It's not an excuse!" The man squealed. "This guy was highly trained, probably ex-military."

"I hired you do to a job and you accepted the terms. My accountant tells me that the funds were deposited into your account. This was a simple business transaction and you failed to live up to your end of the bargain."

"Please, Mr. Dumond, if you give me another chance, I know I can finish the job. Whoever was protecting Randall can't guard him all the time. I just need a few more days and I promise you…"

"I don't have a few more days. Your services are no longer required," Dumond said, pushing another button on his intercom.

The rumpled man turned at the sound of the door opening and flinched upon seeing three burly men file into the room. Two walked to opposite sides of him, while the third positioned himself behind his chair. His eyes wide, he turned to face Dumond.

"Please, you can't!"

"Escort this gentleman out," Dumond said to his guards.

In unison, the three grasped the seated man, yanking him to his feet. They dragged him to the door.

"Please, I have a family!"

"You should have thought about that before you failed to complete your assignment."

The guards hauled the man from the office, slamming the door behind him. Dumond smiled as he heard the man's wailing. He had earned his fate, and Dumond was happy to oblige in providing it. His smile faded, though, as his thoughts turned to Nick Randall. Once again, the professor had eluded him.

How could Randall have beaten him again? It seemed that the professor had an uncanny ability to remain one step ahead of him, despite his planning and resources. Realizing that the ordeal had alerted Randall to his intentions, Dumond knew he had to act immediately if he were to get his revenge. But how? Randall had surely gone underground after the attempt on his life, so finding him wouldn't be easy. His only chance was to draw the professor out of hiding by attacking his weakness.

Opening his drawer, Dumond retrieved his file on the professor. Randall had two children, his daughter Sam and a son named John. He could change his scheme to abduct Sam, but he decided against it. What he had planned for Samantha Randall was too good to change and it was something that only he could do himself. His heart fluttered at the thought of his scheme to repay Samantha Randall for her part in ruining his plan to attain the power source he had sought. *I'll enjoy taking my time with her*, he thought, smiling at the prospect of hearing her beg for mercy.

That left John. He flipped through the information his people had compiled on Randall's son. Apparently, the young man was quite bright. He worked for a company called Alpha Genetics, a bio-tech outfit near Tyson's Corner in Alexandria. It appeared he was creating a drug to erase memories. *Such a drug might prove useful in future ventures.* He would abduct John Randall and hold him hostage to lure his father out of hiding. In the process, he would steal John's research and synthesize the compound for his personal use. Kill two birds with one stone, as the saying goes.

"Get me Ms. Seivers on the line," Dumond said into his intercom.

"Yes, Mr. Dumond."

He had to notify his associate Margaret Seivers about the failed attempt on Randall's life. The only female member of the Alliance, Dumond's business partners on this project, Margaret held a critical role as the buffer between Dumond and the other partners. As such, she would update them about Randall. Although Dumond would have to tell her that he had failed, he'd keep his plan to abduct John to himself. She hadn't been overly enthusiastic about killing Randall in the first place, so it was doubtful she'd approve of kidnapping his son. Although the professor had cost the alliance partners dearly, Margaret had simply written it off as a business loss. A far kinder response than Dumond had in mind.

"Her line is busy, Mr. Dumond. Would you like me to hang up and call her back later?"

"No, put the call through to me. I'll leave her a message."

Chapter Fourteen

August 18, 6:02 P.M.
Hamilton, Bermuda

When Randall returned to Jamie's office, he found her nervously pacing. When he softly called her name, she flinched. After he apologized for startling her, he explained the plan and asked if she wanted to go on the boat with them. Jamie jumped at the offer, forgoing the chance to get dinner first.

Taking a cab to the landing, the two caught a late ferry back to the Maritime Museum. Thirty minutes later, they walked to the Keep and spotted the dive boat.

"Over this way. I see Rob," Randall said.

"Are you sure we can trust your friend?"

"Absolutely. Rob and I go way back. We were roommates in college and worked together at the university for years. He knows this area better than anyone and he also knows about my past research. He's probably one of the most open-minded people you'll meet."

"Okay, if you say so. This has all just happened so fast. I mean, this morning I didn't even know you, but for some reason, I trust you."

"Once I introduce you to Rob, I'm sure you'll feel the same about him."

The two trudged the final few feet to the dock and found Hoffman leaning over a small electrical device.

"Ready to shove off, Captain?" Randall asked.

"Oh, hey Nick, glad to see you. I was just entering the coordinates into the GPS. Give me a minute," Hoffman replied, punching the keys on the Garmin.

Finished, he looked up at his guest. "Who do we have here?"

"Rob Hoffman, this is Jamie Edmunds."

"Pleasure to meet you," Hoffman said, tipping his ball cap.

"It's nice to meet you, Dr. Hoffman. Thank you for your help."

"Please, call me Rob. Any friend of Nick's is a friend of mine. Now if you two will excuse me, I need to finish storing some of the gear. We'll be ready to go in a few minutes."

Hoffman disappeared into the hold of the ship, leaving Randall and Jamie on the deck. The sun was slowly dipping toward the horizon, casting a beautiful pink hue across the western sky.

"Red skies at night, sailor's delight," came a voice from the stairs. Hoffman reappeared on the deck. "Are you two ready to do some exploring?"

"Ready as we'll ever be," Randall replied.

"Nick, untie the rope at the stern for me and I'll get the rope at the bow."

Hoffman slowly throttled the engine and the boat slipped away from the dock, smoothly gliding out to sea. Randall looked at Jamie and sensed her tension. She was standing at the rail of the boat, gazing out over the water. She looked stiff and her mind seemed far away—almost as if she was recounting some long-lost memory. Randall decided to give her some space. Seeing Rob by the boat's controls, he made his way over to his friend.

"Where are we going?"

"There's a little spot northeast of here that I've taken my students to survey the wreckage of a galleon. It's one of the most intact specimens I've ever seen. Just a perfect setting for these kids to get their feet wet surveying a site."

"Why that particular site?"

Hoffman removed his cap and scratched his balding head. He seemed confused by the question, which seemed odd. After a long moment, he responded. "Nick, I wasn't completely honest with you earlier today. Remember how I mentioned that I'd had one trip that was kind of rough and had to make some changes to my program afterward?"

"Yeah."

"Well, it wasn't the weather that was the problem."

"Go on."

"It was the third group I'd taken to this spot. The first two trips went perfectly. We had great weather and the ship was well preserved. Anyway, we'd been at the site for about two hours and were setting up the grid lines for the salvage survey when something happened."

Randall shifted, watching Hoffman's eyes as he relayed the story.

"One of my students spotted something in the ocean off in the distance. At first it just looked like a small disturbance in the water."

ROBERT RAPOZA

"Like an underwater structure causing water displacement? A reef or submerged rock formation?" Randall asked.

"Exactly. I didn't think much of it and we just kept working. The thing is, this disturbance was moving. It kept getting closer and closer to the boat. A couple of the students noticed it and started getting nervous, but I acted like it was no big deal. I was trying to keep them calm, but to tell you the truth, I had the worst feeling," Hoffman said, steering the boat as he spoke.

"What was it?"

"I told the students we had gotten a weather update and were expecting a thunderstorm and needed to head back in. One of my graduate students, Gary, who'd been with me on the other trips, saw through my white lie. Once we got the students out of the water, he came over and asked what was wrong. That's when it happened."

"What happened?"

At first, Hoffman didn't answer, but the look he wore told the whole story. The color had drained from his face, the normal twinkle in his brown eyes replaced by a cold, distant stare.

"Rob, tell me what happened. I won't think you're crazy."

Hoffman shook his head. "The disturbance in the water ... it started to move faster. I increased our speed and it adjusted as well. I made some quick turns to see if I could shake it, but it matched everything I did. It was following us."

"Did you get a look at it?"

"At first it kept its distance, like it was tailing us. By now, everyone on the boat had seen it and they were starting to panic. Then the thing just closed in on us like we were standing still. Whatever it was, it moved quickly and silently, and it was huge—the length of a football field. I could see pulsating, colored lights under the water as it got closer. It came within

92

fifty feet of the boat and then suddenly dove straight down and disappeared."

"What did you do?"

"I radioed the coastguard station and gave them the details. They said they would send someone out to meet me to get a full report."

"Did they?"

"When we pulled back into the dock, there were three guys waiting to talk to us. Two of them pulled my students aside and the other one escorted me back to my office. I can't be sure, but I think they were military."

"Why do you say that?"

"All three of them had short-cropped hair and their demeanor was all business. The guy I spoke with was a tall, gray haired fella. He was an older guy, very full of himself. He told me that we had seen a secret submarine prototype and that I wasn't to discuss the situation with anyone or I could face criminal charges. I tried asking questions, but he just cut me off. He was a real piece of work."

"Did you get a name?"

Hoffman shook his head. "The next day, I was called into the provincial authority's office and was told, in no uncertain terms, that if I wanted to keep coming back here to teach my class, I was never to go back to that place again. Hell, they wouldn't even let me go back and get the equipment we had set around the shipwreck. We had some expensive gear down there."

"Were you able to get any more information from anyone?"

"I asked a couple of guys I know, but when I brought it up, they became really uneasy and wouldn't talk to me. They said they could lose their jobs or worse if they were even seen speaking to me. I'm a hardheaded man, you know that, but I eventually got the message. I had to either let this thing go or I could kiss my program goodbye and maybe even end up in the clink."

"So, when I visited you earlier today…"

"In a way, it was a relief, but at the same time, it was like reopening an old wound. Damn it, Nick, the whole thing didn't sit right with me. Maybe it's my age, but I don't like people telling me its steak when I know it's a shit sandwich. Something's going on out there and some pretty powerful people don't want anyone to know about it. That's not right, and I'm not about to let sleeping dogs lie, especially when it affects some nice kid like her." Hoffman nodded in Jamie's direction. She was still gripping the side rail and staring out to sea.

"That's how I feel, too. Jamie has been through something terrible, and who knows how many other people are experiencing the same thing."

"So, what exactly happens to you when she has her visitors?"

Randall glanced over a Jamie, then back at Hoffman. "At first, it feels like a nightmare, but then it gets too real to just be a dream. I can feel what she's feeling, and I know what she's thinking."

Hoffman's eyes went wide.

"After what I went through in Peru, I knew my life had changed, but I just didn't know what I had to do next. Now I do and I'm glad you're here to help," Randall said.

Hoffman's expression softened, and he cracked a smile. "God help you if you're coming to an old dog like me for help."

"Well, they say that the good Lord looks after fools and drunks. Guess we're the former."

Chapter Fifteen

August 18, 8:51 P.M.
North Atlantic Ocean

Stars twinkled like tiny Christmas lights dotting the night sky. The air was crisp and clear, but the nearly moonless night made seeing into the distance a challenge. Randall strained his eyes, but all he could see was the open ocean.

"How much longer before we get there, Rob?"

"About ten minutes. We're getting close to the spot now. How's our girl?"

Randall glanced toward the side of the boat where Jamie stood facing out to sea. She had barely moved since they left the dock. He had tried engaging her in conversation, but she had been reticent.

"Not much of a change since we pulled out. I'm worried about her. Poor kid has no idea what's been happening to her and now she's out here in the middle of nowhere with a couple of old farts telling her everything's going to be alright," Randall replied.

"Speak for yourself, buddy! I'm still a spring chicken!"

"You keep telling yourself that, Dr. Hoffman."

"On a serious note, what are we going to do if we find what we're looking for? As you so delicately pointed out, we're just two old guys and a young lady. I'm not sure we can take on a bunch of creatures from another planet if it comes down to a good old-fashioned street fight."

"Let's cross that bridge when we come to it."

The words had barely left his lips when Randall heard a faint noise coming from behind the diving boat.

"Do you hear that?" he asked.

"Yeah, sounds like a boat motor," Hoffman replied, scanning the water.

"Someone out for a cruise?"

"I doubt it. Most sailors from these parts like to travel during the day, and if they're out on the water at night, they tend to hug the coastline."

"It's getting louder," Randall said.

"Take the wheel." Hoffman hurried to the aft of the boat and removed a tarp draped over a large cylindrical object. Randall realized it was a searchlight. Hoffman swung the light up and turned on the power. The darkness parted as a bright beam swept out across the waves.

"Sounds like it's coming from the starboard side, off that way," Randall said, pointing off the side of the ship.

Hoffman slowly brought the searchlight around and spotted a vessel closing fast on their boat. "Who the hell is that?"

A cracking sound emanated from the distance as small plumes of water danced around the diving boat. It took Randall a moment to realize what was happening.

"They're shooting at us!"

The cracking noise returned. Some of the bullets finding their mark, striking the hull of the boat.

"Shit! Nick, kill the running lights!" Hoffman turned off the spotlight and ran to Randall as Jamie joined them.

"What's going on?" Jamie asked.

"I don't know, but we have to try and lose them," Hoffman answered.

"Where's the nearest harbor?" Randall asked.

"Back where we came from, three hours that way," Hoffman gestured with his thumb. He banked the boat hard to port, making a straight line directly away from the pursuing speedboat. "If they don't have sonar, we might be able to get away."

"What if they do have sonar?" Randall asked.

"Then we're out of luck."

The dive boat jumped up and down in the waves, the increased speed causing it to bounce on the choppy seas. Randall strained to hear the pursuing ship over the sound of their own motor, which roared under full load. He could still make out the sound of the other boat, growing louder. It was gaining on the dive boat.

"What kind of ship did it look like?" Randall yelled over the sound of the motor.

"I dunno, but it's definitely bigger than ours," Hoffman replied.

The gunfire returned. Randall could hear small, mosquito-like sounds whip past his ears.

"Jamie, get down!" Randall yelled, pulling her to the deck of the ship.

"I'm sorry I got you into this, Nick!" Jamie cried.

"It's not your fault! To be honest, these guys might be after me!"

"You? Why?"

ROBERT RAPOZA

"I had a run-in with a crazy guy in Peru. It's a long story!"

"You'll have to share it with me sometime!" Jamie managed a thin smile.

"They're getting closer, Rob!"

"Jamie, take the wheel, I have an idea!" Hoffman said.

"Okay." Jamie replied, popping next to him.

"Have you ever driven a boat before?"

"When I was younger, my dad took me out a few times."

"Great, here's the throttle. When I give you the sign, throttle down and then kill the engine. After that, head back to the searchlight and get ready to turn it on when I tell you."

"What's the sign?" Jamie asked.

"I'll blink my flashlight twice from the back of the boat," Hoffman replied.

"Right!"

More gunfire raked the air around them. Several rounds crashed into the deck, sending shards of wood and fiberglass everywhere.

"Nick, come with me!"

The two men raced across the deck and into the hold of the ship.

"What are we doing?" Randall asked.

"Grab a wet suit and get dressed!"

"This is no time to go diving!"

"We're not diving, old buddy, but we'll need the suits to keep buoyant in the water."

Randall grabbed a suit, trying to dress by flashlight. The beam weaved up and down crazily as the boat bounced on the choppy ocean.

"Okay, now grab two of those air tanks and follow me up to the deck."

The two men scurried onto the deck, tanks in hand. Randall could see that Hoffman had also grabbed tanks and a heavy

98

pipe wrench as well. Hoffman moved to the back of the boat and Randall followed closely. They set the tanks down near the rear ladder, which lead down to the small deck in the back of the boat. Hoffman turned and flashed his light twice to Jamie, who followed orders and killed the motor. The dive boat quickly came to a standstill.

"I hope you know what you're doing," Randall said.

"Trust me. When I get down the ladder, hand me the tanks one at a time."

Hoffman turned and climbed down the ladder. Randall handed down the first tank, which Hoffman set on the diving deck directly above the water. Although he couldn't see their pursuers, he could hear the engine getting louder. They were quickly closing in on them.

"Rob, I'm by the searchlight!" Jamie shouted.

"Great. There's a big switch on the side, do you see it?"

"Yes!"

"Okay, when I tell you, flip the switch and point it right at the other boat. Nick, climb down here with me."

Randall climbed down the ladder and stood next to Hoffman and the four air tanks. Hoffman was loosening the valves on each tank. The engine of the other boat was louder now, and Randall could make out the image of the ship. They were no more than a hundred yards out.

"Better hurry, those guys are almost on top of us!"

"I'm counting on that," Hoffman said as he lowered himself into the water. "Okay, I'm going to need you to come into the water with me. We're going to lower one tank at a time into the ocean. You'll need to hold it in place for me because it won't float by itself. Keep the valve on the deck and hold it up."

"What are we going to do with the tanks?"

"We're going to give those boys in that other boat a big headache if I can help it," Hoffman replied, raising the wrench above the valve of the first tank in the water.

The pursuing boat moved closer and slowed. Randall could hear voices on the deck and the sound of metal clicking. A light from the pursuing boat flashed on, bathing Randall and Hoffman in light.

"Now, Jamie!"

Jamie flicked the switch and the searchlight came to life. She carefully aimed the beam directly at the opposing boat. The intense beam struck the eyes of their pursuers, causing temporarily blindness. Randall could hear cursing from the men.

"Hold it steady, Nick!"

Hoffman brought the wrench down on the loose valve, sheering it off from the tank, which launched like a torpedo at their pursuers. It glanced off the side of their boat and careened off into the murky water.

"Next tank!"

Randall dragged a second tank into the water. He could see the men on the other boats regaining their sight and training their guns on them. Hoffman raised the wrench and struck a heavy blow on the valve just as a hail of gunfire splattered the water around them. The second tank raced across the water directly at the other boat, the escaping gas creating a rooster tail as it sped toward its target.

"Get another tank, Nick!"

The second tank narrowly missed the other boat, but Randall could see men looking down into the water as it passed.

"They're trying to damage our hull!" a voice yelled from the other boat. More gunfire crackled in the night as bits of fiberglass splattered around the back of the boat. Jamie screamed.

"Are you okay?" Randall asked.

"I think so!"

The spotlight spun wildly in the night air. Jamie tried to regain her footing just as a large wave passed underneath the boat. She was temporarily lifted into the air and then unceremoniously slammed into the deck. Randall and Hoffman fared no better. The two remaining air tanks spilled into the inky water as the two men clung to the ladder on the rear deck.

"Crap, we lost the tanks!" Randall yelled.

Turning, he looked for Hoffman, but saw only crashing waves.

"Rob!"

Randall searched frantically, but Hoffman was nowhere to be found. He considered diving beneath the waves to search for him but was pulled back to his own tenuous situation by angry voices shouting in the darkness.

"Get into the Zodiac and get them! Dumond wants Randall alive!"

"Jamie are you alright!"

No response.

"Jamie, talk to me! Are you there?"

"I'm okay, Nick, but my head…"

Randall heard the high-pitched whine of a small motor growing louder. They were coming for him and would be there soon.

"Jamie, I need a light! Rob's gone, and I need to find him!"

There was only silence.

Randall scrambled onto the boat, hoisting his battered body from the water. The sound of the motor continued growing louder. They were closing in. Randall climbed the ladder and found Jamie curled up on the deck.

"Jamie!" Randall lifted her head gently from the wooden deck. He could faintly see a dark streak coming from her forehead. "Jesus, what am I going to do?"

Jamie stirred, groaning and lifting her hand to her injury.

"Nick! Where the hell are you?"

Startled, Randall turned toward the back of the boat.

"Rob is that you!"

"Yeah, get your ass back here!"

Randall set Jamie back down gently. "Hang in there."

He hustled back to the ladder and looked down into the water. Hoffman was clinging to the back step with one hand and holding a cylinder in the other. Randall raced down the ladder and grabbed the tank.

"Thought I lost you!"

"Come on, we got one more shot here."

The searchlight streamed to life again. Jamie having regained her footing. She aimed it directly at their pursuers.

Randall steadied the tank and Hoffman raised the heavy wrench; the small Zodiac was a mere twenty yards away and bearing down on them. Hoffman dropped the wrench on the valve and the tank launched through the water, narrowly missing the small inflatable craft. The men in the Zodiac turned instinctively as the sound of rushing air and water streaked by their boat. Randall strained his eyes to see the water-borne missile surging through the darkness. It closed in on the larger ship and Randall heard a loud crashing sound followed by the sound of men's voices shouting.

"They hit us! Get your asses back here!" a voice boomed through the darkness.

"Let's get out of here!" Hoffman yelled, hauling himself out of the water and up the ladder. Randall followed close behind, glancing back to see the Zodiac returning to the larger vessel.

"Nick, help Jamie!"

Rob started the dive boat's motor and slammed the throttle as far down as it would go. The boat surged forward.

Randall found Jamie hunched against the side of the boat, having turned off the searchlight. She was holding her head.

"You're bleeding, I need to find the first aid kit."

"I'm okay. But please stay with me." Jamie grasped his hand.

"I'm not going anywhere."

The boat raced through the darkness, bouncing up and down on the choppy ocean surface. Randall looked back over his shoulder, checking to see if they were being followed. After a short while, Rob killed the engine, stopping the boat. Randall listened for the sound of the other craft approaching. There was nothing. They were alone again. He looked up to see Hoffman jogging over to them as they sat against the side railing.

"I think we lost them. Jamie are you alright?"

"I'm fine, thank you for asking."

Hoffman knelt. "You have a nasty cut on your head, we better get you back home."

"Who were those men?" Jamie asked.

Randall and Hoffman shared a look.

Randall sighed. "By the sound of it, Dumond's men. Looks like we have something else to contend with."

Hoffman glanced at his watch. "It's getting late. I think we'd better get back home and figure out what we do next."

Randall nodded. Hoffman walked back to the steering wheel, started the motor, and put the engine into drive. No one spoke on the way back to the dock.

Chapter Sixteen

August 19, 4:41 A.M.
Hamilton, Bermuda

They returned to the marina as the moon hovered above the horizon, the darkness of night still heavy in the sky. Randall dragged his aching body up the front path, following Hoffman to his room while Jamie trailed at a short distance. Randall struggled to stay upright, longing to fall into bed and sleep. He pulled up next to Hoffman, who had stopped a few feet short of the door to pull his keys from his pocket. As Hoffman turned the tumbler of his door lock, Randall noticed that the front window was open.

"That's funny, I thought that was closed when we left," Randall said.

Hoffman pushed the door inward. The lights snapped on. The sudden brightness stung his eyes. "What in the..."

"Where's Nick Randall?" a male voice demanded.

"What's going on here?" Randall said, pushing his way past Hoffman.

As he entered the room, he placed his body directly between his friend and the intruders. He made out the shapes of two figures standing in Hoffman's room, but the light prevented him from seeing their faces. "I don't know who you are or what you want, but Dr. Hoffman has nothing to do with this," Randall said.

"Dad?"

His eyes finally adjusting to the brightness in the room, Randall squinted toward the figures. He finally recognized them. "John? Sam? What are you doing here?"

"We could ask you the same thing," John replied.

Randall sighed in relief.

"Rob, I think you remember Sam and John."

"Sure, Sam and Johnny! How you kids been?" Hoffman reached out and shook hands with John then turned to hug Sam.

"We've been fine, Dr. Hoffman, thanks for asking. So, I see my dad dragged you into his little adventure," John said, casting a sideways glance at his father.

"How did you kids find me?" Randall asked, hugging Sam and then John.

"I still have the password for your online credit card account. I checked recent transactions and found charges to a paid website for UFO research, so I logged into that site and found your search history. That led us here," John said.

"How were you able to see my searches on that site?" Randall asked.

"You used the same user name and password for both accounts. By the way, you might want to think about changing those. I'm guessing they're the same for your bank account."

"Pretty impressive detective work," Hoffman said.

"But how did you know to come here to Rob's place?" Randall asked.

"How many other people in Bermuda do you know?"

"He's got you there, Nick," Hoffman said, elbowing his friend.

"Excuse me? What's going on here and who are these people?" Jamie said, standing in the doorway.

Randall turned to face her. "Jamie, I want to introduce you to my son John and my daughter Samantha."

Jamie walked over and met them.

"Now that I know how you found me, why did you come?" Randall asked.

John explained what had transpired as his father listened attentively. He described the man who had been sitting at his work desk and how he had narrowly escaped.

Randall shook his head. "I'm sorry I've pulled you into this mess. This has to be the work of Francis Dumond."

"I'm not so sure, Dad. I think the men who came after me were military. Several times in the past year soldiers have visited our facility. It turns out they've been funding our research, and I think I know why."

John produced the MK Ultra folder and handed it to his father.

"What's this?" Randall asked.

"I took it from the guys who were chasing me yesterday. It explains why Jacob disappeared and why they're after me ... and possibly you."

Randall walked over to a wooden chair, sat down, and began reading.

"Oh my God..." Randall whispered.

"Guess I'm the one who owes you an apology," John said, looking down at his shoes.

Randall closed the folder. "I'm not sure our problems are related."

"What do you mean?"

"Remember when you were at my house and I called you?"

"Yeah."

"I had just been assaulted by one of Dumond's men."

"How do you know he works for Dumond?"

"The guy who helped me escape told me."

"What do you mean?" Sam asked.

"Without going into too many details, I was cornered by an armed gunman, and if this other fella hadn't arrived when he did, I probably wouldn't be standing here today," Randall answered.

"John, the man asking about your research. You said he was tall and thin, with gray hair. Tell me a little more about him." Jamie said.

John scratched his chin and thought for a moment. "He was tall, maybe six-two, had short gray hair, and chain-smoked like there was no tomorrow."

"Did you catch his name?" Jamie asked.

"No. Why do you ask?"

"I think he's been to my office."

"Wait a minute. The same guy who tried to kidnap John also paid you a visit?" Randall asked.

"Yes. He claimed to be with an insurance company from the D.C. area that wanted information about reinsurance. Said his name was Mr. Shaw. He asked for me directly, but when we met, it was pretty clear he didn't care about reinsurance."

"What makes you say that?" John asked.

"He kept asking me about Bermuda and if any of the stories about weird things happening are true. To be honest, he creeped me out, so I cut our meeting short and told our security detail that he wasn't to come into our offices again."

"Pretty coincidental," John said.

"I'm beginning to think this isn't really a coincidence at all," Randall mused, reversing course.

"What do you mean?" Sam asked.

"Right after I returned from Peru, I started having nightmares, except they weren't nightmares. I was experiencing Jamie's abductions. Then we find out that the military has been funding John and Jacob's research and that this Shaw character tried to kidnap John after visiting Jamie."

"So, Jamie appears to be the common thread," John said.

"Right, and with Jacob's kidnapping and Jamie's more frequent abductions, it sounds like something big is about to happen."

"But what?" John asked.

"Good question. If we can answer that, we'll probably know how the events are linked," Randall answered.

"While we try to figure that out, we need to find a safe place to hide. If John was able to find you, Dad, then Dumond probably isn't far behind. John and Jamie, the same goes for both of you," Sam said.

"I know a place where we can hole up for a while," Hoffman said.

"What did you have in mind?" Randall asked.

"I have a place on an island nearby. It's isolated and only a few close friends know about it. We can stay there until we figure out what to do."

"Sounds good, we should probably get going right away," Randall said.

"Hold on Nick, before we go, I need to get something from my place," Jamie said.

"I don't think that's a good idea. We have the government and Dumond both looking for us," Randall replied.

"I have something that might help us find Shaw."

"What is it?" Randall asked.

"I have a file with contact information he provided: phone number, email address, name of his company. Maybe we can use it to track him down."

"If he's with some branch of the military or government, chances are his contact information is bogus. His name probably isn't even Shaw," John said.

"You're probably right, but it's all we have to go on at this point," Jamie replied.

"How far away is your place?" Sam asked.

"It's not far, just a few miles. I can make it there and back in an hour."

"I'll go with you," John said.

"Okay," Jamie said.

Randall sighed, his eyes bouncing between Jamie and John.

"We'll be okay dad," John said.

"Alright, go pick up the file, and be back here in one hour. No later," Randall said, folding his arms across his chest.

"We will dad. See you all in an hour."

"John," Randall said.

John turned to look at him.

"Be careful."

Chapter Seventeen

August 19, 7:02 A.M.
Nassau, Bahamas

The bright afternoon sunlight spilled in through the window and splashed onto Gabby's desk. It was the kind of day that marketers plastered onto postcards beckoning tourists to spend a few days in paradise. The beauty of the afternoon, however, was lost on Gabby who sat in her chair staring at a blank computer screen, holding her chin between her fingers. Two days had passed since the break-in at the field office, and they had found no additional information. The situation had been surreal, and Gabby still couldn't believe that her friend was dead, or that his murderer had been allowed to walk free.

"You know, if people see you staring at an empty computer screen, it won't be long before rumors start flying that you've lost your mind," Waters said, leaning his tall frame against the doorjamb.

"Maybe they're not rumors. Maybe there's some truth to the idea," Gabby replied, not lifting her eyes from the screen.

"Horseshit! The wound's still fresh, that's all."

Waters walked over to the desk, grabbed a wooden chair, spun it around, and sat down with his arms folded along the back. He did so in one fluid motion and, despite her mood, Gabby couldn't help but be a little impressed.

"We still don't have any more information about the break-in, and forensics wasn't able to tell what the guy was after. Whoever he was, he really knew how to cover his tracks."

"When did you check with forensics?"

"At seven this morning. They were still working on it but didn't seem too hopeful."

"Is that right? Hmmm, well that's not what I heard," Waters said, his crooked smile slowly spreading across his face.

Gabby noticed a sheet of paper carefully folded and dangling from his fingertips. She immediately shot up from her desk, taking long strides toward Waters.

"Is that what I think it is?" she asked hopefully.

"Might be, but then again, might not," he replied.

"Damn it, Charlie, stop messing around." Gabby grabbed the paper from his hand and hastily unfolded it.

"Who's Jamie Edmunds?" Gabby asked.

"Well, it's like I was telling you before you so rudely interrupted me. Apparently, forensics was able to recover part of the file that our friend had copied from our system. He was looking for information on Ms. Edmunds."

"I don't get it. Why would someone risk breaking into the field office to get information on this woman?" Gabby looked down at the sheet of paper, flipping it over to see the back. It was blank. The only information on it was Jamie's name and an address in Bermuda. She looked at Waters.

"I was wondering the same thing, so I called a friend of mine in the Miami office. He checked the records and found something interesting about Ms. Edmunds."

"What Charlie, what did he find?"

Waters lifted his head and propped his chin on his left fist and looked contemplative.

"Charlie!"

"Okay, Gabby," he said, grinning from ear to ear. "Ms. Edmunds had called to report being abducted by aliens about a year ago. Apparently, the agent taking the call thought she was crazy, but filed the report anyway. She asked if we could send someone out to meet with her, but the agent told her it wasn't the type of thing we investigate."

"What would the DOD want with a woman who reported being abducted by aliens?"

"Beats me." Waters shrugged.

"Maybe we need to pay Ms. Edmunds a visit."

"Didn't Agent Spence tell you to drop this?"

"Yes."

"But you're not going to listen, are you?"

"No, I'm not."

"Well then, I guess I have to do what any self-respecting Texan would do in a situation like this."

"And what's that?"

"Come along and protect the lady in distress, of course!"

Gabby shook her head and smiled for the first time in days. "Thank you."

Chapter Eighteen

August 19, 8:49 A.M.
Hamilton, Bermuda

The morning sun hung climbed higher into the sky as John drove the rental car down a quiet street lined with tall, narrow, colorfully painted buildings. The bright daylight bounced off the vibrant facades, hurting the eyes of anyone not wearing sunglasses.

"Turn here," Jamie said.

John swung the car onto her street and slowed down.

"Which building?"

"The white one about three quarters of the way down on the left."

John pulled the car to a stop well short of Jamie's building and on the opposite side of the street.

Jamie furrowed her brow. "Why are we stopping here?"

"After what happened to me the other day, I'm not taking any chances," John said, his eyes scanning the street for signs of trouble. "Is it usually this quiet?" he asked, not seeing anyone else on the sidewalks.

"I don't know. I'm usually at work at this time of day."

John exited the car, went around to Jamie's side, and opened her door.

"Ma'am," John said, extending his hand to Jamie.

"Thank you, kind sir." Jamie took his hand and stepped out of the car.

As she did so, John noted for the first time how beautiful she was. Her sandy blond hair was pulled back into a ponytail, exposing bright blue eyes that twinkled as she watched John's face while she exited the car. Her crooked smile was warm and hinted at a humorous side that she had not displayed back at Hoffman's house. Even in worn jeans and an old t-shirt, she was attractive in a natural manner. So much so that John found himself staring at her.

The two moved casually toward the building, walking at a leisurely pace.

"How long have you lived in Bermuda?"

"Three years. I had a job offer out of college and decided it would be fun to see a new part of the world."

"Where are you from?"

"Santa Barbara."

"Sounds like a nice place."

"It's beautiful. Right on the Pacific Ocean. My mom, dad, and older sister are all still there. I'm the only one who left the nest."

"Do you miss them?"

"Yes. I love the adventure of traveling, but I do miss home. They've come out to visit me a couple of times and I usually head home for the holidays. I'm supposed to be going back next spring for my sister's wedding."

"Congratulations to your sister. How did they meet?"

"In school. They were taking classes together and got to know each other over study sessions at the library. He's a really sweet guy."

John nodded and smiled. "How about you? Anyone special in your life?"

Jamie wrinkled her nose. "No, I guess I've been too busy with work. Besides, I haven't met the right guy yet."

"Oh, and what would he be like?"

"He'll be smart, but not full of himself, and he'll have a good sense of humor. I like someone who can make me laugh. He'll also be warm, you know, someone who's close to his family. They say you can tell a lot about a person by how they treat their family."

As they talked, John noticed Jamie walk a little slower and move closer to him. They stopped outside of Jamie's building.

"This is it," Jamie said.

The building was bright white with black, wrought-iron fencing. Each unit had a small balcony, some furnished with chairs and small tables for their residents to enjoy the warm weather and beautiful views.

"Which one is yours?"

"Come on, I'll show you."

The two walked around the side of the building and up a flight of stairs, stopping at unit 201. Jamie took her keys from her purse, opened the door, and went in. John followed closely behind her.

"The file's in my office, I'll be right back."

Jamie disappeared into another room as John waited in the living room. The room was bright and airy, with a small dining table with four chairs sitting under a large window that looked out over the ocean. In the middle of the table was a picture of Jamie and her family. Her parents looked surprisingly young for a couple with two adult daughters. John walked over to the table and picked up the picture. As he did, the front door burst open.

Caught off guard, John spun to face the door, the picture dropping from his hand and shattering on the hardwood floor.

"Dr. John Randall, I presume."

"Who are you and how do you know my name?"

"Family resemblance. Search the rest of the apartment."

A mountain of a man made his way past the first, heading straight for the office where Jamie had gone only minutes earlier. A third man joined them.

"I've had the pleasure of meeting your father and sister, but this is truly a treat. I didn't expect to find you here today."

"Dumond," John said through gritted teeth.

"Very good, Dr. Randall. I see my reputation precedes me." Dumond motioned for his assistant to approach John. The man did as ordered, pointing a gun at John's chest.

"What are you looking for?" John asked.

"Your friend, Jamie. I understand that your father has an interest in her, and if he has an interest, then so do I. By the way, where is your father? I'm dying to see him again."

"He's gone. I knew he wouldn't be safe here, so I told him he needed to leave the island."

"You're as poor a liar as your father."

The large man who had gone into the office reappeared alone.

"She's not here, Mr. Dumond."

Dumond's eyes narrowed for a moment and then he smiled, turning to face John. "I saw the two of you enter this apartment. Where did she go?"

John shrugged.

Dumond walked over to John, stopping inches from him. He studied John's face. "Well, we have the next best thing. Dr. Randall, would you care to join us?"

Dumond's assistant pressed the handgun into John's ribs, pushing him toward the door.

Chapter Nineteen

August 19, 10:49 A.M.
Cooper's Island, Bermuda

The NASA remote tracking station at Cooper's Island is little more than several trailers and an antennae dish. Opened in 2012, the facility was built to support launches from NASA's Wallops Flight Facility in Virginia. At least that was the purpose of the facility as far as the public was concerned.

Colonel Shaw entered the mobile facility and walked straight into the meeting room.

"Status update on targets," Shaw said.

"Sir, we have been unable to obtain the assets at this time, but believe we may have found them," responded a man dressed in street clothes and wearing a NASA badge.

"Where is Captain Fredericks?"

"He's in the situation room, sir."

Shaw walked briskly down the short hallway. There were no windows in the corridor, but the bright LED lighting washed over the ultra-white walls, creating the illusion of daylight. Shaw stopped at a solid, windowless door and pressed his right hand against the biometric scanner. The device silently identified him and granted access. The air door slid open, revealing a room with a bank of computers not unlike mission control in Houston.

Captain Fredericks was seated at the far-left side, studying something intently. He briefly glanced up upon hearing the door open. "Colonel," Fredericks said, not getting up from his seat. His eyes were locked on the computer screen, which displayed still images of a snowy white plateau.

"What have they been doing?" Shaw asked.

"It's difficult to say. As you know, every time we get a satellite within range to take reconnaissance photographs, they jam it. We've been unable to upload commands and take the surveillance pictures," Captain Frederick replied.

"Are the satellites permanently incapacitated?"

"No, just a temporary blackout. Once the satellites are out of their range, they resume normal operations."

"Do we know how they're doing it?"

Fredericks shook his head. "Our scientists theorize that they're utilizing some type of energy beam, possibly an electromagnetic pulse, to temporarily shut the satellites down. Unfortunately, they're using technology we've never seen before."

Shaw removed his hat, ran his fingers through his short, gray hair, and let out a sigh. "We're running out of time," he said, looking into the distance. "What's the status on apprehending the Randalls?" Shaw demanded.

Fredericks hesitated. "Our men were unable to secure them," he responded, not making eye contact with his superior officer.

Shaw set his jaw. "How did they elude our men?"

"Lieutenant Sanders said that Randall's party used some sort of weapon to damage their boat. They were barely able to get back to port. That's all I was able to get from him."

Shaw grasped Fredericks by the collar and jerked him to his feet, holding him in his gaze. He said nothing for a full ten seconds and then growled. "First you screwed up the intelligence gathering mission at the FBI, and now you're telling me you still haven't been able to locate and apprehend John or Nick Randall. I'm losing patience with you very quickly. You have twenty-four hours to capture them or I'll have you sent to a place where no one will ever see or hear from you again. Understood?"

Fredericks could only manage a curt nod, at which time Shaw released his grip on him. Shaw placed his hat back on his head and strode toward the door. He opened it and stopped in the doorway, facing outward.

"Twenty-four hours Fredericks, the clock is running."

He walked out the door, leaving the captain to his thoughts.

Chapter Twenty

John stood with his eyes blindfolded and his hands tied behind his back. Although he couldn't see it, he could feel that he was shackled to a large metal pipe. By touch, he determined that the diameter of the pipe was approximately three inches — far too large to break. He could also hear water lapping against something solid nearby. The sound seemed to come from over his head, giving him the unpleasant sensation that the room could become inundated with water at a moment's notice. If that happened, he would be unable to escape and would drown. John tried to push the thought from his mind, but being blindfolded only added to the uncertainty, allowing his mind to paint the unnerving portrait in sickening detail.

John strained to hear additional noises, trying to capture any sound that might help him identify where he was. He thought he heard a boat engine strumming in the distance, but the lapping water made it difficult to hear anything clearly. His heart jumped when he heard a door open on squeaky hinges and the sound of boot steps approaching him. Worse, he heard the unmistakable sound of splashing water as the stranger approached. There was water on the floor of the entire room, not just his little spot. The steps grew louder, and he could sense someone getting closer. Suddenly the steps stopped, and there was silence again. John cocked his head back and to the side, trying to hear anything, but whoever was here wasn't speaking.

"Is someone there?"

There was no answer. John waited a minute and tried again.

"Is some…" He was cut off by a wave of water crashing over his face, the liquid forcing its way down his open throat in mid-sentence. John convulsed in response, gagging on what seemed like gallons of water, which burned his lungs. He coughed uncontrollably and turned from his visitor. After a few moments, he regained normal breathing.

"Who are…?"

More water rained down on him, once again flooding his throat and lungs. He felt like he was drowning. Unable to breathe for what seemed an eternity, he coughed reflexively, struggling to rid his lungs of the water. John dropped to his knees, the metal cuffs biting into his wrists. Searing pain issued from the ragged wounds, caused by the metal tearing into his flesh. The salt water added to his suffering, burning his wrists as he struggled to breathe.

He cursed internally, unable to force the words out. Finally, the coughing subsided.

He thought about addressing his captor, but his instincts kicked in. He forced his jaw shut and turned his head down and away from whoever was dousing him with water.

"You learn quickly, Dr. Randall. Good for you."

John stood again, careful to keep his head turned away from the voice that was addressing him.

After a few moments, his captor spoke again. "What is your father's interest in Jamie Edmunds?"

John recognized Dumond's voice but stood motionless.

"Again," Dumond said.

A torrent of water rained down on John's head. This time, though, he prepared himself, forcing his mouth shut and tilting his head down to minimize the amount of water that entered his lungs. His strategy was met with strong hands forcing his head back, making it impossible to keep the water out. John struggled to breathe, coughing uncontrollably. After a moment, he composed himself again.

"I'm waiting, Dr. Randall," Dumond said in a singsong voice.

"What's your interest in her?"

"I will indulge you for a moment. I understand that Ms. Edmunds and I may have shared a common experience and I would like to hear more about what she has gone through. Now, why has your father sought her out?"

"You mean you've been abducted?"

"I'm losing my patience. What is your father's interest in her?"

"Same as yours. Since he returned from Peru, he has been having nightmares."

"Go on."

"The nightmares have involved abduction at the hands of some creature he's never seen before," John said, carefully choosing his words.

"But why his interest in Ms. Edmunds? He could have seen a psychiatrist, astrologer, or any number of people. Why did he come here to Bermuda and seek her out"?

John didn't reply.

"Again," Dumond said. Once again, a strong set of hands forced John's head back and a torrent of water hit his blindfolded face.

"We can do this all day, Dr. Randall."

The sensation was overwhelming. John forced out the water, coughing spasmodically.

"She was in his dreams. Dad was experiencing the abductions through her." John forced the words out.

"Fascinating. Your father is somehow connected to Ms. Edmunds. Perhaps telepathically? Exactly what happened when your father met the creatures in Peru?"

"I don't know," John replied, sucking air in big gulps. "He said he communicated with them and they told him Sam was in danger."

"Where are Ms. Edmunds and your father now?"

"We were supposed to meet some time ago at her office, but we knew you were near and when we didn't show up, they left," John lied.

"I made a mistake by not killing your father and sister when I had the chance. I won't do the same with you. By now I'm sure you've heard the ocean from your cell. This is a special room I had designed for negotiating with my enemies. There is an open-grated window several feet above your head. It keeps out the rising ocean until high tide, which will occur in two hours and thirty-two minutes. Enjoy your stay."

Chapter Twenty-One

Randall paced the floor of Hoffman's room, frequently checking his watch. It had been over three hours and there was still no sign of John and Jamie.

"Something's happened to them," Randall said.

"We don't know that for sure. Let's give them a little more time," Hoffman said.

"You don't know John the way I do, he's always been very punctual. Even as a kid he hated being late for anything."

As Sam was about to comment, the door to Hoffman's room opened and Jamie stepped through the doorway. Her face was flush, and she was out of breath as she leaned on the door jamb.

"They have John," she managed to say between breaths.

"Who has John? What happened?" Randall replied, helping her to a chair.

125

"We were in my apartment and I went into my office to get the folder. Three men burst through my front door and grabbed John."

"How did you get away?"

"I had opened my window and thought about climbing out but didn't have time. I pushed a lamp out the window and I hid behind a chair in the corner of my room. They heard the breaking noise and thought I had escaped. It was Dumond! He's looking for you, Nick!"

"How do you know?" Randall asked.

"I heard him talking with John."

"What do we do now?" Sam asked.

Randall felt like he had been punched in the gut. He staggered over to a chair, placing a hand on the back for support. He steadied himself.

"We need to get out of here. With Dumond on the loose, I can't take a chance of anything happening to the rest of you," Randall said.

"Okay, we'll go to my boathouse and stay there while we figure out what to do about John," Hoffman said.

Randall nodded, staring out the window. "Take Sam and Jamie with you."

"What about you?"

"I'm going to find my son."

Chapter Twenty-Two

Still blindfolded, John could hear the ocean water lapping in through the open window. At first it had been a slow trickle, but now it was coming in large gushes. Salt water filled the room up to John's knees as he struggled to free himself from his chains. He had rubbed his wrists raw. The worst part was not being able to see what was happening. John had tried shaking the blindfold off, pulling it with his teeth and even rubbing it against the wall to remove it from his eyes. All he got for his effort was a skinned forehead.

Despite the pain, John wouldn't give up. It wasn't in the Randall DNA to quit, but the situation was becoming bleak. His thoughts kept turning to Jamie. Had she escaped from Dumond and his men? Was she safe? John wanted nothing more than to break out just, so he could find out if she was okay.

There had to be a way out; he just had to concentrate. His hands were bound to a pipe that ran along the wall. He tried to pull against it with all his strength, hoping that the sea air and water had weakened the attachments enough, so he could pull a section of the pipe away from the wall. But the pipe wouldn't budge. He tried kicking it loose. That failed as well. Hoping that the shackles were loose enough for him to wriggle free, John tried to ball up his left hand and push the shackle off with his right. All he accomplished was cutting his hand even worse. He cursed his failures.

"Damn it!"

John had a sudden thought. Dumond had forgotten to remove the contents of his pockets. He still had his phone and could call for help, but how could he reach it? The water had risen well past his knees now. John realized he needed to get to his phone before it became submerged. He struggled to get his hands into his pocket. The pipe ran parallel to the floor at chest height, making it too high for him to reach his phone. He judged that his reach was short by more than a foot. He needed a way to elevate his legs or lower his arms.

Continuing to struggle, he realized that he hadn't tried sliding the shackles. He walked to his right, dragging them behind him. They moved! John walked faster, pulling the shackles along the wall, splashing water as he went. He moved about three feet, and the cuffs suddenly stopped. John pulled, but they wouldn't budge. Cursing, he walked back the other way, trudging slowly through the deepening water. It was nearly to his waist now. Frantic to get to his phone, John dragged the chains along the wall as quickly as he could. They moved freely for a while, but then stopped again.

"Shit!"

John composed himself and felt along the pipe where his chains had snagged and found the cause. The shackles were jammed on a protruding pipe connection. John felt along the pipe and discovered that they dropped down right after the connection.

John frantically tried to work them free as the water climbed up his body. The flow of water was steady now, the tide having fully breached the bottom of the window. John tugged in all directions. No luck. Salty water washed over the ragged wounds on his wrist. The burning was intense. John stopped and breathed deeply. With every remaining ounce of energy in his body, he pulled to the left. With a sudden jerk, the chains broke free and slid two feet down the pipe.

John scrambled to remove his phone from his pocket. Groping along the material, he finally reached his pocket, grabbed his phone, and pulled it free. His hand and phone were underwater. John jerked the chain back up the pipe, dragging his hands and phone behind. He finally got his phone above the incoming water level and held it gingerly behind his back. He couldn't see the screen. The blindfold was still blocking his view.

He wriggled his face against the pipe, trying desperately to get the blindfold off. Cold, bare pipe scraped at his forehead as he tried to uncover his right eye. John winced in pain as the salty water splashed into the self-inflicted wound on his face. He caught a glimpse of light. His right eye was half exposed. He tried harder, rubbing again and again at the pipe until the blindfold finally succumbed and his right eye was clear.

John craned his head, to view his phone. He saw it out of the corner of his eye. It was still working.

He strained against the shackles, trying desperately to extend his reach. He just needed a couple more inches.

He pushed the phone to the tips of his fingers. It slipped from his wet hands and dropped. John plunged his hands under the water, blindly trying to catch the falling phone. He gripped it momentarily only to have it slip away and drift to the floor of his cell.

"No!"

He tried to feel for the phone with his feet but had no luck. Surely it had suffered irreparable damage by now and John realized that his last hope had skittered away.

Steeling himself against the inevitable, John accepted his fate. His mind flashed over the loved ones in his life and settled on the simple fact that he would never get a chance to tell them how much he cared about them.

The water was shoulder high now. He only had minutes before it would cover his head. He stood quietly as it slowly rose higher and higher until it was nearly to his chin.

A strange clanging noise came from his right. John glanced over with his exposed eye and saw the submerged door, which looked like a ship's hatch with a round, metal wheel in its center. He wasn't certain, but it looked like the wheel was slowly turning. Suddenly, the hatch opened outward, releasing a torrent of water from the cell. The deluge caused the water to drop quickly, from his chin to his chest and then to his knees. Finally, it came to rest once again at his ankles as the raised threshold kept the remaining water from spilling out.

"That's quite a bit of water, mate," a man's voice called out from beyond the hatch. A figure stooped through the opening and into the room. "Those aren't proper togs to go for a swim, lad," the man said, slowly making his way toward John. The towering hulk hovered over John, who stood dumbfounded by the appearance of his savior.

"Who are you?"

"Michael Thompson, at your service," the behemoth responded, producing a large pair of bolt cutters. He sliced through the shackles with ease.

John immediately removed his blindfold and examined Michael. He was easily six and half feet tall and nearly as wide. His dark brown hair was medium length and loosely tussled as if a woman has recently run her fingers through it. His face was long and narrow, with defined cheekbones and jovial brown eyes.

"Looks like I got here just in time."

"I'm confused … how did you find me and why are you helping me?"

"That's a long story, mate, why don't you take a seat," Michael said, motioning to a concrete step. John obliged.

Michael explained that he had once been a member of Dumond's team of mercenaries, serving under their recently deceased leader Colonel Frank Ackers. The former British Secret Forces member cast his eyes downward as he related his displeasure and apparent regret over past indiscretions.

"I just didn't agree with the things Dumond was having us do. It's one thing to face a fellow soldier on the field of battle, it's quite another to murder a helpless civilian who doesn't know a thing about combat."

"How did you get away? I'm pretty sure Dumond didn't just let you walk out the front door."

"It took a lot of time and planning, but I was able to make a powerful friend who helped me."

"Who's powerful enough to take on Dumond?"

"That's a tale for another day. Right now, you need to get back to your group. Dumond is after your dad and your lady friend."

Chapter Twenty-Three

Randall slid his rental car into a spot behind a black Mercedes, several blocks from Jamie's apartment building. With a pair of Steiner marine binoculars, he had borrowed from Hoffman, he surveyed the streets and buildings nearby. After satisfying himself that neither Dumond nor his men were in the vicinity, he exited the Jeep Grand Cherokee and slowly wound his way toward Jamie's building.

Climbing the stairs, he made his way to Unit 201, and stopped outside the door. He listened carefully for the sounds of someone inside. Hearing nothing, he slid the key into the lock, turning it gently to minimize the noise of the tumbler rotating. He slowly opened the door and scanned the room. There were no signs of life. He slipped inside, closing the door behind him.

Broken glass littered the floor near Jamie's dining room table and Randall noticed the fallen picture frame, shattered on the hardwood floor. The room was a mess. Paper and books were strewn about haphazardly as were chairs and other furnishings. Randall hustled into the office, where Jamie had told him the Shaw file was hidden. He needed to find it. It was the only lead they had to find either Shaw or Dumond.

The office was in no better shape than the living room. Dumond's men had clearly gone through the desk and bookshelf looking for something. Randall's body tensed with the fear that they had discovered the file. Without it, they were lost. He drew back the closet door. Jamie's shoes were scattered, but the carpet was still in place. He tugged on the corner of the rug, lifted it up and revealed a floor safe. He placed his finger into the small hole on the front panel and lifted it open. He sighed in relief to find that the safe was still closed. He probed his pocket for the small piece of paper containing the combination Jamie had provided and went to work opening the safe. The folder was safely tucked away inside.

Randall smiled at his good fortune. But the moment was short lived.

"Federal agents put your hands above your head and don't move."

Randall felt a pair of strong hands grasp his right hand and force it behind his back and into a pair of handcuffs. His left hand soon followed. He was then jerked to his feet.

"Turn around."

Randall found himself face to face with a man and a woman he had never seen before. They were well dressed, the woman in a navy-blue suit and white shirt, the man in a gray suit with a bolo tie. The woman had a Glock 23 handgun trained on his chest.

"Who are you?" the woman asked.

"Nick Randall, who are you?"

"Charlie, check him for I.D."

The man reached into Randall's pocket, retrieving his wallet.

"Yep, he's who he says he is," Waters said.

"I'm Federal Agent Gutierrez. What are you doing here?"

"My son was kidnapped by the men who tore through this apartment. I'm looking for something that might help me find him."

"What's your relation to Ms. Edmunds?"

"I'm friends with Jamie. Are you FBI?"

"Where is she?" Gabby demanded.

"Look, Jamie is in trouble and I'm helping her, but now my son has been taken by a crazy man named Frances Dumond who wants to kill me. We need your help."

"Never heard of him. My only concern is finding Ms. Edmunds. Where is she?"

"She's with a friend of mine."

"Where?"

"I don't know, I told them not to tell me where they're going in case I got caught by Dumond's men. You have to believe me!"

"Take him down to the car, Charlie."

"Let's go, Randall," Waters said, grasping him by his handcuffed hands.

"You're making a mistake! If Shaw finds Jamie before I can find John, he'll kill her!"

"Wait! What did you say?"

"A man named Shaw is looking for Jamie and I need the folder in that safe to help us find him first," Randall said, nodding toward the closet. "For some reason, Shaw is after Jamie and my son John. He tried to kidnap John a few days ago. We think he has ties to the military, but we're not sure."

"What does Shaw look like?" Gabby asked.

"He's a tall, thin guy with short gray hair. Probably about my age. John says he chain smokes like there's no tomorrow."

"You said you think he has ties to the military?"

"Yes, John was working on a government project that was funded by the military. His research partner Jacob disappeared, and when John went to work, Shaw was waiting there and tried to kidnap him. We also found out that Shaw visited Jamie a few months ago, claiming to be with an insurance company from D.C."

Gabby lowered her gun. "That sounds like the guy from the DOD. Randall how were you going to get back in contact with your friends?"

"I told them to call me at 4:30."

Gabby looked at her watch. It was 3:58 p.m. "Grab a seat, we're going to be here a little while."

Chapter Twenty-Four

The afternoon sun hung low in a brilliant cobalt sky dotted with wispy clouds as John made his way back from his ordeal. A cool ocean breeze caressed his face and he could hear waves crashing in the distance. He trudged up the walkway toward the barracks, making his way to Hoffman's corner unit. Dripping wet, his body felt like a lead weight. It took each ounce of energy to keep moving. Every square inch of his being ached from the torment suffered at the hands of Frances Dumond, and his mind was awash in a sea of questions. But at this moment, all John wanted was to rest. He yearned for a bed or even a comfortable couch or chair to collapse on. He finally made it to the unit and opened the door. He was greeted by three armed men, one of which he immediately recognized.

"Shaw!"

"Glad you remember me."

"You son of a bitch! What did you do with my family and friends?"

"What are you talking about?"

"They were here waiting for me and now they're gone. You fill in the blanks."

"I don't know what happened to your friends, but I'm glad to know they might come back." As Shaw spoke, three more armed men appeared behind John, surrounding him.

"I trust you have the folder that you stole from the office a couple days ago? I want it back. Now!"

"Sure, it's right here in my pocket. Oh wait, that's right, I left it in my other pants. I don't have your stupid folder!"

Shaw nodded his head and one of his men smashed the butt of his hand gun across the back of John's head, knocking him to the ground. John rolled on the ground clasping the back of his skull.

"Get him up," Shaw ordered. "Next time, you'll think twice before opening your mouth, smart ass. Now, where's Jamie?"

"I told you, I don't know," John said, rubbing the back of his head. "They were supposed to be here waiting for me. Dammit! Dumond must have them."

"Who's Dumond?"

"He's the one who did this to me," John said showing his injured wrists. "He kidnapped me and tried to get Jamie, too. He knocked me out and tortured me to get information about Jamie, but I got away."

"What did he want with Jamie?"

John explained the situation, too tired to hide the details. Shaw's gaze was transfixed on him while he spoke. Despite his best poker face, Shaw's eyes went wide at times, hearing the details of John's harrowing escape from Dumond.

"For your sake and hers, we better find Jamie before Dumond and his men do," Shaw said.

"You expect me to help you? Why would I do that? How do I know you'll treat her any better than Dumond?" John said, recoiling from Shaw.

"You don't have any choice," Shaw said, stepping closer to John. "If I say jump, you say how high. Do I make myself clear?" Shaw moved closer to John. "I didn't spend all of this time on you and your partner just to lose out to some French punk who's upset because he was anal probed by an alien. I'm going to finish my mission, and that means you're coming with me."

Shaw motioned to his men, who pushed John toward the parking lot and a black SUV with heavily tinted windows and a bulbous satellite dish protruding from the top. As they approached the vehicle, the rear door opened and a man clutching a snub-nosed machine gun hopped out. The man scanned the area as they approached. John glanced back at Hoffman's place and wondered if his dad and the others were safe. He hoped they were and that they didn't come back here looking for him.

Chapter Twenty-Five

August 19, 5:27 P.M.
Bern, Switzerland

Michael Thompson sat in the lobby of the administrative wing of the Composite Materials Corporation. Having changed outfits since saving John, he was now impeccably dressed in a charcoal gray Armani suit. To an outsider, he appeared to be nothing more than another stuffed shirt, drawing a fat salary from the multinational firm.

Outward appearances can be deceiving.

He smiled as he watched the office workers mill about. Although the fat salary part was accurate, his compensation was the result of his unique skillset. One that no one else in the company had. Not even his employer, Margaret Seivers.

Thompson propped his chin on his fist as he surveyed the office, taking careful note of everyone and categorizing them into groups. Although he seriously doubted that anyone here posed a threat to his wellbeing, it was still a useful exercise, one meant to keep him sharp. He started at the far end of the room and slowly scanned the area until his eyes came to rest on Seivers' attractive assistant. He allowed his eyes to linger on her finer features as he waited.

"Mr. Thompson, Ms. Seivers will see you now."

"Thanks, Love," he said, flashing her a crooked smile and wink. She blushed at the attention, then shook her head as a broad smile spread across her lips.

Thompson walked into the office and closed the door behind him. Seivers sat behind her desk, her back to the door, reading from a file she held in her lap. She sat motionless, focused on the document in hand.

"How are things, Boss?" he asked, taking a seat opposite her desk.

"I hear you've been busy," Seivers said, turning to face him.

"Just doing what you pay me for."

Seivers looked up at Thompson, studying him from behind a pair of black-rimmed metal glasses. She cocked her head to one side as if looking at him from a different angle might reveal something new.

"I read your last update and I'm pleased that Randall and his son are safe."

"Thank you. We're continuing to track them, but Dumond hasn't made this easy."

"If it were easy, you wouldn't be paid so handsomely," Seivers said, now looking over her glasses, pushing them to the end of her slender nose.

"What would you like me to do next?"

"Monitor them. They're our best chance of obtaining the compound we need to advance our plans."

"And what exactly are our plans?"

Seivers sat back in her chair. A momentary frown appeared on her face, but a neutral expression quickly returned. Her brown eyes narrowed as she locked onto Thompson's face.

"Mr. Thompson, I hired you for a very specific job, which you have completed to my satisfaction. I provide you with precisely the information you require to complete the tasks assigned to you. If, in the future, the work requested of you requires additional information, I assure you, pertinent details will be provided. Until that time, however, I suggest you focus on the task at hand."

Thompson nodded, turning to look out the window. While her outward appearance was that of a well-groomed business executive, he knew that beneath the veneer Margaret Seivers was a dangerous woman whose influence stretched well beyond the confines of a multinational company.

"Do I make myself clear, Mr. Thompson?"

"Yes, ma'am," Thompson said, turning back to face her. He forced a smile, knowing that it fooled no one.

"Very good. I have to return a call to Mr. Dumond now. Please keep me updated on the situation."

The mention of Dumond's name sparked Thompson's attention. "Is there anything I should know?"

"Not at this time. He was simply informing me about his failed attempt on Randall's life. But I believe you already knew about that."

Thompson smiled. "Like I said, Ms. Seivers, just doing what you pay me for." He stood and exited the office. Despite her stern manner, there was one thing he appreciated about his employer: she made her wishes clear. And Thompson had no intention of disappointing her.

Chapter Twenty-Six

August 19, 5:57 P.M.
Nonsuch Island, Bermuda

The setting sun cast a long reflection across the glittering surface of Castle Harbor as a breeze wisped through the trees surrounding Hoffman's home on Nonsuch Island. Randall, Gabby, and Waters had landed their boat on a small stretch of sandy beach on the southern side of the island and made their way through the dense foliage until they reached a clearing that opened to reveal Hoffman's home. Having spoken with him earlier, the three now joined Hoffman, Sam and Jamie. They sat in the study, which offered a view across the water and directly into the Cooper Island Nature Reserve. The scenery was beautiful, but the mood inside the home was anything but peaceful.

Wanting to be a good host, Hoffman fetched his guests several cold bottles of Barritt's Ginger Beer. He also brought out a bottle of dark rum to mix a "Dark and Stormy" for anyone in need of something stronger. A preferred drink of true Bermudians, the "Dark and Stormy" had seemed like a good choice, and Hoffman had decided the moment they arrived that he would be having several. The group sat in a circle watching Gabby as she absorbed all the information they had shared. Randall, no longer considered a suspect, sat by Sam, staring out the window as she conversed with the agent.

"You and your father faced Dumond in Peru and narrowly escaped, aided and abetted by a local tribe?"

"As crazy as it sounds, yes, Agent Gutierrez," Sam answered.

"Call me Gabby."

"Okay, Gabby, yes, my dad and I fought Dumond and his men in an underground city in Peru and barely escaped with our lives. Dumond also escaped, and I can't say I'm surprised that he's back. Apparently, we threw a serious wrench into his plans to create a super weapon and cost him a lot of money in the process. To put it simply, he was pretty angry with us and I'm sure he'd like to finish the job he started."

"And now you think Dumond wants Jamie because he was abducted by the same creatures that have been abducting her and he wants revenge on them. You also think he has captured your brother John."

"Exactly," Sam said, nodding.

"Rob, I'll have one of those drinks," Gabby said, rubbing her eyes.

"I know this sounds crazy Gabby, but it's all true," Randall said.

"I want to believe you, but it all sounds so far-fetched," Gabby replied.

"Even if you don't believe we're telling you the truth, we all want the same thing. To catch Shaw and stop Dumond," Randall said.

Gabby shook her head.

"What do we do now?" Hoffman asked, mixing Gabby's drink and raising an eyebrow in anticipation of the answer.

A hushed silence fell over the group. Hoffman glanced at his old friend who looked at the ground, clearly feeling defeated. He handed off the cocktail to Gabby, who nodded in appreciation and took a long pull from the glass. Hoffman sat down at his desk, folded his hands across his lap and waited.

Just as he did, Waters walked into the room, sliding his phone into his jacket pocket.

"Any news, Charlie?" Gabby asked.

"News?"

"The phone records from Jamie's file. You were calling the sub-office to trace the call Shaw made to Jamie, remember?" Gabby said, grinning at her partner of five years.

"Sorry, no news yet, but hopefully we'll hear something soon," Waters said, a tinge of embarrassment in his voice. He slid his lanky frame into an empty chair near his partner.

Almost as if on cue, Gabby's phone rang, the noise startling everyone back to a sense of reality.

"Gutierrez," Gabby said into the phone. Everyone's eyes fixated on her as they listened to one side of the conversation.

"Are you sure about that? Okay, thanks." Gabby ended her call and took another long sip from her drink.

"Well?" Randall asked.

"Shaw's call to Jamie came from a burner phone, a pre-paid phone that is untraceable," Gabby said, watching Randall sink deeper into his seat.

"But they were able to pull records from local cell towers to see if we had a hit on the number, which we did. It appears

144

that the call originated from nearby. Our techs were able to triangulate the location to Coopers Island."

"Coopers Island? The only thing over there is the NASA tracking station," Hoffman said.

"That's correct. Jamie, have you had any contact with anyone from NASA?" Gabby asked.

"No," Jamie responded, unable to hide the surprise in her voice.

"That's what I thought. I think we've found Shaw."

"Great, what do we do next?" Randall asked.

"Nick, do you play poker?" Gabby asked.

"Yeah, why?"

"How good are you at bluffing?"

Chapter Twenty-Seven

August 20, 6:15 P.M.
Cooper's Island, Bermuda

The morning sun slowly crawled into the eastern sky over Cooper Island, revealing a nearly cloudless stretch of light blue as far as the eye could see. The green trees stood in sharp contrast to the sky and the air felt crisp and cool. The NASA facility was comprised of three semi-truck trailers, arranged in a U-shaped formation, with the fourth side of the square enclosed by a small building. Another small structure in the center of the square completed the complex. A large satellite dish rested on the west end of the formation near the building, and further beyond the satellite dish, the land fell away to Castle Harbor in the direction of Nonsuch Island.

Randall shifted restlessly, waiting for them to put their plan into action. He had barely slept, worrying if John was all right and if they would find him. He could only hope that Gabby's plan would work and that they could get information from Shaw to help them locate John.

"Are you ready to go?" Gabby asked.

"As ready as I'll ever be," Randall replied.

The plan was simple. Waters had an agent friend place a call to the Cooper Island facility, asking about the whereabouts of a man named Shaw. Gabby and Randall would then show up at the facility, confront Shaw, and tell him they had indisputable proof that he was behind the break-in at the FBI sub-station and murder of Agent Hernandez. Gabby would then threaten him with a non-existent task force of FBI agents waiting to storm the facility if he failed to cooperate with the investigation. They had to hope that would be enough to make Shaw crack and that he wouldn't call their bluff.

Randall and Gabby walked down the gravel path toward the lead trailer and immediately spotted surveillance cameras. As they drew within ten yards of the trailer, its door opened, and a single uniformed man stepped out and walked down the steps to greet them. He appeared to be unarmed.

"This is a United States government installation and you're trespassing. Turn around now or you'll be taken into custody."

"I'm a Federal Agent," Gabby said, removing her badge from her pocket, "and I'm here to investigate the murder of a fellow agent at the Sub-Office at the U.S. Embassy in Nassau. Interfering with this investigation is a federal offense, punishable by a long prison term in a federal correctional facility. Unless you'd like to trade this beachside Shangri-La for a four-by-six concrete room with bars, I suggest you take us to your boss."

The soldier held his hand up to an inconspicuous listening device in his ear and, after a moment, spoke.

"This way, Agent Gutierrez."

Gabby and Randall exchanged glances before walking up the metal steps and into the trailer. The soldier held the door open as they walked into the trailer.

"This way," the soldier said, leading them down the narrow hallway. They stopped at another door that led into the courtyard and the soldier once again held the door open, so they could walk down the steps, toward the small building in the middle. The soldier removed a small, plastic ID card from his front shirt pocket and waved it in front of a rectangular black card reader. The door slid open.

Randall and Gabby followed him to a small windowless door, which he opened in the same manner as before. He motioned for them to go in.

"Where's your boss?" Gabby said, standing in the doorway.

"I'm right here," Shaw replied from inside, sitting by a desk with a cup of coffee and several files in front of him.

Gabby and Randall walked into the room and stood on the opposite side of his desk while Shaw remained seated. The room was completely windowless and painted drab gray. There were no pictures on the walls. In fact, there were no personal effects anywhere in Shaw's office. Just somber empty walls and a single desk with a computer and an ash tray on top. The ash tray was overflowing with discarded cigarette butts. A single lit cigarette burned almost to a nub sat on the edge of the ash tray with small wisps of blue smoke trailing into the air.

"Sergeant, has Captain Fredericks reported for duty?" Shaw asked.

"Negative, sir. We've tried calling him twice, but his line goes straight to voicemail."

"Keep me posted," Shaw said, making no attempt to hide his displeasure. He looked up at Randall. "To what do I owe the pleasure of your visit?" Shaw asked.

"Drop the act, Shaw," Gabby said. "I want answers about John Randall's disappearance and why you're after Jamie Edmunds. I know that you're the one who orchestrated the break-in at the Sub-Station. You're complicit in the murder of a federal agent."

"I see, and I'm sure that you have a warrant?"

Gabby leaned onto the desk, her face a foot from Shaw's. "I could get one if you like."

"Really, and what would be the charges?"

"How about attempted murder and the kidnapping of John Randall and Jacob Taylor, for starters? I'm sure we could toss in conspiracy for your role in the murder of Agent Hernandez as well."

"Sounds serious. Of course, if you had wanted to charge me with those crimes, you wouldn't be here warning me, would you? What is it you want, Agent Gutierrez?"

"I want to know what you're up to. I want to know why you want Jamie Edmunds and John Randall, and what you plan to do with them. There's clearly something larger happening here, otherwise the DOD wouldn't be involved in breaking into an FBI sub-office and trying to kidnap government researchers. I want a signed confession from you, and I can offer you immunity from prosecution if you're willing to turn over the people who ordered the break-in and are responsible for the murder of Agent Hernandez."

An evil grin crept onto Shaw's face as he sat listening to Gabby. He took a heavy draw from his cigarette, then crushed it into his ash tray. He blew out the smoke and locked eyes with Gabby. "Now let me tell you something. You don't have proof of anything and you have no idea how in-over-your-head you are. If you really think I'm going to roll over for some punk agent coming into my facility making empty threats, then you really are naïve."

"I'm warning you, I have a task force ready to tear this place apart if you don't comply."

"Call them."

Gabby pulled the radio from her pocket.

"Charlie, come in, this is Gabby, get ready to send in the team."

There was only silence as Shaw's grin grew wider.

"Charlie, are you there?"

After another moment of silence, Shaw opened his desk drawer and removed his own hand-held radio. "Send them in."

The door to his office swung open, and to Randall and Gabby's horror Jamie, Sam, and Hoffman walked in with their hands held behind their heads. Bringing up the trail was Waters, who had a gun trained on them.

"Charlie, what the hell are you doing?" Gabby asked.

"Sorry, Gabby, the DOD pays better," Waters said. "What do you want me to do with them, Colonel?"

"Lock them up with the other one."

Chapter Twenty-Eight

The small group walked down the hall toward the holding cell with a soldier in front, Waters in the back, and the rest as prisoners in the middle. Gabby walked slowly to be sure she was within earshot of Waters.

"I can't believe you're doing this, Charlie. You're a goddamned traitor!" Gabby seethed.

"It's not what you think, Gabby, there's more going on here than you realize. This situation is a lot bigger than the field office and what we do there daily," Waters replied.

"Is that what you'll tell Raffi's family? Is that going to bring back those little girls' dad? You can lie to yourself all you want, but don't tell me this is about anything other than a bigger payday for yourself. Like you said, the DOD pays better. To think, I used to really care about you and think you were something special."

As they approached the door to the holding cell, the soldier in front held his ID up to the card reader and the door slipped open. While he ushered the others in, Waters grabbed Gabby's arm and pulled her aside.

"This is much bigger than anything you can imagine. Most folks are kept in the dark about what's really happening in the country — in the world for that matter. There are things kept from the public eye that would tear society apart. You must trust me on that. I never wanted anything to happen to you and I'll make sure that you and your friends are safe, but for now, you need to do what you're told."

"Don't you dare tell me what I need to do," Gabby said, pulling her hands back from Water's grip. "As far as I'm concerned, you're a dead man, Charlie. As a matter of fact, the Charlie Waters I knew never even existed." Gabby stomped into the holding cell, staring daggers at Waters. She could see in his eyes that her words had hurt him, and she was genuinely happy that they had.

"Hey guys, can't say I'm glad to have company, but I'm happy to see you!" John said, jumping up from his chair and coming over to greet everyone.

"Son! Thank God you're okay!" Randall said, rushing over to John, throwing his arms around him, and squeezing with all his might.

"How did you get here?" Jamie said, hurrying to give John a hug as well. "Last time I saw you, Dumond and his men had trapped you at my building. How did you get away from them?"

John told them about his ordeal at Dumond's hands.

"Who helped you get away?" Sam asked.

"Some guy I've never met before. He used to work for Dumond and Ackers, but he didn't agree with what they were doing and found a way out. He works for someone pretty powerful but wouldn't tell me who."

"Well I'm just thankful that you're alive," Randall said, putting his hand on John's shoulder.

The feel-good moment was loudly interrupted by a thunderous clap followed by men screaming orders. Before another word was spoken, the holding cell's door slid open.

"We're under attack, I'm under orders to —"

Debris and flames engulfed the soldier, before he could finish his sentence, as another explosion rocked the facility and reduced a section of the wall to rubble.

"Run for the door, we need to get out of here!" Randall yelled.

John led the way, followed by the others. As they exited the room, their eyes were blinded by sunlight streaming through a gaping hole in the exterior wall.

"Get down!" a soldier screamed as a hail of gunfire poured through the hole. Everyone ducked for cover.

"What's happening?" Randall shouted.

"Someone's attacking us with RPGs and automatic weapons. They have us pinned down inside the facility," the soldier replied.

"Who is it?"

"We don't know, but the colonel gave explicit orders to protect all of you. You need to follow me!" the soldier said, grabbing Randall's arm and motioning for the others to follow. They sprinted down the corridor toward the satellite dish.

"Stay here!" the soldier barked, pushing Randall and the others behind heavy office equipment and heading for the exit door. As he reached for the handle, an explosion caved the door inward, knocking him off his feet as shards of metal from the door ripped through his body, slamming his lifeless form to the ground. Three men dressed in battle fatigues rushed through the opening, their assault rifles at the ready.

"Back the other way!" Randall screamed at the group.

As they ran, the intruders rained bullets into the hallway behind them. Bits of wood, metal, and plastic showered the air and littered the ground.

The group raced back past the opening in the exterior wall. Another explosion detonated near the opening just as Gabby ran by, knocking her to the ground.

"Gabby!" Hoffman screamed, turning to help her. As he did, the gunmen turned the corner and unleashed an unrelenting torrent of bullets. Hoffman dove for an open door just in time to avoid being ripped apart.

The gunmen closed in on Gabby, who writhed on the ground in pain. The lead gunman reached her and trained his weapon on her. Gabby looked up defiantly. A sharp cracking sound was followed by the gunman's head bobbing up and then down. A stream of blood trailed down his face and his body slumped to the ground. The other gunmen spun, training their weapons in the direction of the gunshot blast. They were cut down by a ribbon of metal. Gabby craned her neck to see the source of the gunfire and saw her partner standing at the opening in the wall. He sprinted over by her side.

"Charlie!"

"Let's get you out of here!" Waters set down the assault rifle and lifted his friend. "Are you able to walk?"

"Yes!"

Without warning, a camouflaged man entered through the opening in the wall and turned his gun on Gabby. Waters instinctively threw his body between the gunman and Gabby just as the soldier fired. Waters' body shook viciously as the automatic weapon unloaded into him. He collapsed to the floor.

Gabby grabbed Waters' weapon and fired at the gunman as he reloaded. Several rounds found their mark and his body slammed against the wall, leaving a crimson streak as he slid to the ground.

Gabby grabbed Waters, turning him over. "Charlie!"

It was too late; his lifeless eyes stared up at her. She pulled him close to her and cried.

"Gabby, we need to get out of here!" Hoffman yelled as Randall appeared by his side.

The two men grabbed her and lifted her to her feet as Waters' body fell away.

"This way!" Sam yelled down the hallway.

The three sprinted in her direction as the sounds of the battle raged on.

They reached Sam and found John and Jamie trying to extricate someone from a pile of wreckage. As they drew close, they realized that it was Shaw. He was severely injured.

"Rob, Dad, help me try to move this beam!" John yelled.

The three men tried heaving the smashed girder lying across Shaw's abdomen, but it wouldn't budge.

Shaw grabbed Randall's shirt and pulled him within earshot.

"Under my desk, there's a panel on the right side. Push it. There's a flash drive with information about Operation Ice Hammer. Take it and read it! Find General Flores. He must know that we failed here! Hurry!" Shaw released his grip, pointing at his desk.

Randall crawled under the desk and groped for the panel. Finding it, he pressed. A section at the bottom of the desk sprang open to reveal the flash drive. Randall secured it in his wallet.

"Desk drawer … keys to my Jeep!" Shaw cried out.

Randall retrieved them, running back to Shaw's side.

"It's parked by the satellite dish … go!"

The group exited the room with Randall at the rear.

"Randall!" Shaw called out.

Randall stopped, turning to look at Shaw, who motioned for him. Randall knelt by Shaw's side, his eyes wide with confusion. Shaw's breathing was labored as he struggled for oxygen.

"Caroline … remember Caroline." He pushed Randall away from him and pointed for him to go. Unsure of what Shaw's cryptic message meant, Randall staggered to the door and turned to face Shaw. The men's eyes met. Shaw gave a curt nod. Randall looked on helplessly, then left.

One by one, they bolted through the door toward the satellite dish. Reaching a small section of standing wall, they dropped to the ground to take cover. The scene was utter mayhem. Bloodied bodies littered the tiny courtyard, and entire sections of buildings and trailers had collapsed or were missing. What was left of Shaw's small contingency of soldiers was trying desperately to repel the attackers. They were clearly failing.

"This way!" John yelled, pointing to several vehicles parked in a small clearing.

Randall judged the vehicles to be twenty-five yards from the edge of the satellite building. They would have to traverse the open space to reach them, making them easy targets. Randall grabbed John's arm. "You wait here with them."

"No way! I'm going to the Jeep, you stay here under cover!"

"Son, I can't let you. If something happens to me, you've got to get everyone else to safety."

"I'm younger and faster than you; I'll have a better chance."

"There's no way I'm letting you go."

John was about to speak when he felt a soft touch on his arm. It was Jamie. She looked into his eyes.

"You have to let your dad try."

John looked at Jamie and then his Dad. The shooting was intensifying. More attackers were closing on the facility.

"Please," Jamie said

John nodded.

Randall stood, ready to go, but was dragged back to the ground by his son.

"Be careful," John said.

Randall smiled. "I'll be right back."

Randall sprinted for the cars. Lines of tracers danced wildly about his feet as the attackers tried to pepper him with bullets. He moved in quick bursts, changing directions frequently. He was sweating profusely, and the smell of smoldering wreckage filled his lungs as he dodged the relentless gunfire.

He closed on the first vehicle parked in the opening, a Yamaha motorcycle. He ran past it, ducking behind it for cover. Next up was Audi A-4 Coupe, but three cars beyond it, Randall saw his target. A silver Jeep Wrangler Rubicon, its convertible top removed.

Randall quickened his pace. He was closing on it when he saw a man pop up from behind several small bushes, just beyond the vehicle. The assailant was holding an assault rifle. Randall slid like a base runner trying to avoid a tag. Several rounds pierced the air above his head.

He rolled under a white Land Rover, emerging from the other side. He couldn't see the gunman anywhere. The windows of the Land Rover exploded above him.

Randall ducked behind the vehicle and crawled toward its rear, away from the shooter.

The gunman emerged from the brush and strode toward Randall, firing in small bursts. Randall could see the man's legs and boots from under the vehicle. He was closing on him quickly.

Randall leaped to his feet and dashed for cover behind the Audi, a trail of gunfire following close behind. He knelt next to the side of the vehicle. Seeing the quickly approaching gunman, he rolled onto his back and under the car. The gunman moved closer. Randall crawled on his belly, trying to exit from under the opposite side of the Audi. His belt tugged back. He was caught on something under the car.

The gunman came to a stop by the vehicle and knelt. He wore a sickening grin as he stared at Randall, his face only inches away. He lowered his gun.

A sudden jackhammer-like sound reverberated, and Randall watched as the gunman was ripped from the ground like a rag doll, the earth around him exploding in great chunks.

Randall pulled his belt free and slid out the other side of the Audi just in time to see an Apache attack helicopter fly over the compound, heading in the direction of the attacking main force. Reinforcements had arrived.

He sprinted to the Jeep, yanked the door open, and started the car. He jammed his foot on the accelerator and the Jeep lurched forward, smashing the motorcycle out of his way. Randall drove directly toward John and the group, coming to a skidding stop right in front of them.

"Get in!"

Everyone piled into the Wrangler.

"Go!" John yelled.

Randall spun the Jeep back in the direction he had come, driving directly away from Dumond's men. As he did, a huge explosion materialized from the direction of the helicopter. He glanced over his shoulder in time to see a fireball crashing to the ground. The helicopter had been obliterated. It would be his final memory of Shaw's ill-fated command post as they escaped down a fire road, away from the complex.

Chapter Twenty-Nine

The sound of gunfire had diminished to an occasional popping sound.

The tide of the battle has turned against us.

Shaw danced on the edge of unconsciousness. The world was blurring at the edges as he tried to stave off impending death. He no longer felt the weight of the great iron beam that was resting on his mid-section—a sure sign that his senses were failing. He had lost a great deal of blood and knew his time was limited.

Two figures appeared at the doorway to his office. He didn't recognize the first, but immediately knew the second.

"Fredericks ... you son of a bitch ... I'll ..."

"You're not going to do anything but bleed to death."

"Where's the information you've been hiding from Randall?" the second figure asked Shaw.

"Who … the hell … are you?" Shaw asked, his vision obscured by his condition and a ribbon of blood flowing freely from a gash on his head.

The stranger knelt next to him.

"I'm Francis Dumond."

"Dumond … I've heard of you." Shaw snorted.

Fredericks began rummaging through Shaw's desk.

"You won't find it there." Shaw said, drifting in and out of consciousness.

"What do you mean?" Dumond asked.

"The flash drive is gone. And so are your chances of finding the base," Shaw snarled, his lips parting into a grin.

"Where is it, Colonel?" Dumond snapped.

Shaw was fading quickly. Dumond grasped his face and shook until he opened his eyes. "Where is the flash drive?"

"I gave it to them," Shaw replied.

"To who? Randall?"

Shaw smiled again, his eyelids sliding shut.

He was slipping away quickly, but he heard Dumond and Fredericks conversing as they walked out of his office.

"What do we do now?" Fredericks asked.

"We find Randall and his brood, and this time, I intend to finish the job I started in Peru."

Chapter Thirty

August 20, 1:17 P.M.
Hamilton Harbor, Bermuda

The boat gently bobbed in the water, following the rhythmic ebb and flow of the currents. After escaping from Shaw's base, the group had driven directly to Hoffman's boat. They had set out to sea and Hoffman had dropped anchor in Hamilton Harbor hoping to be lost amongst the throngs of other small vessels docked nearby. The sun was almost directly overhead as the morning gave way to afternoon.

The group sat hunched around the small screen of Rob's laptop, anxiously waiting to discover what information they would find on Shaw's flash drive. Randall sat directly in front of the computer, his hand hovering nervously over the trackpad, ready to click open the files his former enemy had so carefully guarded. As he waited, Randall couldn't help but consider how quickly fortunes could change. In a matter of minutes, Shaw had gone from being his kidnapper to entrusting him with his life's work.

The computer whirred to life and Randall wasted no time inserting the flash drive into the USB port. He discovered a single folder named *Operation Ice Hammer,* just as Shaw had described. He clicked on it. The file was password protected.

"Great, what do we do now?" Hoffman said.

At first, Randall stared at the screen in disbelief. To come this close and not be able to read the files was overwhelming. Then he remembered Shaw's final words to him.

"Wait, I think I know the password." Randall typed the word "Caroline" into the computer. The computer sprang to life as the folder opened, revealing two files. The first was a word document, the second a video. Randall chose the video first. After an interminable wait, the video finished loading and began to play.

A handsome man with a thick mop of sandy blond hair and piercing blue eyes appeared on the screen wearing a wetsuit unzipped and folded down to his abdomen. He was thin and wiry with a face that would have looked at home on the cover of a fashion magazine.

My name is Dr. Charles Vernon, and this video is classified Top Secret by the Department of Defense, requiring appropriate security clearance to allow viewing. The information I'm about to share is the result of over six years of research by my team, which culminated with the discovery made on March 3, 2017 in the Sistema Sac Actun underwater cavern. The cave system is situated along the Caribbean coast of the Yucatán Peninsula with passages to the north and west of the village of Tulum. Out of respect for the contents of the discovery, we refer to it as La Caverna de la Piedra de Rosetta Cósmica, The Cavern of the Cosmic Rosetta Stone.

After a comprehensive review of the literature retrieved at Roswell, we felt certain that this was the location spelled out in the translated material. *My partner, Dr. Bill Kim, and I made initial dives on the site beginning in July, 2016, but we were unable to confirm the exact location of the cavern until March of the following year. That was when Dr. Kim discovered the cavern with the same writing uncovered in the wreckage. Although some of the symbols were undecipherable, we were able to read enough of the message to determine that the tablets in question were in a previously undiscovered cavity running perpendicular to the cavern with the writing.*

Our team found a small fissure located deep within the outer cavern and was able to fit a small hand-held submersible with a nose-mounted camera into the opening. The submersible was able to confirm the existence of La Caverna de la Piedra de Rosetta Cósmica.

Bill took a team back in the following day and was able to get into the fissure to look for the tablet. Sadly, before he was able to recover it, the cavern suffered a massive cave-in, trapping Bill. We discussed using explosives to create a big enough opening to get him out, but it was determined that the area was already too unstable and that the use of such a charge would further endanger Bill's life, as well as the lives of others. We then attempted to clear the debris manually, but another diver was seriously injured during a secondary collapse. After multiple delays, we were finally able to remove enough debris to reinsert our smallest submersible unit. Unfortunately, Bill didn't make it. We were forced to terminate retrieval operations to get our injured diver to a medical facility.

A special rigging system is being built to provide support within the cavern for a second expedition and additional heavy underwater equipment and greater manpower will be utilized to retrieve Bill's body. We estimate it will take six to nine months before we will be able to return to the site, but now, we're all struggling with the loss of our good friend. Bill was not only a wonderfully talented scientist, he was also a great friend to all of us and he will be dearly missed.

The video continued with Vernon looking down, placing his hand on his head. He was clearly shaken at the loss of his colleague. A moment later, the video ended. Everyone stood in silence trying to grasp the enormity of what they had just heard.

"This is impossible," Hoffman said. "Charles and Bill died in 2011 testing a new deep-water submersible in the Marianas Trench. The submersible was utilizing a new, low friction propulsion system. According to the report I read, they had successfully passed below the seventeen-thousand-foot mark when they reported mechanical trouble, then the system suffered a catastrophic failure."

"Jesus, what happened to them?" John asked.

"The crew of the command ship reported that they maintained contact for another thirty-eight minutes as the submersible sank below nineteen-thousand feet. Then they heard the outer hull failing as Bill and Charles tried to restart the system. A full search and rescue mission was launched but they were unable to locate anything. It was assumed that the submersible suffered a complete hull breach and took Bill and Charles to the bottom of the trench."

"You think it was all just a ploy, so they could disappear to work on this?" Randall said, pointing a thumb at the computer screen.

"I dunno, I guess it was."

"Let's take a look at the other file," Randall said, clicking on the second document.

The contents of the Word file were equally startling.

The file explained the existence of a secret underground military facility in Dulce, New Mexico, which was the headquarters for Operation Ice Hammer. Randall's blood ran cold as he read the name of the commander of the base.

"Am I reading this correctly?" Hoffman asked.

"I'm afraid you are," Randall replied.

"I guess we know where to find General Flores."

"What's next?" John asked.

After a moment of thought, Randall spoke. "John, you, Gabby, and Sam head to New Mexico to speak with General Flores. We need to find out exactly what Operation Ice Hammer entails and how it relates to what's happening to Jamie."

"Do you really think they'll talk to us?" John asked.

"The only way to find out is to go. I'm sure they know by now that their base was destroyed, and Shaw was lost. If they ask for proof that we're working with Shaw, show them these files and tell them his password."

"What are you, Rob, and Jamie going to do?"

Randall turned to face his friend. "How do you feel about going for a dive, old buddy?"

"Just like old times," Hoffman said, sporting a large grin.

"Jamie, we'll need someone on the boat while we're in the water."

"You know I'm here for you, Nick."

"Okay then, let's get going."

Chapter Thirty-One

August 21, 6:15 A.M.
Albuquerque, New Mexico

The American Airlines jet touched down in the pre-dawn darkness at Albuquerque International Sunport. John, Sam, and Gabby had spent more than half the day traveling from Bermuda to Miami and then to New Mexico. The airport was a small sea of lights in an otherwise desolate expanse of darkness, punctuated by other tiny islands of brightness in the New Mexico landscape. Most of the city was asleep as the 787 Dreamliner lazily taxied to the loading gate outside of Terminal 5.

After a few hours of restless sleep, John was deep in thought as he stared out the window into the darkness. He felt a hand touch his forearm. He turned to see Sam slowly rubbing the sleep from her eyes.

"Are we in New Mexico?"

"Just landed. We should be at the terminal any minute now. Where's Gabby?"

"I was just speaking with the flight crew," Gabby said, pushing her way past passengers retrieving their bags, as she approached John's seat. "They said Dulce is about ninety miles from here. We can rent a car outside the terminal and be there in a couple of hours."

"Sounds good, but how do we find the base? Remember, this is a secret facility so it's not like we can just open a map and put our finger on it," Sam said.

"I have an idea that might help, but we'll need to make a stop on our way," John replied.

A short time later, the three approached the rented Ford Fusion.

John turned to Gabby. "You drive."

"Where to?" Gabby asked.

"We need to make a stop at Andy's Card and Comic Lair in Las Cruces."

Sam and Gabby shared an amused look.

Grinning, Sam faced her brother. "John, don't you think it's an odd time to browse for comic books?"

"You realize that's about 180 miles in the opposite direction. Exactly who do you want to speak with and how do you know him?" Gabby asked.

"His name is Andrew Bauman and we were in the same dorm wing in college. Andy was a computer science major — he helped me with a computer programming class and I helped him with organic chemistry. He was brilliant when it came to writing code and advanced algorithms. He eventually graduated with a double major in computer programming and mathematics and went on to earn his PhD in math."

"Why would a guy like that open a comic book store? He could have gone to work for the CIA, NSA, or any number of agencies and made a great living."

John pursed his lips as a crooked smile crept across his face. "Let's just say that Andy marches to the beat of his own drum. He did his doctoral dissertation on advanced mathematic algorithms and their application for breaking and creating advanced encryption. As part of his study, he worked with the NSA for a little over a year and caught wind of what they wanted him to do with his technical expertise. He politely declined, so they pulled the plug on his project and threatened to have him imprisoned if he ever talked about his work."

"Okay, but that still doesn't explain why we're going to see him," Gabby persisted.

"After his brush with the NSA and some of the things he learned while working with the government, Andy became a believer in government conspiracies and started conducting research into some of them. With his knowledge and contacts in the computer field, he's been able to uncover some interesting facts that the government has tried very hard to conceal. If anyone knows where to find the Dulce facility, it's Andy."

"Found the shop on my phone, it says his store opens at 10:00 a.m. Looks like we'll have some time to kill. Any ideas?" Sam asked.

"I don't know about the two of you, but I'm ready for breakfast," John replied as Gabby pulled the rental car onto the highway.

Chapter Thirty-Two

August 21, 6:35 A.M.
Sistema Sac Actun, Yucatan Peninsula

Utilizing the coordinates provided in the documents on Shaw's flash drive, Hoffman programmed the GPS on the boat they had rented in nearby Cancún. The system guided them to the entrance of the sea cave leading to La Caverna de la Piedra de Rosetta Cósmica. Once they arrived, Hoffman, Jamie, and Randall found themselves floating on the glassy surface of the Caribbean Ocean. The sun was just rising, painting the Eastern sky a beautiful shade of deep blue as the new day shook away the cobwebs of the recently passed evening.

Randall and Jamie busied themselves preparing the diving equipment while Hoffman brought the ship to a stop directly over the mouth of the cave and dropped anchor. He studied several underwater depth charts he had picked up along the way and confirmed the depth of the opening.

"Are we in the right place, captain?" Randall said with a grin.

"You know it, buddy. If there's one thing I can do, it's pilot a ship and stop her right where I want to be."

"I have complete faith in you. There's no one I would rather have driving this boat."

"Jamie, I'm going to need you to monitor our progress from above. Come over here and I'll show you how to operate the boat." Hoffman said.

Jamie did as instructed, standing next to Hoffman while he explained the controls to the ship, the weather monitor, and communications system.

"I checked the forecast — we have 4-5 hours of clear skies before a tropical storm front rolls in," Hoffman said. "We'll take extra tanks to increase our total dive time. I'll need you to maintain the ship's location by firing up the engines occasionally to move us to compensate for the current, which will carry us due east. I'll also want you to keep an eye out for updated weather news to let us know if we need to cut the dive short."

"Got it."

Hoffman smiled a broad knowing smile. "That's why I like working with bright people, no need to repeat instructions."

The two men donned their spring suits and masks, and dove into the water, carrying their extra tanks with them. The weight of the tanks served a twofold purpose. First, they would allow the men to extend their dive time by providing additional breathable air, and second, their added mass served as ballast to assist them with their descent. Once in the outer cave, they would set the extra tanks aside to allow them to move about more freely while they explored.

The descent to the cave went without incident and the two men soon found themselves immersed in the darkness of the cavern. Having affixed a safety line, they switched on their diving lights and began searching for the writing Charles had spoken about in the video. Hoffman carried a Sony Z100 Ultra HD camera with its Gates housing to record the experience, so they could review it on the boat to see if they had missed anything on the dive. He also figured it wouldn't hurt to have the dive recorded on video as insurance, in case the stone was too large to retrieve.

The experience was otherworldly as the lights revealed the intricate and beautiful features of the rock formations existing nearly forty meters beneath the surface. Hoffman was the first to find the cryptic symbols, which confirmed that they were in the correct location. Next, the two men began probing deeper into the murky darkness, searching for the fissure. As they entered the bowels of the underwater cavern, Randall noticed what appeared to be a recently created debris field. Chunks of rock ranging in size from a man's fist to the size of a bathtub littered a section of the tunnel. He immediately recognized that the fissure must have been somewhere nearby.

Randall motioned to Hoffman. "Here's the debris field. The fissure Dr. Kim entered must be nearby," he said into the Divex microphone built into his diving helmet.

Hoffman nodded and the two continued their search. It didn't take them long to find the fissure and, as expected, it was littered with debris from the cave-in, but Dr. Vernon's team had cleared away most of the larger stones. The two men set up a small winch and pried the remaining rocks away from the opening until there was a gap large enough for a man to fit through.

Randall looked at Hoffman. "I'm heading in," he said, pointing into the fissure.

Rob tapped his watch to remind his friend to pay attention to his oxygen supply and time limit. "Don't forget to set your dive watch."

Nodding, Randall slipped through the opening.

The initial gap into the inner cavern was a long tube-like structure that started wider and slowly tapered to the point where Randall could barely fit through. As he reached the end of the tube, Randall shone his light into the inky darkness. He could only see several feet into the cavern and couldn't make out any details. Holding his light in one hand, Randall grasped the edge with the other, kicked his fins, and passed into the inner cave system.

The darkness was all consuming. Without his light, Randall couldn't see his hands in front of his mask. He lifted his beam in front of him. A ghostly figure materialized from the darkness. He lurched back, startled by the sight. His heart raced as he put his hands up in defense. The figure floated past, swaying with the light current.

The face was mostly white and bloated, except for streaks of red from jagged flesh near the left eye, which stared vacantly into the cavern. He had found the late Dr. Kim. Randall took several deep breaths, trying desperately to calm his nerves, his hands shaking.

He gently pushed the floating apparition away and examined the cave. The cavity itself wasn't very large, perhaps twenty feet in length with the floor falling away to a maximum depth of about twelve feet. The sides and floor of the cavern were relatively smooth, but stalactites drooped from the ceiling, creating the look of a jagged-toothed monster closing its mouth on its prey. As he shone his light on them, they cast long shadows over the back wall of the cavern.

Randall swam deeper into the cave, searching for the stone that could help to explain the cryptic message they sought to decipher. He moved his beam in sweeping motions over the floor and soon discovered Dr. Kim's smashed goggles. They were sitting in silt, frozen in time since Bill Kim had met his untimely death.

As he swam up for a closer look, Randall's fins stirred up the silt, creating a great cloud that filled the open space. He stopped momentarily, waiting for the disturbed dirt to settle so he could see again. Randall floated patiently, occasionally looking back in the direction of Dr. Kim's body. He shivered as he waited, unsure if it was the coldness of the deep water penetrating his suit or the discomfort he felt at being so far beneath the surface of the ocean in this dark, foreboding place. He decided at that moment to bring back Dr. Kim's remains. No one deserved to suffer such a horrible fate as to be left in this watery tomb.

Randall checked his dive watch. After allowing time for decompressing on the trip back up to the dive boat, he estimated that he had another fifteen minutes of air left for exploring the cave. The cloud of silt finally settled, and Randall was once again able to see. He trained his light where he had seen the goggles and tank and was surprised to find another object beside them. The sharp corner of what appeared to be a piece of stone was protruding from the sediment on the floor of the cavern. Randall swam slowly so as not to disturb the silt again and finally reached the stone. He carefully brushed away the debris and found a black, rectangular piece of rock with strange symbols carved into it. He had found the Cosmic Rosetta Stone.

He grasped it with both hands and gently lifted it. The tablet was no larger than two text books set side by side and offered little resistance, its weight lighter since it was underwater. Randall swam clear of the bottom and headed for the tube back to the outer cavern.

Without warning, the earth shuddered, knocking stalactites and other pieces of stone loose from the roof of the cavern. Randall searched for cover from the falling debris, but there was nowhere to hide. Reflexively, he dropped the stone and shone his light toward the ceiling just in time to see a jagged spike of rock falling directly on top of him. He kicked his fins, propelling himself to avoid the falling dagger of rock, which dropped inches away from his goggle-clad eyes.

More debris rained down on him and Randall was forced to move in a crazy zig-zag fashion to avoid being impaled. As the first pieces of debris hit the cavern floor, silt kicked wildly into the air. A debris cloud soon formed on the bottom of the cave, its plume extending ever upward and outward. Randall swam for the opening, racing to stay ahead of the falling rocks. He slipped into the tunnel just in time to avoid being smashed by another large boulder that had broken free of the ceiling.

The shaking subsided, but Randall waited in the tube, his breathing fast and shallow. He slowly backed out of the tunnel and returned to the cave. He shone his light toward the ceiling; there were no additional objects falling. After once again waiting for the silt to settle, he searched the floor for the tablet and found it amongst the debris field. It was lodged between several rocks. Still jittery from the shaking, Randall swam quickly to the stone. Moving several rocks aside, he picked it up, and propelled himself back out of the cavern.

The tunnel seemed longer going out than it had coming in. Randall held the tablet to his chest and kicked as hard as possible. In the commotion, he had forgotten about Hoffman and was now concerned for his friend's safety. Hopefully, he had avoided injury in the outer cavern.

The tunnel widened as Randall approached the exit into the outer cavern but there was something different. As he approached the end of the tube, his heart sank. There was debris in front of his exit. Randall set the stone on the floor of the tube and pushed at the rocks. They wouldn't move.

"Rob, are you there?" Randall called into his helmet microphone.

No reply.

"Rob, it's me, I'm trapped in the tunnel!"

Only silence.

"Jamie, can you hear me, I can't reach Rob!"

Jamie didn't reply either. Randall assumed that something was interfering with their communication system, hoping that this was the cause for Hoffman and Jamie's lack of response.

He checked his dive watch. Assuming that he could not reach or find an external air tank after the cave-in, he only had enough air to slowly ascend to avoid nitrogen poisoning. He couldn't afford to waste precious time in the tunnel.

He pushed with all his strength on the rocky debris blocking his way, but there was no movement. He was trapped.

Chapter Thirty-Three

August 21, 9:58 A.M.
Albuquerque, New Mexico

The sun had climbed high into the sky as Gabby pulled the rental car to a stop on South Solano Drive in Las Cruces. She stared out the window at an incredible view: Highway 10 stretched out into the distance, running in an almost perfectly straight line toward the Organ Mountains. Having spent the better part of the past eleven years in the Bahamas, she was taken by the stark beauty of the desert landscape. Pulling herself away from the view, she checked the thermometer, which already read 91 degrees.

"Going to be a hot one," John mused. "Looks like the shop should be open in a few more minutes."

The three exited the Ford Fusion and walked up to the door of the comic shop. John pulled the door handle, but it wouldn't open.

"I guess they're still closed," John said, knocking on the door.

At first, nothing happened, but after a moment they saw movement inside the shop as a young woman made her way to the door. She glanced through the glass door and, after fiddling with the lock for a moment, opened it.

"Hi, welcome to Andy's Comic Lair, please come in," she said, motioning for her three would-be customers to enter the business. "Good timing, we were just opening. Can I help you with something?"

"I'm an old friend of Andy's from college. I was in the area and thought I would stop by to see him. I didn't call ahead but was hoping he would be here. My name's John Randall," John said, extending his hand to the woman.

"Nice to meet you, John, I'm Melinda. Andy's in the back taking inventory, I'll go get him."

Melinda disappeared into the back of the store and reappeared shortly with Andy in tow. Bauman was small in stature, about five and half feet tall, with long chestnut brown hair tied back into a ponytail. He wore round, metal-rimmed glasses that hung off his sharp, beak-like nose. His face was largely hidden underneath a well-trimmed goatee that extended down to a crisp triangular point.

"Johnny, how have you been? When Melinda told me you were here, I thought she was kidding! What have you been up to?" Bauman said grasping John's hand and pulling him close for a hug.

"I've been good, Andy. Remember Jacob? He and I are research partners working for a biomed company in D.C."

"You and Jakester are research partners, huh? Makes sense, he's a great guy. Did he come with you?"

"Unfortunately, he didn't."

"Well that's okay, it's good to see you anyway. How about your two friends here? Do they work with you?" Bauman said, turning to face Sam first.

"I'm Sam Randall, John's sister. It's nice to meet you," Sam said, extending her hand.

Bauman gripped it tightly and shook with vigor. "John talked about you a lot in school, nice to finally meet you." Next, he turned to Gabby.

"Special Agent Gabby Gutierrez, nice to meet you."

Bauman smirked at her greeting, clearly caught off guard, but he still shook her hand enthusiastically. "Special Agent? Am I in some kind of trouble?"

"Andy, you've probably guessed that this isn't really a social call. Do you have somewhere we can speak in private?" John asked.

Bauman furrowed his eyebrows. "Sure Johnny, we can speak in my office in the back. Oh, where are my manners? John, Sam, and Gabby, this is Melinda, my fiancée. She's the best thing that's ever happened to me," Bauman said, smiling over his glasses at Melinda, who blushed with embarrassment. "Mel, do you mind watching the shop while I talk with my old buddy here?"

"Sure, hon. Nice to meet you all."

Bauman lifted a fold-up section of the counter and led the group to his office in the back. The shop was filled with boxes labeled with familiar comic book titles and other memorabilia. John noted that there were several thousand dollars of merchandise on one shelf alone. They passed through the inventory section and into Bauman's office, which was sleek and modern. The floor was carpeted with a gray and navy blue striped pattern and the walls were putty colored with tall khaki file cabinets spaced evenly on two of the four walls. Bauman's desk was a functional wrap-around unit with solid wood desktops and overhead hutches. His desk was completely bare except for a black, cylindrical device situated in the rear center portion of the counter. Upon seeing it, John recognized it as the latest incarnation of the Apple Mac Pro. Mounted on the wall directly above it were dual Apple Thunderbolt 27-inch displays.

"Nice set up," John said, nodding toward the futuristic computer.

"Thanks, John, I only own the best," Bauman said, smiling broadly. "Please sit down."

The four sat around a circular table with four black rolling chairs situated in the corner of his office.

"What's up? It's not every day my old college roommate pays me a visit with two beautiful women, especially one that works for the FBI."

John took a deep breath. "We're here because we're in trouble and we need your help. Jacob was kidnapped and we're not sure where he is, but we have reason to believe we can find the answers nearby in Dulce."

Bauman raised an eyebrow. "Go on."

John summarized the events that had led them to this meeting while Bauman listened attentively.

"Right now, my dad and his friend Rob are searching for the tablet and we're trying to find the base at Dulce. I know you used to dabble in this kind of stuff and thought you might be able to help us find General Flores."

Bauman stared at John through squinted eyes. He shot up from the table and settled down at his desk, tapping at a hidden keyboard. His monitors flickered to life. John and Sam shared a look while Gabby watched Bauman closely.

"Come over here." Bauman waived them to his side as aerial images appeared on the dual screens above his desk.

"What's that?" Sam asked.

"Satellite images of the alleged Dulce base, taken within the last 72 hours. The first one here was taken three days ago," Bauman said, pointing to the left monitor. The image showed a small complex that looked like a mining facility complete with banks of fans emanating from one hillside. The photograph of the facility showed very little activity. "This one was taken 48 hours ago, and you can see a small convoy of vehicles staged in this general area, to the east of the access road. Clearly there's something happening with all of these people entering or exiting right here." This time, he was pointing to the right monitor, which showed an entrance to what appeared to be a tunnel in the side of an earthen mound.

Bauman punched the keyboard again, causing the image on the left to change. "This final image was taken 24 hours ago."

"I don't see anything except a single truck in this one," John commented.

"How about now?" Bauman said, zooming in on the vehicle.

"My God, is that what I think it is? It can't be," John said, staring at the screen.

On the monitor were three armed men leading a fourth, whose head was covered, and hands were bound, into the tunnel.

"Based on your story and the timeline you provided, we may have found Jacob. If not, this must be someone else who's involved in this secret government plan. The timing of this activity probably isn't a coincidence."

"How did you pull up these images so quickly and where did you get them?" Gabby asked.

"Let's just say … I like to keep close tabs on what the government is doing nearby. As for where I got them, our country isn't the only one to have orbital imaging systems. There are other groups who have an active interest in what's taking place in Dulce. Whatever you're involved in is big and the secret is out. Something major is going to happen soon and we need to get you in there as soon as possible."

"We?" Sam asked.

"Yes. I'll help you. We'll need to get you close enough to contact General Flores directly. If you get picked up by the exterior guards, you'll end up in a holding cell. By the time you speak to the general, if you ever get the chance, it'll be too late. We need to get Flores' attention, so you can speak to him directly."

"How do you propose we do that?" John asked.

Bauman's face wrinkled into an impish grin as he tented his hands and peered over his beak-like nose.

"Why don't you let me worry about that?"

Chapter Thirty-Four

August 21, 10:20 A.M.
Sistema Sac Actun, Yucatan Peninsula

Hoffman stood on the deck of the diving boat, his hands in the air, and his body dripping salt water. After the cave-in, he'd been unable to reach Randall or Jamie, so he'd made his way to the surface to get additional tools to help free his friend. He was greeted by six uniformed men toting guns who had boarded their boat while he and Randall were in the cave. The soldiers had clearly been monitoring their whereabouts as demonstrated by the timing of their actions. Now, with Randall trapped by the cave-in, Hoffman and Jamie were powerless to help him. Of the six assailants, three had their weapons pointed at Hoffman and two covered Jamie. The sixth man, clearly the leader of the group, approached Hoffman.

General Keung was nearly six feet tall with short black hair tinged with silver edges. His dark brown eyes conveyed his razor-like focus on completing his mission. His face was round with the long, deep creases that came from years of bearing the responsibility of safeguarding his country.

"What did you find in the cavern?" he asked with a thick accent, holding Hoffman's dive camera in his hand.

"Nothing. We didn't find anything," Hoffman replied.

"Do you take me for a fool? I know that you and your friend found the stone and filmed it to study later. All of the information I need to find the base is on this," the general said, holding up the camera. "Put this in my cabin so I can examine the footage when we are done here," he said, handing the device to a young soldier.

"You can't keep me here; my friend is still down there, and he's trapped in the cavern. If I don't clear the debris blocking the tunnel, he'll run out of air!"

"That is not my concern." Keung looked past Hoffman and smiled as his own divers climbed up the ladder on the rear of the boat and made their way to him.

"General, we have set additional charges above the cavern as you ordered. When they detonate, they will destroy the cave and everything inside," the lead diver reported.

"How long before the charge detonates?"

The diver glanced at his watch. "Fifty-six minutes and counting, sir."

"Very good. Take the prisoners to our ship and prepare to return to base."

"You can't do that, you're signing Nick's death warrant by destroying that cave system!" Hoffman yelled.

General Keung motioned downward with a swipe of his hand and Hoffman was rewarded with a stinging blow to the back of his head by one of the general's men.

"Rob!" Jamie yelled, trying to move in his direction. Another guard jabbed the end of his weapon into her chest to block her movement.

Hoffman staggered to his feet, rubbing the back of his head.

A large, black inflatable craft, carrying additional soldiers, pulled alongside the anchored dive boat. The crew hurried off the vessel, securing the two boats together. The general walked to the black inflatable, motioning for his men to prod Hoffman and Jamie to join him.

"After you," he said, gesturing for his prisoners to climb aboard the sleek black craft.

Once the prisoners were secured, the rest of the military detail piled onto the inflatable. They sped away from the dive boat, leaving Randall to his fate.

Chapter Thirty-Five

The black Escalade roared down the desert highway as the late afternoon sun sank into the west. Their destination grew closer as they approached the location Bauman had identified as the Dulce base. Bauman drove the vehicle while explaining the plan to his friends.

"So how are we going to get by the primary gate guards?" John asked.

"The main gate guards have one simple assignment: keep out anyone who doesn't belong. They do that by screening all personnel that come to the gate, to confirm that they have authority to access the compound. The only ones authorized to enter are military personnel and contractors hired by the government to work at the facility. The guards verify their clearance by checking these," Bauman said, holding up a plastic ID card with his right hand while steering with his left.

"This is a Department of Defense contractor's badge," he continued. "All information about the contractor is coded into

185

a chip within the card. The guards take the badge, scan it into a card reader that's tied into the DOD database and, voila, they know whether or not the badge holder has business on the base."

Gabby craned her neck from the backseat. "Where did you get the badge?"

"When I used to work for the DOD, I got to know some folks. Let's just say there are a few staffers who don't entirely support the agency's agenda."

"That takes care of you, but what about us?" John asked.

"Open that glove box in front of you," Bauman said.

John did as instructed and retrieved three additional badges, one for each of his accomplices.

"So that's what you were doing before we left on this little road trip," John commented, turning to distribute the ID cards.

Their SUV wound deeper into the desert, crested a small hill in the road, and followed the road as it bent to the left. In the distance, John saw a large installation materialize on the horizon. They had arrived at the Dulce base.

As they approached the perimeter guard gate, a burly man in military fatigues waived them to a stop. The entrance was precisely what John would have imagined for a heavily guarded military complex. A hefty gate blocked the entrance into the base, followed by double strips of metal spikes that protruded several inches from the ground. As if this wasn't enough, the access road was also protected by large metal pylons set three feet apart on center. If a picture could paint a message, this one would say *Stay Out*.

John stared at another soldier clutching his assault rifle as his partner approached their truck. The soldier strode to the driver's side door as Bauman opened his window.

"How's it going?" Bauman asked cheerily.

"Card," the soldier replied, his expression set in stone.

"Here you go," Bauman said, handing over his ID card. "Nice weather we're having today. Not too hot, not too cold."

The soldier shot Bauman a disdainful glare before examining the card.

"We need your ID cards as well," the guard said to the rest of the group. He collected them, never breaking eye contact with Bauman.

"Wait here," the soldier said, disappearing into the guard station. His partner walked directly in front of the Escalade, staring them down.

The soldier with the ID's emerged a moment later, handing the cards back to Bauman.

"Pull forward when the gate opens."

The gate slid open — the metal spikes and pylons retracting into the ground — allowing the SUV to pass. Bauman drove the vehicle fifty yards past the guard house and pulled to a stop.

"Switch with me, John," he said, exiting the driver's side and walking around to John's door. Stunned at first, John hopped down from the passenger side, walked around to the driver's side, and began to drive, noting that the guards had apparently seen them switching and were now glaring at them as they pulled away.

"I don't think they liked seeing us switch like that."

"We really didn't have a choice. I didn't think you could pull off the lie like I could. Now there's something else I need to do," Bauman said, pulling a laptop from under the passenger seat.

John glanced back over his shoulder toward the entrance. "One guard is calling someone on the radio and another one is running to a Humvee. What exactly is your plan again?"

"Keep driving toward that building right over there," Bauman said, pointing to a semi-circular, windowed building built into the hillside. "I need to get close enough to access their network."

"The Humvee's closing on us," Sam said.

Several other vehicles appeared from an underground structure and were bearing down on them from multiple directions. John accelerated, closing in on the building Bauman had identified. "How's it going there?"

"I'm still trying to access their network, they've improved their encryption since the last time I hacked their system."

Gabby glared at Bauman. "You've hacked the DOD system before?"

"A few times," Bauman replied, typing furiously.

John glanced nervously in the rearview mirror and then scanned to his left and right. The soldiers were closing in from all sides. They would soon be boxed in. All John could do was make a beeline for the building and hope that Bauman's plan worked.

"Assuming you hack their network, what's next?" John asked.

"I'm going to get the general's attention," Bauman replied, still tapping on his keyboard.

The chase vehicles closed to within twenty yards as John drove onward. The building was no more than forty yards in front of him now. They were running out of real estate. He gunned the engine for the final run and skidded to a stop ten feet short of the building. The military vehicles formed a ring around the Escalade as heavily armed soldiers poured out from them. They encircled the SUV, guns drawn and ready.

"In the car, turn off the engine and put your hands where I can see them!"

John shut off the engine. "Andy?"

"Almost done, just need a few more seconds."

"Exit the vehicle. NOW!"

Armed soldiers were now standing directly outside the doors on both sides of the SUV, their guns trained on the occupants.

"Get out of the car and put your hands on your heads!"

Bauman smiled and put his hands up, just as a soldier opened the passenger door from the outside. They all exited the Escalade.

"Face the vehicle!"

The four stood, facing the SUV, remaining motionless. The soldier who had barked the orders stepped away from them. He reached for his earpiece and listened to someone speaking to him. John tried to see where he went, but another soldier blocked his view. John didn't dare turn for fear of acquiring new ventilation holes in his outfit. It had never occurred to him to question Bauman about his plan. Now he wondered if trusting his old friend had been a mistake. His question was soon answered.

"Who's responsible for playing the video of Dr. Kim?" a gruff voice called out from behind John. He strained to see who was speaking, but the man was out of his view.

"I'm the guilty party," Bauman replied.

"Bring him to me," the voice said calmly.

"Yes, General."

Chapter Thirty-Six

Randall backed out of the tunnel and into the inky blackness of the inner cave, leaving the Cosmic Rosetta Stone inside the tube. He shined his flashlight to assess the damage and look for other ways out. The cave-in had subsided, but the agitated silt still clouded the water. Randall had no choice but to wait for the water to clear. He suddenly felt very cold and alone. Although his spring suit was designed to maintain his body heat, the long-term exposure to the cool water at this depth had slowly gnawed at his core body temperature. Making matters worse, he was running out of air.

Realizing that there was nothing he could do at the moment, Randall switched off his light to save the battery, casting himself into total darkness. He was no stranger to being alone, having spent large stretches of time conducting research, but this was an entirely different feeling. He was wholly cut off from the outside world and his mind dwelled on being trapped in this watery crypt for eternity. Knowing that Dr. Kim had suffered a similar fate only made the situation worse. Panic crept into his mind and he had to force himself not to lose hope.

His thoughts then turned to concern for Hoffman and Jamie. There were three possible reasons he hadn't been able to reach them: something was interfering with his signal, they had left him, or they were in trouble. Randall was certain that they wouldn't have left him unless something had happened to them, which meant there were really two possibilities. Floating in the dark, Randall's mind raced, and he arrived at a frightening prospect: Dumond had learned of their discovery, had followed them and had captured Hoffman and Jamie. If this were the case, Dumond would simply wait for Randall's oxygen to run out and then send a team of divers to retrieve the stone. Once they had it, there would be no need to keep Jamie and Hoffman alive. Randall steeled himself against the thought of remaining trapped in the cavern and losing his friends. He had to find a way out, so he could rescue them.

With a renewed sense of purpose, Randall made a mental checklist of the steps he needed to take. The first order of business was his oxygen supply. He and Hoffman had brought additional bottles, but they were on the other side of the blocked tunnel. Randall switched his light back on and was relieved to see that the water had cleared significantly. He surveyed the cavern, looking for possible fissures that had developed after the ceiling collapsed, but found none. His eyes then fell upon the ghostly outline of Dr. Kim. His body had settled on the floor of the cave, weighed down by fallen debris, near the spot where the stone had been.

An idea struck. Dr. Kim was still wearing his oxygen tank. If he had been killed prior to emptying his tank, there might still be oxygen for Randall to use. Randall swam toward the body, careful not to stir up the silt again. He gingerly rotated the body and found the tank's pressure gauge. It was empty. Deflated, he gently released the body and let it float back to the cavern floor. As the corpse settled back to rest, another object nearby caught his eye. It was a black mesh diver's bag. Dr. Kim must have brought it with him on his fateful dive, and the recent jarring of the silt had revealed it.

Randall grabbed the bag and lifted it, swimming back to the tunnel. The bag was too small to contain a pony keg of additional breathable air, but he hoped that the scientist had brought other tools that might help him dig his way out. He rummaged through the mesh container and withdrew several small cylindrical metal objects. Randall was stunned when he realized that Dr. Kim had brought underwater explosives into the cavern and wondered if the researcher had accidently killed himself by detonating one within the chamber.

Randall checked his dive watch. He had seven minutes of air left. There was no time to waste, he had to break through the tunnel and hope that the extra tanks were still on the other side. He grabbed the Rosetta Stone and set it on a rocky outcrop directly below the tube. He then swam back into the tunnel and searched for an opening large enough to lodge one of the canisters. He placed the charge and flipped the switch. Unsure of how much time he had until detonation, he slipped back out of the opening and swam to the lowest part of the cave.

He covered his head and waited. The detonation came moments later, sending sound waves and bubbles trailing out of the tube. Randall wasted no time—he retrieved the stone and swam up to the tunnel and shone his light directly into the opening. The gap was littered with smaller fragments of rock and the water was cloudy. Randall glanced at his watch. He had a little more than four minutes of air remaining. He swam into the cloudy water, pushing past the debris. The shaft was larger now, due to the blast. He pushed forward, feeling his way through the murky water, clutching the stone with his free hand.

He swam forward, jamming his hand into a rocky outcrop. He paused momentarily, shaking his injured limb. His hand was badly scraped, but he managed to hold onto the light. The water was clearing, but visibility was still poor. He gingerly groped for the rock he had struck and, finding it, began feeling for a way around it. His hand moved down the jagged face for half a foot and then broke free. There was an opening under the rock. He pushed forward, but the opening was smaller than the rest of the tunnel and his trailing hand caught as he tried to pass through. Backing up, he jammed the stone through the breach and, extending both arms above his head, he slipped through the opening, scraping his arms as he passed through.

Randall found himself in the outer chamber, but Hoffman was gone. Worse, he couldn't find the spare air tanks. He rechecked his watch. Less than two minutes of air. He dove for the spot where they had left them, shining his light to search for the tanks. There was nothing but silt and debris.

Damn it, the cave-in must have buried them.

He dug at the dirt, knowing time was short. He heaved handfuls of grainy sand out of the pit, each time failing to find anything. He reached in again, and again, still finding just dirt.

His air tank was empty. He was out of time.

Randall dug faster, blindly digging through the silt.

More sand, more digging.

He was becoming lightheaded but had to keep going.

He thrust his hand into the sand and struck something hard, jamming his fingers once again.

There was no time to focus on the pain.

He groped through the sand, feeling for the tank valve. He found it. He unscrewed the regulator from his spent bottle and blindly tried to attach it to the new air supply. His lungs burned from oxygen deprivation. He needed air.

His regulator finally caught on the threads of the new canister. He twisted it until it sealed then opened the air supply, gulping deeply.

Calming himself, Randall slowed his breathing, allowing him to think clearly again. He had to retrieve the stone and find Hoffman and Jamie. He swapped tanks and began searching for the relic. Finding it, he exited the cave system and began his slow ascent back to the surface, careful not to climb too quickly to prevent decompression sickness.

Finally breaking through the surface of the water, Randall welcomed the sight of the sun sitting high above the horizon. He looked around the ocean surface until he located the dive boat. There was no one on the deck. He kicked his way to the back and climbed the ladder, lifting the stone onto the swim deck. Cautiously, he peered over the stern of the boat, unsure of what he would find. There was no movement or sound coming from the pilot house. He hoisted himself onto the deck and quietly slipped his tank and flippers off.

Searching the entire boat, Randall found no trace of Hoffman or Jamie. They had vanished. He had to get back to John and the others and hope that whoever had taken his friends needed the stone. It was his only bargaining chip. Randall pulled up the anchor, throttled the motor, and started his long journey back to land.

Chapter Thirty-Seven

John watched a soldier lead Bauman over to the man giving orders.

"Where did you obtain this video?"

"From a colleague of yours. I didn't actually get it, my friend over there brought it to me. He can explain everything," Bauman said, pointing to John.

The soldier guarding John brought him to the elderly soldier dressed in combat fatigues. John recognized his rank as general from the insignia on his lapel. The man was nearly bald, and his face was round with craggy wrinkles. His light blue eyes were sharp and focused, but the bags under them spoke to a man under great stress who had slept very little recently.

"What's your name, son," the general asked.

"John Randall. May I ask yours?"

"I'm General Flores, the base commander. Your little stunt put a lot of people on edge."

"Sorry, we needed to make sure we got your attention."

"Consider yourself successful and very fortunate you didn't get killed in the process. Where did you acquire the video? You realize this is classified information and I could easily have you and your friends sent to a federal penitentiary for possessing it," Flores said, his voice steady.

"I don't believe you want to do that, sir. I can explain, but I'd feel better if my friends weren't held at gunpoint."

Flores turned to look at the soldiers guarding the rest of the group. He nodded, and the soldiers lowered their weapons.

"Thanks. Would it be possible to speak inside?" John asked.

"Captain, escort our guests into my office."

Flores' office was the perfect confluence of high tech and old-world charm. The walls were decorated with photographs of the general with various high-ranking government officials from both the United States and international allies. John stopped counting when he reached the fourth picture of Flores with a former president. The man was obviously well connected.

The general held a chair for Sam and then for Gabby and motioned to two other leather-bound chairs for John and Bauman while his captain stood watch at the door, scowling at them. Flores walked around his mahogany desk and sat down in his high-back executive chair. Resting on his desktop were several pictures of a beautiful older woman with short brown hair and a gleaming smile. Alongside the woman were two strapping young men. One was in combat fatigues, the other in civilian attire.

"My wife and sons," Flores commented, watching John as he studied the pictures. "I met her when I was the base commander at the Air Force Academy. She was a civilian lecturer for a series of classes on abnormal psychology. The one on the left is Michael, he's stationed at Ramstein Air Base in

Germany, and the one on the right is Anthony, he followed his mother's lead and teaches psychology at Vassar."

John smiled. "You must be very proud of them."

Flores nodded. "Now about the video: I need to know how it came into your possession. There are only three copies of it. I have one and just spoke with the owner of the second copy. That leaves one possible source."

"Colonel Shaw gave this copy to my father. We were being held captive at your Cooper Island facility when it came under attack. Shaw gave it to us for protection and told us to contact you."

"And what became of Colonel Shaw?"

"He's dead, but I think you already know that."

Flores studied John. "Do you know who attacked the base?"

"Francis Dumond. He's the owner of an energy consortium who had a previous run-in with my father. He's a ruthless killer and he wants the serum that Jacob and I created."

Flores raised an eyebrow. "How did he hear about the serum?"

"He tortured and nearly killed me, shortly after your men tried to kidnap me." John paused before continuing, wanting to see Flores' reaction.

The General's face remained emotionless. "You say Shaw gave the video to your father. Where is he right now and why didn't he bring it to me?"

"My father is looking for the tablet that Dr. Vernon described in the video. Once he has it, he'll contact us."

"Was your father alone or were there others with him looking for the tablet?"

John gripped the arm of his chair and set his jaw. "Why do you ask? I'm not sure I want to answer any more of your questions, but just to make myself clear, your men tried to kidnap and kill me, then they took my family and friends hostage. When Dumond tried to destroy your base, Colonel Shaw gave my father a flash drive with the video and told us to find you because you needed to know what had happened. We came here to help you and now I feel like I'm being interrogated. With all due respect, my father better be safe right now because if your men have done anything to him, I'll find a way to make your life a living hell." John leaned forward in his seat.

Remaining calm, the general turned away from John and typed into his keyboard. He rotated his desktop monitor for John and the others to see.

"This video was taken from an aerial drone near the cave site. After losing Dr. Kim, we keep constant surveillance on the area. You can see a dive boat pull up here." Flores pointed to the screen. "There are three people on board. I'm assuming this is your father and friends. Two enter the water and while they're diving, another ship arrives on the scene. You can see that the second vessel carries armed individuals, who board the dive boat, then detonate a small, underwater charge while the two divers are still submerged. A short time later, a single diver surfaces and is captured by the armed men, who take your two friends with them, at gunpoint, and depart the area."

"My God. Can you tell who the two hostages are?" John asked.

"Captain Keane, can the video be enhanced?"

"This was an aerial based platform, we could only get overhead shots and couldn't get facial recognition. We have confirmed that one hostage was female, and one was male," Keane replied.

"Do you know who took them? Are there any identifying marks on the second ship?"

"We believe the kidnappers were part of the Red Dragon brigade, a faction of the People's Liberation Army. We have reason to believe they're seeking the tablet as well."

"The PLA? How did the Chinese army know about the tablet?"

"Unfortunately, we discovered a mole in our operation who was feeding information to the Dragons and helped them get information about the tablet and most of your research."

"Why do they care about my research?"

"We have reason to believe that a small bloc within the Chinese government is trying to develop a mind control drug based on the secretions retrieved at Roswell. We also have reliable intelligence that the Red Dragon Brigade is actively seeking what we believe is an alien base in the Antarctic."

John's mouth fell open. "A base?"

"Correct. Drs. Vernon and Kim were trying to locate the tablet, which we believe holds the key to finding that base. If the Chinese find the base first, they'll attack and try to take a creature alive to get the secretions. If they're successful, we believe they'll try to synthetically reproduce the drug, possibly in aerosol form."

"And if they do…"

"They'll have the ability to deliver it in mass quantities, thereby controlling huge portions of any population. This would be a game changer. If they utilize it against our troops in battle, we won't stand a chance. We can't let that happen," Flores said, switching off his monitor.

John sat speechless, trying to comprehend what the General had shared. "They could start an interspecies war," John commented.

Flores nodded in agreement. "John, I'm sorry about Jacob and the incidents with you and your family, but I think you can understand why we took the course of action that we did.

We needed your research to help create an antidote to the mind control substance. We had to prepare for the worst-case scenario in case the Chinese contingent successfully synthesized the secretions."

"You only showed the Chinese taking two people hostage, do you know what happened to the other diver? Did he make it out alive?" John asked.

"I apologize, but we don't know. Once the two hostages were taken, we re-tasked the drone to follow the Chinese vessel."

"Can you send a satellite overhead or have another drone fly by the area to check it again?"

"Captain Keane, how long before we get eyes on the cave area?" Flores said, revealing that he had already had the same thought.

Keane turned and spoke into a hidden microphone as they waited.

"Sir, we will have a live video feed in forty-three minutes."

Chapter Thirty-Eight

The wait was interminable as the Northrop Grumman MQ-4C Triton unmanned aerial vehicle (UAV) made its way from Tyndall Air Force Base near Panama City, Florida southwest to the underwater cave system. Complicating the situation further, the most direct route involved flying the drone through Mexican airspace. Not wanting to cause a flap with his neighbors to the south, Flores had to route the vehicle in an indirect manner.

Still technically in the testing phase, the UAV had been developed for the United States Navy as a surveillance aircraft under the Broad Area Maritime Surveillance (BAMS) program. The system was intended to fly real-time intelligence reconnaissance missions (ISR) over vast ocean and coastal regions, providing continuous maritime surveillance, as well as assisting with search and rescue missions. As such, it seemed like the perfect tool to use to search for the dive boat.

"Sir, live feed coming online from the drone."

"Put it on the screen."

The clarity of the video was amazing as the open expanse of turquoise water filled the screen. The boat, however, was nowhere to be seen.

"Have we confirmed the coordinates of the last known location of the craft?" Flores asked the technician.

"Affirmative, sir. The area in view is the last known position of the diving boat."

"Widen the field of view and search for traces of wreckage."

Speaking into his headset, the technician relayed the general's command to the drone pilot, and the UAV began utilizing its full sensor suite to detect signs of the dive boat or possible wreckage.

"Sir, still no sign of the dive boat or any wreckage. Should we begin a grid search?"

"Yes, plot probable courses based on known variables and begin the search. Report back to me when you have an update."

Flores turned to the group, who sat in stunned silence. Flores plopped down behind his desk and massaged his temples, closing his eyes as he contemplated his next steps.

"I'm sorry about your father and friends, but we have to assume that they're either dead or will be soon. We also must assume that the Chinese have the tablet. We'll continue to search for the dive boat as long as we can, but we need to develop a contingency plan based on worst case scenarios."

"I just can't believe this is happening. Dad's survived so many close calls over the years, especially in Peru last year with Sam. To think he might be trapped in that underwater cave..."

"I know this is difficult, but there are even more lives at stake. In fact, if the Red Dragons have possession of the tablet and can find the base and extract the mind-control substance, the entire free world is in jeopardy. I can't allow that to happen. Please excuse me." General Flores stood up from his desk and disappeared from the office.

Gabby placed her hand on John's. "I'm really sorry about your dad. Maybe he found a way out."

John looked up at her, then glanced over at Sam, who was white as a sheet. Her eyes were red, tears forming in the corners.

They all sat quietly for some time until Gabby finally spoke again. "What do we do now?"

"I guess we wait to hear what General Flores has in mind," John said quietly.

Time passed slowly as the group sat in the office waiting for more news. A somber mood had settled over them, fueled by a lack of sleep and the letdown the body feels after being in a heightened state for too long.

Finally, Flores rejoined the group.

"We're going to relocate you to temporary quarters while we determine our next steps. I'll have Captain Keane escort you. Again, my deepest sympathies to all of you," Flores said, nodding to his captain, who stood and opened the door to his office.

They exited the building in single file, shuffling along in silence. As John stepped into the bright sunlight, his phone began to beep as it found a cell signal. At first, the sound didn't register with John, who was still in a state of shock.

"John, check your phone," Gabby said.

John looked at Gabby and then at his phone. The expression on his face turned from numbness to anticipation as life resurfaced in his dark brown eyes.

"It's dad, he's alive! He tried calling but couldn't reach me, so he texted me. He's on his way to Dulce and he has the tablet! Captain Keane, we need to speak with General Flores!"

Keane spoke into his headset, then said, "Follow me, the General's in his office."

They scrambled back inside.

"General, my father is alive, and he has the tablet. He's on his way to Dulce now and said he'll call when he arrives."

"Did he say how he'd get here and how he escaped?"

"No. My father's a careful man and probably didn't want to tip his hand in case someone intercepted his message. He just said he had the package and was on his way."

"Thank God! Do you have any idea when he'll get here?"

John glanced at his watch. "I would say in 2-3 hours, but that's just an educated guess."

"Captain, send a team to each airport and have them stationed at each gate with a flight arriving from Mexico. I want Dr. Randall escorted by our men the moment he emerges from the boarding ramp."

Chapter Thirty-Nine

The caravan of Humvees pulled to a stop in front of the main building as John and General Flores waited impatiently. A small cadre of uniformed soldiers sprang from the vehicles, taking protective positions around their important guest as Captain Keane barked orders. A single soldier opened the rear door of the third Humvee and Randall exited the vehicle looking somewhat bewildered by the amount of attention afforded to his presence. Slung over his right shoulder was a faded, brown leather courier satchel, which he clutched by his side.

Seeing John, Randall smiled, and jogged over to him.

"Good to see you, pops!" John said, embracing his father in a long hug.

"Good to see you too, son," Randall replied, smiling broadly. He turned to the general. "General Flores, I assume?"

"Pleasure to meet you, Dr. Randall. If you wouldn't mind, let's discuss the situation in my office," Flores said, gesturing to the main building as a large soldier held the door open and saluted the group. Captain Keane trailed behind, deferring to his guests and the General.

"Where's everyone else?" Randall asked.

"Sam, Gabby, and Andy are having dinner. The general felt it would be better if just the three of us met. Sam is dying to see you. She was nearly in tears when we heard you were missing."

"I'm glad you're all okay. I wasn't sure how this situation would play out. By the way, who's Andy?" Randall asked.

"He's my old roommate from college, remember?"

"That's right. I just forgot."

"He helped introduce us to the general," John said, grinning.

They entered Flores's office and took seats around the desk.

"Dr. Randall, I understand you have the tablet?" Flores said, a trace of anticipation in this voice.

"Yes, it's right here," Randall said, tapping the bag. "But first, what happened to Rob and Jamie?"

"They were captured by the Red Dragon brigade, a small group comprised of former soldiers of the PLA," Flores replied.

Randall turned to look at John, who was nodding.

"We saw the video feed. Apparently, these men are trained soldiers who split away from the People's Liberation Army. They captured Jamie and Rob and rigged explosives to trap you in the cavern. When they got Rob, they took his video camera too, so they have any information you recorded."

"My God. We have to rescue them, and this is the key," Randall said, gingerly removing the tablet from his courier bag. He stared at the stone intently. "In the midst of the commotion, I never really had a chance to examine it."

"Did you film the stone? We need to know what information the Red Dragons might have acquired when they captured your friends," Flores said.

Randall shook his head no.

"And you say you didn't study the stone on the plane?" Flores asked.

Randall's face went flush at Flores's infatuation with the artifact and his apparent lack of concern for Rob and Jamie.

"No. I was concerned that taking it out of my bag would draw attention, and I've become somewhat paranoid about people trying to harm my family and friends for possessing such items," Randall replied, glaring at Flores.

"Message received, Dr. Randall, and I assure you, no harm will come to your children and friends while you're on this base. The markings, they're smaller than I had expected," Flores said.

"Yes, and by the crisp nature of the symbols, they appear to have been created by a machine and not by hand," Randall said. "The translation key is in Sanskrit, which I happen to know well. This stone will let us translate messages written in the foreign dialect to Sanskrit and then into English. I'm assuming that there is a message to interpret?"

Flores shifted uncomfortably and sat back in his chair. He strummed his fingers on his knee, clearly mulling something over in his mind. Randall held his tongue, waiting for Flores to reply.

"I'm in a precarious situation. This operation is highly classified and only a handful of people are aware of the current situation. We strongly feel that this information must be shielded from the public or it could cause panic and a possible collapse of our social structure."

"But…?" Randall asked.

"Time is of the essence and you possess the skill to translate a message of critical importance to the success of our mission."

"I think I know more about this subject than you imagine, and so do my son and daughter. There's nothing that you can show me that'll be earth shattering at this point. Besides, my friends are being held captive by a group of thugs and there's no way on God's green earth I'll sit by and let them be harmed."

Flores just stared.

Randall scooted to the edge of his seat, locking eyes with Flores. "To be frank, you don't seem to be too concerned about them, and that bothers me. They both risked their lives to get this artifact, and if you're not going to do something, I will."

Flores flinched at the comment, letting Randall know he had hit the mark. The General quickly recovered his poker face.

"I appreciate your candor, but I believe the best way we can help your friends is to translate the message on that stone and get to the base before the Red Dragons. If they don't know where to find it, they'll hold your friends as insurance."

Randall nodded.

Flores folded his arms in his lap. "The next step is to show you the message, so you can help translate."

"I want to see my daughter first."

Now it was Flores's turn to glare at Randall. The senior military officer clearly wasn't accustomed to having his authority questioned. He relented, however, and took Randall to see Sam. After receiving a hug from his daughter and letting her know he was fine, Randall turned to Flores.

"Okay, let's go."

Flores escorted Randall down the hall as John followed behind. The General stopped abruptly.

"Dr. Randall," Flores said to John, "this is a highly classified area that I'm taking your father to, and I will only take him."

The elder Randall shook his head. "I won't go without my son."

Flores' face turned red, his bottom lip curling over the top. His eyes narrowed as they locked on Randall's face. Randall stood expressionless, crossing his arms over his chest.

"Do you realize how many laws I'm violating by taking one of you into this section of our facility?" Flores asked.

"About the same number of laws, you'd be breaking to take both of us," Randall replied.

"I could be court-martialed for my actions and spend the rest of my life in prison."

"Either both of us go or we leave you to figure things out for yourself."

Flores looked like an overfilled balloon ready to pop.

John spoke, breaking the tension. "General, I think you might need my expertise with this situation. Jacob and I created the serum you wanted, so I know more about it than anyone. You mentioned earlier that you'll need to create a compound to counteract it and I can help you with that. You thought enough of my abilities to fund my research for years, let me finish the job with my father."

Flores exhaled a long, slow breath, and nodded to the security detail to allow John to follow. They traveled to a heavily fortified section of the main building and arrived at an entrance guarded by two very large and well-armed soldiers. Flores placed his hand into the biometric reader, which confirmed his identity. The thick metal doors slid open to reveal an elevator car into which the three men entered.

Flores tapped at a keypad embedded in the elevator wall and entered his ID badge into a thin slot adjacent to the pad. The elevator car began to descend at a rapid pace. As they dropped deeper into the earth, Randall and John exchanged glances about the depth they were traveling.

"How far underground are we going?" John asked.

"That's classified."

Once again, father and son shared a glance, a smirk spreading across John's face. Randall smiled, shaking his head.

After a short while, the car slowed and then came to a stop. The doors peeled back, revealing a long hallway with an arching roof hewn from the bedrock. Along the spine of the arch ran a solid bank of lights, which bathed the hallway in brightness. The walls of the hallway were made of smooth, gray painted concrete stretching three-quarters of the way up until meeting the arched natural stone that comprised the ceiling. Lining each side of the hallway were sturdy metal doors, some with small windows, others simply solid steel. Randall assumed that the latter were meant to keep prying eyes from looking in ... or something inside from getting out. He shivered involuntarily.

Flores stepped out of the elevator car first, striding past two guards who saluted as he walked by. He flipped them a quick, stiff salute and marched past them as Randall and John followed. A million thoughts swirled through Randall's brain as visions of a thousand rumors about the complex churned through his mind. The internet was filled with whispers of secret and sinister things happening in this deep underground facility, and he was certain that he was about to discover if at least one of them was true.

The general paused outside one of the windowed doors, running his ID through the scanner. The door opened, and the three men walked into what appeared to be a medical office. A man in a white lab coat greeted the general.

"We'll need three clean room suits," Flores ordered.

The man in the lab coat disappeared into the back room and returned with three neatly stacked outfits.

"You'll need to put these on," Flores said, handing suits to Randall and John before donning one himself.

Properly attired, the three men exited the room, turned left, and walked to a sturdy windowless door. Flores placed his hand into another biometric reader. A small opening in the wall appeared, revealing a black keypad with green glowing alpha-numeric buttons. Flores tapped in a sequence and stepped back as the three-inch-thick metal doors slowly peeled open, revealing the secrets within.

The room was long and narrow, nearly fifty feet wide and three times as deep. Small teams of scientists in clean suits and dust masks hovered over small work benches studying pieces of twisted metal, sheets of iridescent material, and high-tech gadgetry. Overhead, large light fixtures provided ample illumination for the researchers to conduct their work, and air ducts filtered any remnants of dust from the environment, ensuring that contaminants were summarily removed. Flores walked down the main aisle, which traversed the middle of the room, affording an excellent view of the research taking place on both sides. He strode past the work stations, ignoring them all.

Randall was astonished at the sheer amount of material being evaluated. He glanced over at John, who was similarly mesmerized by the sight. He spied one work bench with a perfectly smooth section of metallic material with strange markings like the ones found on the stone from the undersea cavern. It wasn't Flores' destination.

As they finally reached the end of the walkway, Flores stopped in front of the last work station in the room, which was attached to the wall. Perched upon it was a rectangular black box with several wires running out of it and into ports embedded in the table. Mounted on the wall above the box was a large piece of curved glass that Randall estimated was ten feet long and six feet high.

"Turn it on," Flores said to the technician, who punched a command into his keyboard.

The glass instantly transformed into a display that showed a large, 3-dimensional map of the earth rotating in space with strange symbols filling the screen next to it.

"This looks like a heads-up display from a fighter plane," John commented.

"That's where we got the idea," the technician replied, smiling. Flores shot the man a harsh stare.

Randall gestured to the many work stations. "How long have you had these pieces of wreckage?"

"We've acquired these pieces over many years, but the item in front of you came into our possession in 1947. After several years of examination, our scientists figured out how to operate it. Then it took several years to reverse engineer the component that operates the system and many more years until our equipment was advanced enough for us to interface with it. We developed a rudimentary understanding of this new language and were able to decipher parts of the messages encoded within the machine."

"That's how you knew about the existence of the base."

"Correct. However, we couldn't decipher the entire message. Our linguists were able to crack parts of their language, but not all of it. This posed a serious problem. The solution came when one of our team members deciphered a message telling us about the Cosmic Rosetta Stone and its location."

"That's why you sent Drs. Vernon and Kim to retrieve the tablet."

Flores nodded. "But they were unsuccessful."

As he spoke, a tall woman with straight black hair and piercing green eyes approached and stopped next to the general. As she waited, she studied Randall and John closely, her eyes shifting between them.

"Dr. Randall, this is Dr. Melika Chandra. Dr. Chandra is the linguist responsible for translating the parts of the language we understand. Melika, Dr. Randall and his son have retrieved the Rosetta Stone. I would like you to work with them to determine the location of the base. Please share your full research with them."

"A pleasure to meet both you," Chandra said.

"I'll leave the three of you to your work. Good luck," Flores said, turning to leave.

"Thanks, we'll need it," Randall said.

Chapter Forty

$\mathbf{D}$r. Chandra led the group to a small lab just outside of the main facility, explaining that it would afford them privacy and direct access to her research. Unlike the main research area, Dr. Chandra's space had a much more personal feel. Pictures of her family and friends adorned the room, which was nicely appointed with overstuffed cloth chairs, rosewood furniture, and beautiful landscape lithographs of quaint Mediterranean villages overlooking the ocean.

Chandra led Randall and John to the main workstation in the center of the room, where several ancient maps and other assorted documents were neatly stacked on one end of the table. Randall gingerly removed the stone from his courier bag, setting it on the desk under an examination light. As he did, Chandra retrieved three pairs of examination gloves, donning a set before examining the Cosmic Rosetta Stone. Randall and John followed suit. The stone itself was a dark, charcoal color with thin white bands of lighter colored rock embedded at irregular intervals. The writing was small and precise, requiring magnification to read it.

"It's a beautiful specimen," Chandra said, gently stroking the smooth stone. "It's much smaller than its terrestrial counterpart."

Dr. Chandra carefully moved the rock under a magnifying tool, which was attached to the workstation. Next, she opened a recessed compartment in the workstation, revealing a keyboard and power switch. She hit the switch, and one of two monitors above the workstation flickered to life. With a few clicks of the mouse, she accessed a file showing various symbols on the stone side by side with their English translation.

"I see you've been busy," Randall commented.

"It's been a long and difficult process, but we've been able to decipher a great deal of their language. However, there are still major holes in our ability to translate. I'm hoping this stone will help fill those gaps," she responded.

Dr. Chandra opened another compartment in the workstation, removing a long, hand-held device that resembled a flat curling iron. She pushed the magnifying glass aside and slowly ran the wand over the stone. The second monitor now became active, the symbols from the stone appearing on the screen in tandem with Chandra's movement over the rock. Within minutes, she had scanned the entire contents of the stone into the computer.

"Neat trick. Did you create a program to read the language and translate it based on your research of the wreckage?" John asked.

"Yes, this algorithm lets us translate anything we find much more quickly than doing it by hand, but it's not perfect. The process still requires a human touch to make sure the translation is correct. I'm not fluent in Sanskrit, that's why the General asked for your help."

"Glad to do whatever I can," Randall said.

Chandra typed at her keypad. "I'll have to adjust the code based on this new information. This stone will make deciphering these messages exponentially faster and with greater accuracy," Chandra said, her voice rising and her eyes opening wider as she spoke.

Randall nodded. "How long do you anticipate the programming to take?"

"It'll take the better part of the day," Chandra replied.

Randall looked over her shoulder and realized that she was staring into a screen mounted into the workstation. On occasion, she asked Randall to clarify certain Sanskrit symbols to ensure she was translating it correctly. Together, the two worked for several hours ensuring that the new language was properly matched with its corresponding Sanskrit counterpart. From there, the final step was to translate the Sanskrit language into English.

"That should do it."

The first monitor above the workstation still showed the scanned image of the stone while the second monitor showed the translation to English in progress. The entire process took several minutes to complete, after which all three scientists began reading the message. Their initial excitement turned to disappointment.

Chandra cupped her chin in her hand. "This can't be..."

The stone, while providing the ability to translate the unknown language, did not disclose the location of the base. Instead, it referred to another document hidden in another part of the world. The message on the tablet was simply another clue in the puzzle. Randall shook his head and rubbed his aching eyes.

"What do you make of it, dad?" John asked.

Randall considered the question, shrugging off the initial shock. "The writing refers to Agharti, which—if I remember correctly—was a legendary underground world alleged to have existed at the center of the Earth with access somewhere in Asia. According to legend, there are tunnels that run under the Himalayas with entrances somewhere near Tibet. It's the home of a race that possesses some great, forgotten knowledge. Supposedly, Buddhists know the location of the city."

"Okay, so we go and find it," John said.

"It's not that easy. Most scholars believe Agharti is just a myth and the Buddhists are mum on its existence, so no one really knows how or where to find it."

"We've reached a dead end," Chandra stated.

"Maybe not. I think I know someone who might be able to help us. Unfortunately, I don't know if he'll want to," Randall said.

John turned to his father, a look of surprise on his face. "Who are you talking about? I thought I knew all of your old friends."

Randall sighed. "You and Sam know most of them, but not this one."

"Who is it?"

"That's a long story."

Chapter Forty-One

August 22, 9:45 A.M.
Oxford, England

After several hours of broken sleep, Randall and John sat in the back of a C130 transport as it traveled across the Atlantic to London. Back at the Dulce base, Randall had explained to Flores that a former colleague, Mark Talley—a professor of ancient history at Oxford—specialized in the folklore and culture of Asia and was their best chance of finding Agharti. What he failed to mention was the reason he was reluctant to contact his former friend.

Making matters worse, Randall couldn't bring himself to explain the situation to John. It wasn't for a lack of effort on John's part. He had tried to discover what had happened, but Randall had completely shut him down. Now, nearing the end of the transatlantic flight, the tension between father and son was palpable. John glared at his father, tapping his index finger on the top of his laptop in metronome fashion.

"I don't know why you won't tell me what happened between you and Dr. Talley. It was clearly something big and now we're going to see him, and I have no idea what to expect. If you can't trust your own son, who can you trust? I just don't get it, Dad," John said, shaking his head and looking out the window.

Randall squirmed in his seat, feeling every bit like a teenager hiding a secret from his parents while they grilled him about what had happened the previous night.

John turned back to face his father. "If Sam were here, would you tell her?"

Randall stared at his hands, unsure of what to say. He had wanted to tell John on multiple occasions since they left Dulce, but each time he had started to speak, he had thought better of it. Now his son was justifiably angry with him and he had no defense other than it was his own business and no one else's. Of course, this thin veil of an excuse would only last until they arrived at Oxford, at which time the details of the past would be on display for John and everyone else to see.

"Buckle your seatbelts, gentleman, we're preparing for landing," the pilot's voice called over the loudspeaker in the cargo hold.

The plane began its descent to Royal Air Force Station Lakenheath, Suffolk, United Kingdom about 70 miles northeast of London. Randall checked his seatbelt, trying to avoid eye contact with his son.

"Still won't talk? Okay, Dad, that's fine. I'll be sure to remember this when you start in with one of your lectures about the virtues of honesty and openness," John said, mumbling something else under his breath.

The plane taxied to the end of the runway, turned, and headed to a covered hangar on the far north end of the field. As they descended the ramp, Randall and John were greeted by a squad of Special Air Service (SAS) soldiers who escorted them to a waiting Humvee, which then took them to the base commander's office. After a brief meeting with the CO, it was decided that the situation warranted a low-key approach so as not to draw attention to the American visitors. A pair of non-uniformed officers chauffeured their guests to the university and waited in the car while Randall and John walked into the university offices.

The grounds of the oldest university in the English-speaking world didn't disappoint. With its Gothic towers thrusting into a radiant blue sky, a sense of reverent awe overwhelmed Randall as he gazed upon the incredible architecture that more resembled a medieval cathedral than a school campus. Students scurried about the expansive grounds, which were covered with luscious green patches of grass interspersed between the university's many halls. Randall, always excited to educate, considered telling his son that teaching had been taking place at Oxford since 1096, but one look at John told him that now would not be a good time for small talk. Sighing, he entered the main administration building while his son held the door for him. All the while, Randall could sense John's laser-like focus burrowing into the back of his head.

The two were directed to the Dean's office, where they were seated at a small meeting area near the back of the room. John resumed staring at his father, occasionally shaking his head from side to side while muttering.

"The secret will soon be out. Sure you don't want to come clean before I find out from a stranger?" John asked in a sing-song tone.

Randall remained impassive, staring directly ahead as the minutes ticked by. Beads of sweat formed at his temples then ran down the sides of his face. He wiped them away with one hand while nervously tapping on the arm of his chair with the other.

A voice suddenly broke the silence.

"If I weren't seeing this with my own eyes, I wouldn't believe it."

The sudden sound of his former friend caught Randall off guard. He flinched in his seat. Randall looked up to see the face of a man he had not seen since graduate school, many years ago. He stood and walked over to Mark, his hand extended.

"What do you want me to do with that?" Mark commented, his gaze moving from Randall's outstretched hand to his face.

Randall stopped in his tracks. "We need your help, Mark. We're trying to find Agharti."

The serious expression on Mark's face morphed into one of amusement as he wagged his head at his former colleague.

"I haven't seen you in over twenty years, and the first words out of your mouth are that you're looking for some imaginary city that only exists in the minds of old men and even older texts. I'll give you credit for having the guts to come here, but that's about it," Mark said, a frown returning to his face.

"Look, I know we didn't leave on the best of terms—"

"The best of terms? Are you kidding me? You steal my girlfriend, run off and get married, and that's all you can say? We didn't leave off on the best of terms? I should punch you in the mouth, you stupid bastard!"

John cringed. The cat was officially out of the bag.

"I didn't mean to hurt you—you were my best friend—but things just happened. Anne and I were young and in love. I tried to deny it, but couldn't, and neither could she."

"So that justifies you screwing over your friend? You leave me crushed and run off to live your dream and now you expect me to just help you out of a jam."

"Anne's dead. She died four years ago."

"What?"

"Things haven't exactly been easy for me, either," Randall said, locking eyes with Mark, whose hard outward appearance wavered.

"What happened?" Mark asked.

"She died in a car accident. I was away on fieldwork and she was picking up a package when her car was run off the road by a semi-truck. There weren't even proper remains to identify her," Randall replied, turning away and wiping his eyes.

"Jesus, I'm sorry Nick. I had no idea. It's still a sore subject with me," Mark said, walking over to a chair and plopping himself down. Randall followed suit, taking a seat by Mark and John.

"Mark, this is my son John," Randall said, using the back of his hand to wipe his eyes and motioning to John.

"Nice to meet you, Dr. Talley," John said, shaking his hand.

"Please, call me Mark. I must look like a real ass right now," Mark commented.

"Not at all," John said, casting a glance in his father's direction. "Dad can have that effect on people sometimes."

"Do you remember Rob?" Randall asked, eager to change the subject.

"Sure, I do. Good old Rob, always a smile on his face. How's he doing?"

"He was kidnapped, along with another friend of ours named Jamie. That's the reason we came. The only way we can help them is to find Agharti and locate an artifact that can help us find what we're looking for," Randall said.

222

Mark looked at Randall and then at John, his eyes wide and his mouth hanging open. "Kidnapping? Old legends? Jesus! What have you gotten yourself into, Nick? This sounds serious and I'm more than a little concerned that you think I can help you. I'm a professor of ancient history, not a cop."

Randall raised his hands. "I apologize, but I can't go into more detail about the situation. I can tell you that we have the backing of some important people and it's imperative that we find Agharti. I believe you're the best chance we have. You know more about Tibet and the ancient legends surrounding the area than anyone in the world and, more importantly, I trust you," Randall said.

Mark sat back in his chair, his mouth still hanging open. He cocked his head to one side, staring off into space. His lips moved slightly as if he were talking to someone. He turned back to face John and Randall.

"Let's assume for a minute that the legends are true and Agharti exists — and that's a big assumption — finding it won't be easy. The entrances have been a guarded secret for thousands of years. I have some general ideas of where they're supposed to be, but even with a limited number of possibilities, it could take months, if not years to properly explore them all. I'm guessing you don't have that kind of time."

"You're right, we don't, but I have something that might help narrow down the possibilities," Randall said, removing a slip of paper from his coat and handing it to Mark. "I have solid information that points us in the direction of something called 'The Valley of the Angel's Wings.' Does that help?"

Mark took the slip of paper with the words written in Sanskrit. He studied it, confirming that the translation was correct. He looked up from the paper, his eyes narrowing as he studied Randall. "Where did you get this information? I've studied every piece of literature and lore about Agharti and have never seen or heard anything like this before."

"It's from an ancient tablet recovered from an underwater cavern in Mexico. I know what you're thinking. It's authentic, but I can't tell you any more than that." Randall shifted in his seat. "Does it help narrow the possibilities?"

Mark studied Randall's face then shrugged. "Yes. If this is true, then there's only one possible location for the entrance you're referring to, and I know exactly where it is."

"So, you'll help us?" Randall asked.

Mark sat back in his chair, staring at the ground. His head bobbed up and down while he massaged the beard on his face.

"I haven't seen or heard from you in years, you pop in with a crazy story about legendary cities, tell me Rob's been kidnapped, and expect me to just drop my life and go on an adventure with you?"

"I know I'm asking for a lot, but it's not just for me, it's for Rob. Besides, I know this is something you've always dreamed of doing, and I'm offering you a chance to find Agharti. What do you say?"

"I'd say you're nuts."

Randall set his jaw. "There's more to the story, but I've been instructed not to tell you."

"Then it sounds like you've hit a dead end."

Randall closed his eyes and sighed. "Without your help, Rob and Jamie are doomed. You're the only person I trust to help us find this information and we're running out of time."

Mark squirmed in his seat. He was feeling the heat now.

"I'd have to find someone to cover my classes for the upcoming term."

"We'll have you back before classes start."

Mark furrowed his brow. "Are you serious?"

"Yes, I promise you'll be back in time. How about it Mark?"

Mark sighed deeply. "You're sure you've found credible information on the entrance to Agharti?"

"Nothing's ever one hundred percent, but I believe we have extremely credible evidence."

"Okay, I'll do it for Rob. He helped me out a jam when I was younger, and I've been waiting for a chance to return the favor. I have a friend whose brother works for the Chinese foreign ministry who can fast-track our paperwork. We can be ready to travel in 48 hours."

"The Chinese government can't know about this, but I have a different way to get us in. We'll need you to be ready to leave as soon as possible."

Once again, Mark's eyes went wide, and he shook his head. "Fine, we'll do it your way. I'm assuming we at least have the backing of the American government on this."

"Yes, we do. Thanks for agreeing to help us. How long before you'll be ready to go?"

"I have to wrap up a couple of things, pack a bag. I can be ready in four to six hours."

"Perfect. We'll meet you back here."

Chapter Forty-Two

August 23, 3:58 P.M.
Tibet Autonomous Region, China

Twenty-four hours after their initial meeting and a military transport flight into Afghanistan, the group found themselves skimming the tree line in a specially modified Blackhawk helicopter. General Flores had arranged for the three to be flown from London to Incirlik Airbase in Turkey. From there, it was a short hop to the base in Afghanistan where their Blackhawk was fueled and waiting for them along with a squad of Navy Seals led by Captain Mike Steele. This particular stealth variant of the famed chopper featured special modifications rendering the aircraft virtually silent until it was nearly overhead. To allow for greater range, additional external fuel tanks were added to the helicopter, at the expense of its normal armaments.

With Mark now officially on board, Randall filled him in on everything that had transpired, while Captain Steele looked on.

"My god Nick, what the hell have you been up to since I last saw you? This sounds more like some crazy conspiracy story than a research project," Mark said.

"I know. But I swear I never intended for any of this to happen."

After adjusting to the shock, Mark settled into teacher mode and explained where they were going and why. He studied the maps and pointed to the geological features from which the location derived its name. Their goal was simple. They needed to find the document referred to in the stone, and hope that it would identify the exact location of the alleged alien base.

"You can see from these aerial photos why this area was nicknamed 'The Valley of the Angel's Wings.' The stratification of the stones and the weathering gives them the grooved look of wings in flight around the center of the valley. Based on my research, the entrance to the underground tunnel system would be here, where the wings meet along this ridge," Mark said, pointing to a raised band of stone running along the spine of the mid-point of the joined wings. "If you follow along here, you'll see a depression at the base of the ridge."

"So, you think the entrance to the tunnel system is somewhere in the depression?" John asked.

"Yes. The entire area surrounding the depression is granite, but this area right here is dirt. In fact, it's the only soil within a half mile of the spot in any direction. If there's a tunnel anywhere in the region, it would have to terminate here," Mark responded, tapping the map with his index finger.

Captain Steele scanned the map. "That puts the entrance less than a mile from the landing zone. My men will take the point to navigate to the entrance and the rear to cover our flank. Drs.

Randall and Talley, we'll have you take the lead once we reach the depression, so you can search for the entrance."

The helicopter snaked its way along a winding river, as they made their way through the country of Nepal and approached the Chinese border. Moments later, the aircraft quietly entered Chinese airspace. The tension in the chopper ratcheted higher.

"We're approaching the landing zone. When we touch down, my men will form a perimeter. When I give you the signal, hop out, crouch down, and make your way over to me."

The Blackhawk departed from its river route and detoured toward a small, oval-shaped patch of prairie grass. With pinpoint precision, the pilot brought the chopper down and landed with a soft thud in the center of the clearing.

"Let's move!" Captain Steele yelled over the thumping of the chopper blades. His men hopped down from the side doors, fanning out into a circular defensive position.

Randall watched as the soldiers performed their maneuvers with Swiss watch-like precision. After a few minutes, Steele gave the sign and Randall, Mark, and John hopped out into the open field. Following the Captain's orders, the three men stayed low and jogged over to his side. The helicopter lifted off, leaving the team to their mission.

"Espinosa, take point. Greene, bring up the rear. The rest of you fan out and keep an eye out for Chinese regulars. Let's move!"

The team silently made their way along a rocky outcrop that afforded them some cover. To their right, the grassy terrain sloped upward toward a peak. To their left was a rocky, boulder-strewn field. The late afternoon sun was dropping toward the horizon, causing a severe drop in temperature. The bitterly cold air tore through Randall's thermal jacket and he clapped his hands together, trying to keep them warm inside his Gore-Tex gloves.

Private Greene motioned for them to get low. They all dropped to the ground. Greene flipped open the scope on his assault rifle, slowly panning the horizon to their left. After several tense minutes, Greene returned to his feet and waved them forward.

The group continued marching with John finally breaking the silence. "Mark, what do you think the entrance will look like?"

"That's a good question. According to the legends, the guardians of the tunnel were simple people who had a distaste for lavish things. In fact, the reason they went underground was human greed. Based on that, I would expect the entrance to be simple and probably made with natural materials found on the mountain, but that's completely a guess on my part."

As he finished speaking, Espinosa called out over their helmet-mounted microphones, "Drs. Randall and Talley, I'm at the coordinates you provided on the flight. Move to the forward position to begin your search."

Upon hearing the news, Randall, Mark, and John jogged up the trail to join Espinosa. The contour of the land matched what they had seen in the aerial photographs and they found themselves staring at a dark patch of dirt, which stood in stark contrast to the mottled, gray rocks surrounding them. The patch started off wider and then narrowed to a small, arching semi-circle that fed into the mountain. The feature resembled an earthen funnel terminating at the valley's apex. As they approached, the dark earthen spot grew taller. When they finally reached Espinosa's side, the entrance into the rock face was clear.

"It's a cave," John said, stopping next to his father. Captain Steele and his men were close behind.

"Fan out and create a perimeter," Steele said. "I'll lead the way in."

The four men slowly made their way into the cave with the captain in front. Steele made short, sweeping arcs with the barrel of his gun, illuminating the cavern with his gun-mounted light. They traversed thirty yards into the cave, which terminated in a sheer rock face. The captain shined his light from side to side. There were no other openings.

Randall approached from behind, stopping next to Steele. He trained his light directly ahead. He walked several paces past the soldier and stopped, shining his light up the rock face and then directly down. An eight foot-wide opening, spanning the length of the cave, sloped downward at a sharp angle. Two steps further and he would have tumbled directly down.

"It's an illusion designed to trick people into thinking the tunnel terminates," Randall said.

"The slope is too steep, we'll need to rappel down," Steele said, keying his mic. "Espinosa, bring us the climbing gear."

Minutes later, Espinosa appeared in the cave with a bag of ropes, harnesses, and carabineers. He assisted his captain in setting up the equipment and then hustled back out to his defensive position.

The men rappelled down, one by one, to the lower level of the underground cave system with Mark being the final team member to join the others. The cavern wasn't large, the ceiling less than ten feet high. Captain Steele once again took the lead, carefully working his way back into the tunnel. This time, he searched the ground, assuming they may find another sharp drop. After moving forward another twenty yards, the group hit a dead end. Randall moved to the front and studied the wall, which was solid rock. It was perfectly smooth. He turned to face the group.

Captain Steele, who was to his left, frowned. "Are you sure this is the right location?"

Randall didn't answer him; his eyes were fixed on the wall behind the captain. Randall brushed by him, shining his light at the wall. Working his way from the top down, he noticed a small seam in the stone, nearly filled with dirt.

Randall looked over his shoulder, "Can someone give me a brush?"

John flipped his backpack to the ground and removed a small brush from his father's tool kit. "Here you go."

Shining his light at the seam, Randall meticulously ran the brush over the seam, slowly revealing a perfectly cut rectangular outline in the wall. Handing the brush back to John, he then began pushing on the rectangle. At first, nothing happened, but after applying pressure to the bottom, a panel rotated outward, revealing an alcove about three feet off the ground. Sitting in the center of the alcove was an intricately carved wooden box. Randall sensed the others closing around him as his light illuminated the container.

"Hold this," Randall said to Steele, handing him his flashlight. Randall studied the area surrounding the box.

"What are you looking for?" Mark asked.

"Trip levers. I want to make sure we don't set off any devices that were designed to protect the box from outsiders."

Not finding any, he stepped back, retrieving his flashlight from Steele. "Mark, would you like to do the honors?"

"If you insist," Mark said, grinning broadly.

The two men stood shoulder to shoulder as Randall illuminated the wooden box. Mark gingerly lifted the lid, revealing a cloth-lined interior on which rested a twelve-inch cylindrical container. Mark lifted the container out of the box and held it in both hands. He cradled it for a moment, like a proud father holding his newborn. Randall shone the light on one end of the cylinder, revealing a rolled document inside.

"Let's take it back up and examine it in natural light," Mark said.

John retrieved a foam-lined metal box from his backpack and Mark placed the tube inside for protection. The four men rapidly made the ascent up the ropes and back out the mouth of the cave.

The sun had nearly set, but there was still sufficient light to examine the contents of the cylinder. A flat rock served as a makeshift workstation. Mark held the tube in one gloved hand, peering into the open end. He slowly tilted the container and the document slipped out into his other gloved hand. He carefully set the paper down on the cloth-covered rock, holding it gingerly but firmly, lest the wind blow it off. He carefully unrolled the document, finding the material to be in relatively good shape despite its age. The writing matched that of the stone Randall had retrieved from the underwater cavern.

John opened his bag, removed a translation sheet Dr. Chandra had created, and set it down next to the scroll, allowing his father and Mark to translate the document together. Randall, peering over a set of glasses, read the scroll, a smile slowly spreading across his face. Almost in unison, he and Mark turned to face each other, both men grinning like children who had just discovered that school had been cancelled due to heavy snow.

"We have the location of the base," Randall announced, removing his glasses.

Mark rolled up the document, placing it back into its protective cylinder. He then tucked everything inside the metal case. He fished a notepad from his pocket, recording the location of the base. As he did, Greene joined the group.

"Radio for our ride back to base," Steele said to Greene.

"Bird Dog, this is Bravo 1-6, package delivered, repeat, package delivered, over," Greene said into his radio. There was no reply.

"Sir, there appears to be some sort of interference..."

"You, in the cave, lay down your weapons!" a loud voice called out from the distance.

"Shit! Everyone down! Espinosa get eyes on that target!"

Shots rang out as Randall and the team hit the dirt.

"I have fire coming from the river, Chinese regulars!" Espinosa called out.

"Fire team, I want cover fire for assets, repeat, cover fire for assets!" Steele yelled into his throat microphone.

"We're pinned down, sir," Greene replied.

Gunfire erupted from multiple directions as the Chinese soldiers closed in. Each time Steele and his men attempted to move, they were met with a shower of bullets. They were trapped.

"I need information, people, where is the main fire coming from!" Steele said into his mic.

"Sir, we have unfriendly fire coming from the rubble field to your left. I count at least twenty troops moving your way."

"Mark, you said there was a monastery nearby, which way is it?" Randall asked.

Mark frowned. "It's along the ridgeline up and to the right, why?"

"Captain, what do you think?" Randall asked, turning to face Steele.

"We can give you cover fire and hold them off. That should give you time to make a break for it. Greene, escort them to the monastery and try to reach Bird Dog," Steele ordered. "Fire team, on my signal, I want cover fire on approaching force. Ready, go!"

The Americans fired in unison, unleashing their own show of force. Caught off guard, the approaching Chinese soldiers were forced to drop for cover. The moment they did, Randall, John, and Mark sprinted in the direction of the monastery, with Greene taking the rear to offer cover.

The four men sprinted up and to the right, covering twenty yards before drawing the attention of the Chinese. Spotting the four Americans making a break, the soldiers trained their weapons on them and began shooting again.

"Take cover!" Greene shouted, and the men dropped to the ground, searching for boulders large enough to hide behind.

"Mark, how much farther?"

"A couple hundred yards up and over that rise. The monastery is at the peak of this ridge."

"We should have a clear line of sight to communicate with the chopper from there. I should be able to reach them with no trouble. Once they get here, you boys need to hop on board and get out of Dodge as fast as you can!" Greene barked.

"There's no way we're leaving you guys behind," Randall protested.

"We knew what we were getting into when we signed up for this mission, and right now, you're my priority. My job is to make sure that you and the document get on that transport and back to Dulce. We need to move before they close in on us," Greene said. "Captain, we need another round of cover fire, over."

"The captain's down, Greeny. I'll radio the team. Go on my mark!" Espinosa responded. "Now!"

The remaining soldiers concentrated fire on the advancing Chinese soldiers, offering several moments of cover. The plan worked as the Chinese regulars turned their attention to the remaining armed resistance, giving Randall's group enough time to race up the slope toward the monastery. The ridgeline offered some protection as they stretched the distance between themselves and the approaching force. They covered more than half the distance to the peak, but once again the Chinese soldiers regained their mark on them. Resuming fire, they struck Greene as he covered their flank.

Randall, trailing Mark and John, saw the soldier go down and ran back to his side.

"What the hell are you doing," Greene said through gritted teeth. "Get your ass up that hill!"

"I'm not leaving without you," Randall said, lifting the soldier, who threw his arm over his shoulder for support. Greene groaned in pain and struggled along, aided by Randall. John and Mark, having now seen what had happened, ran back to help. John grabbed Greene on the side opposite his father, Mark taking the gun and firing shots back at the Chinese while they moved up the hill. After struggling the remainder of the way, they finally reached the monastery.

What they didn't know was what kind of reception they would receive.

Chapter Forty-Three

The four men approached the monastery's steps, but there were no monks in sight. They reached the huge wooden doors and set Greene down on the ground. From their vantage, they could see the valley below where Steele's men had been fighting the Chinese army. The gunfire had been reduced to an occasional cracking sound. It appeared that the American force had been largely neutralized. Greene gathered himself and reached for his radio.

"Bird Dog, this is Bravo 1-6 come in, over," he spoke into his microphone. The only reply was static. "Bird Dog, we need immediate evac. We've taken casualties and need to be air-lifted immediately. Do you copy?"

Nothing.

"It's no good, something's interfering with our signal. I don't think we can count on the cavalry coming to the rescue. We need to find another way out of here," Greene said, tossing the radio aside. He grasped at his stomach as blood gurgled from his wound.

Randall pounded on the huge monastery doors with his fist. "Is anyone in there?" After a few moments, he pushed on the door, which folded inward. He craned his neck, peering into the compound, checking for signs of life. The monastery appeared to be deserted.

"Let's get you inside," Randall said to Greene. "John, give me a hand." Both men grabbed Greene under his arms and lifted him to his feet while Mark held the door open. The four men entered the monastery, closing the door behind them.

"We don't have much time before the Chinese get here. We need to look for a place to hide or some sort of transportation," Randall said.

The four men stood in a meticulously maintained courtyard with carefully manicured gardens and a fountain in the middle. Several stone stairways led to buildings within the main structure and each building was capped off with long sloping eaves that curled up to a point in every corner. The architecture was strikingly beautiful and stood in stark contrast to the sparse and barren landscape surrounding the monastery.

Randall scanned the grounds and found what he was looking for: several heavy wooden benches were neatly arranged in the garden to allow for thoughtful contemplation by the monks.

"Help me move these in front of the door," Randall said, setting Greene on the ground and walking over to the nearest bench. Even with the three men working in unison, the bench was a chore to move, easily weighing two-hundred pounds. They placed it directly in front of the gate they had entered only minutes earlier. The three men then repeated the exercise with three additional benches, stacking them two high and two deep right in front of the opening.

"That should slow them down," John commented.

They lifted Greene and moved toward the main building in the center of the courtyard. Mark pushed the door open, holding it while Randall and John hefted Greene inside. As they had done with the gate in the courtyard, they barricaded the door.

"John, wait here with Greene while Mark and I scout the building," Randall said.

The main room was ornately decorated with painstakingly crafted murals covering the walls and an eight-foot-tall statue of the Buddha serving as the area's focal point. The smell of incense filled the air, clearly signaling that the monastery was inhabited, but there was no other sign of the monks. Randall and Mark walked toward an opening that led to a hallway with multiple doors feeding into the main part of the building. They slowly made their way down the long corridor, straining to hear any sounds emanating from deeper in the building. There were none.

Randall stopped short of the first door and peered around the doorframe and into the room. It appeared to be a study with a single desk situated against the far wall. Wall-mounted sconces held lit candles, providing light for the desk, which held several well-worn books and a single ceramic cup. It seemed that someone had recently been in the room, but whoever had been here was now gone.

The men continued down the hallway and came to the next room. Randall again peered across the threshold to look into the room. This one had a large carpet runner in the center and little else besides small paintings hanging on the walls. The two men shared a look.

"Where is everyone?" Mark asked.

Randall replied with a shrug.

As they reached the end of the hallway, they discovered a flight of stairs leading to a lower level of the building. The two made their way down the steps, which creaked under their weight. The stairs ended, and the men found themselves standing in another small hallway that led into a main room, with a second open doorway to one side. This time, they heard the distinct sound of chanting.

Randall went first, tiptoeing down the short passageway, stopping at the entrance to the room. He leaned forward into the open doorway, seeing many orange-clad men kneeling on the ground. Facing away from the opening, their heads were bowed down in front of their bodies.

"Can I help you?"

Randall jumped, his heart thumping wildly in his chest. He turned to see the smiling face of an elderly man wearing glasses, his head shaven completely bald.

"Are you lost?" the elderly man said, his hands folded across his chest and a thin smile on his lips.

"Our friend is hurt and needs medical attention," Randall blurted.

"I'm sorry, we don't have medical staff here, but we would be happy to see if there is some way we can help him," the monk responded.

Randall took a deep breath. "Thank you. That would be great. He's upstairs with my son."

Randall and Mark walked with the monk back up the stairs and into the main room where John waited with Greene. Greene looked up at them, his eyes drooping and face ashen. Upon seeing Greene, the smile on the monk's face evaporated, replaced with a serious look.

"Thank God you're here, Greene's lost a lot of blood and I'm having a hard time keeping him awake," John said, cupping the man's head in his lap.

The monk knelt to look at the injured soldier, who was moaning in pain, fading in and out of consciousness.

"Your friend's condition is more serious than I thought. He requires attention that I cannot provide here. May I ask what happened and how you came to be at our monastery?" the monk asked softly.

Randall was in a bind. On the one hand, he realized that Greene needed immediate medical attention and that the Chinese could arrive at any minute. On the other hand, if he told his host that they were in possession of a document created by a secret society, which most people thought was only a legend, the monk would likely have him taken away in a strait jacket. Realizing he had no choice, he explained their predicament.

"We're explorers seeking a scroll kept by the inhabitants of an ancient civilization that used to call this area their home. We hoped it would help us find our friends who were taken prisoner by a group called the Red Dragons, a faction of the People's Liberation Army. We found the scroll, but the Dragons attacked us and shot our escort. We escaped and are trying to keep them from getting this document because we're afraid they'll destroy it. Unfortunately, we've also lost contact with the rest of our team who can get us out of Tibet. Can you help us?" Randall asked.

The monk paused for a moment, his head tilted to one side, his hand on his chin. He looked directly into Randall's eyes as he spoke, his body perfectly still.

"Wait here," the monk said. He rose to his feet and walked down the hallway and out of their sight.

Randall looked at his son and then at Mark.

"I don't like this one bit," Mark said. "The PLA will come through that door at any minute and we have no way of defending ourselves or escaping from this place. We're in over our heads." Mark got to his feet and paced the room.

As he did so, the monk returned with two others who lifted Greene and spirited him away from the group. The monk approached Randall and the group huddled together.

"What do you know of the residents of Agharti?" the monk asked.

Randall and Mark shared a look of surprise at the monk's mention of the fabled land.

As the resident expert of the group, Mark replied. "Mostly what was relayed in Plato's stories. The inhabitants of Agharti are gentle people who have no desire to harm others or to take part in the material world. They seek only wisdom and truth and will one day return to power to help relieve mankind from its need to constantly acquire material wealth."

A broad smile spread across the monk's face. "Very good. You understand the essence of my people."

Mark's mouth fell open again. "That's ... not ... possible."

"Our ancestors went into hiding when they realized they could do nothing to contain mankind's avarice, but they swore they would return when humans were ready for true change. The members of my order are the sworn guardians of the entrances to the great city and this monastery is a gateway to that world," the monk said calmly.

"What will become of Private Greene?" Randall asked.

"My brothers will heal and watch over him until he is well enough to re-join his people. I assume you have the sacred scroll in your possession and have learned the information you sought?"

"Yes, it's right here," John said, removing his backpack and retrieving the document from its protective case. He handed the cylinder to the monk, who nodded in appreciation.

"Very good. Come, it is time to lead you out of this place as your pursuers are near," the monk said. Heavy pounding commenced on the gate outside. He led Randall, John, and Mark to the wall on the far side of the room. He stopped for a moment, chanting as he nodded his head at a small piece of paper, hanging six feet from the floor, directly above a section of wall.

A loud crashing sound came from the courtyard. The Chinese had arrived. The three men shared a look of concern.

"I apologize, but if we're leaving, I think we need to go now," John said.

The sound of boots flooding the courtyard grew louder and culminated with a loud thud on the door to the main building. Soon, the shouts of the Chinese soldiers could be heard through the walls. The only thing separating the PLA from John, Mark, and Randall was a single piece of wood.

The monk continued the chant for a few more moments and then abruptly stopped. When he did, a small section of the wall, just large enough for an adult to fit through, opened in front of them. His hands clasped in front of him, the monk walked into the opening. Randall waited as John and Mark entered after the monk. He then followed them in as well. The monk turned and placed his hand on the wall, causing the panel to close.

"What will happen to your brothers when the Chinese find that we're missing?" Mark asked.

"Although we are a peaceful people, we will fight if given no alternative," the monk replied, grabbing a lit torch from a holder on the wall. He led the men down a long pathway toward a circular stone staircase, which fed into an underground tunnel system. The first part of the tunnel had torches illuminating the path every fifty feet.

"Take this path directly ahead for two hundred yards. You will pass three openings on your right; do not take any of them. When you reach the forth opening, it will be on your left. Enter it and continue walking. It will take you in the direction of the Valley of the Angel's Wings."

Mark shook his head in disbelief.

The monk smiled. "You will reach a solid, smooth wall at the end of the path. There will be an ornate notch in the wall. This key fits into that notch to operate a hidden door. The door will take you into the cave in which you found the scroll. You can exit and radio your compatriots," the monk said, removing a small wooden token from his robe and handing it to Randall.

"We cannot repay you for your kindness. Thank you for saving us and for helping us return to assist our friends," Randall said.

The monk simply bowed. Rumbling began in the distance from the direction they had come.

"Hurry, you must move quickly," the monk said, turning to go back toward the monastery.

Chapter Forty-Four

Randall, John, and Mark jogged through the passageway and arrived at the fourth opening just as the monk had described. They entered it and moved quickly until they came to the wall. Randall removed the wooden key from his pocket and placed it into the groove. He twisted the key and heard a loud click. The wall opened in front of them. They scurried through the opening and back into the chamber where they had found the scroll.

The ropes from their previous descent still hung where they'd left them. They shimmied up the ropes and out of the cave, into the open field. The valley was dark now and the only sounds were those of the animals and insects near the cave.

John removed the radio from its cradle. "Bird Dog, do you read me?"

"Roger, please confirm your identity."

"This is John Randall. Captain Steele and his men are dead. We need you to pick us up from the cave entrance immediately."

A different voice came on the radio. "Dr. Randall, did you get the information you needed?"

"Yes, we have it, but the Red Dragons ambushed us and are chasing us. We need you to pick us up ASAP!"

"Roger that, we're on our way. ETA is approximately 20 minutes to the landing zone."

"That might be too long. We're at the entrance to the cave right now and the Dragons are only minutes behind us. What should we do?" John asked.

"Head back to the landing zone where we dropped you off. In the time it takes for you to get there, we should be on the ground waiting to pick you up. Do you copy?"

"Got it. We'll be there waiting," John said.

"Bird Dog out."

"Well you heard them, we better get going," Mark said as John packed up the radio.

The three men looked back at the cave, sharing an unspoken thought. *How far behind are the Red Dragons?* They worked their way back down the earthen cone they had traversed earlier in the day. Now traveling in the dark, they used their flashlights to guide them. They had advanced about three hundred yards when the first noises started coming from the cave— thundering boots and men screaming orders. The Chinese had arrived and were in pursuit.

Small arms fire crackled in the distance, the bullets flying wide of their mark. While they had a good lead, they weren't out of danger. The Chinese soldiers were younger and in far better shape than Randall and Mark. They were also highly trained killers.

All these thoughts swirled through Randall's mind as he watched his son pull ahead. Wisely, they had given the notes containing the location of the base to John.

John looked back at his father and Mark. "Come on guys, we have to pick up the pace! I know you can do it!"

Smiling at his son's encouragement, Randall put his head down and ran as hard as his legs allowed. The uneven terrain made keeping a steady pace difficult. On multiple occasions, Randall felt the loose gravel giving way under his feet, almost causing him to fall over. As he struggled to stay upright, he heard a loud crashing sound behind him, followed by cursing. Randall turned and watched as Mark lost his footing, his body toppling over and skidding down the embankment.

"John, Mark's down! We have to help him!" Randall yelled.

John turned to look and immediately changed directions, making a beeline for Mark who lay near the bottom of the hill. He wasn't moving.

Randall picked up his own pace and turned toward Mark as well. A few seconds later, he arrived by his side, John having arrived just before him. Mark was conscious, but writhed in pain, holding his right knee.

"My knee, I can barely move it and it hurts like hell. I don't think I can run," Mark said through gritted teeth.

John yanked a knife from his bag and cut away Mark's pant leg. His knee was swollen to the size of a softball. Randall glanced back toward the Chinese soldiers, who had cut the gap between them nearly in half and were gaining ground quickly.

"Help me get him up," Randall said, hoisting his friend to his feet. John grabbed Mark on the opposite side, jarring his injured knee, causing him to wince in pain.

"Let's get going," Randall said as the three men scrambled forward toward the landing zone.

246

The Red Dragons were still too far away to shoot with accuracy, but that didn't stop them from firing occasional bursts from their assault rifles. Most of the bullets missed wide, but some were getting closer. It was now a race against time to see if they could maintain a wide enough margin to prevent their pursuers from taking a long-distance kill shot.

Randall, John, and Mark struggled forward, fighting for every inch of progress. Clearly in pain, Mark hopped on his good leg, cursing with every step. Randall's legs burned with exhaustion, the added weight of supporting his friend sapping his body's strength. He knew that stopping to rest was a luxury they couldn't afford, but his energy was waning.

"I have to stop for a moment," Randall said finally, straining to get the words out.

The three men pulled up to a large rock, setting Mark down behind it for protection. Randall placed his hands on his knees, sucking in as much air as he could. Sweat poured from his brow in sheets and his shirt looked like he had jumped into a lake.

John looked back at their pursuers, the expression on his face telling Randall everything he needed to know.

"We need to move, Dad."

"You guys go without me," Mark said. "I'm holding you back and that's not right. Besides, you need to get back to help Rob." Mark held his injured knee.

"No way! We're not leaving you!" Randall said, grabbing Mark and hoisting him back to his feet before he could argue. John didn't wait to be told, he grabbed Mark from the other side and they were off to the races again.

The three men pushed forward. Energized by the short break, they moved more quickly, but were still losing ground to the Chinese. The gunfire was coming faster now, and with greater accuracy. It wouldn't be long before their pursuers were close enough to shoot them.

They cleared the rubble field and entered the grassland. The even terrain and lack of rocks made running easier, while the Chinese dealt with the harsher terrain.

The landing zone was getting close. Randall caught sight of the chopper, making its way toward the open area.

The blades of grass whipped at their legs, the cold night air biting their exposed faces. Twenty more yards and they would be safe.

A single gunshot pierced the temporary silence and a puff of smoke rose from the ground near John. He tumbled to the earth, taking Mark and Randall with him. Mark yipped in pain as he fell onto his injured leg.

Randall hit the ground hard, rolling and striking his head, arms, and torso on the rocky landscape. Branches and thorns tore at his clothing and skin, inflicting a hundred tiny injuries. He finally rolled to a stop. Without checking himself, Randall popped up and sprinted past Mark, arriving at John's side.

"Son, are you alright? John, talk to me!"

John writhed on the ground.

Randall searched for an entry wound. "Where were you hit?"

John sat up, blood trickling from a gash on his left cheek as he rubbed the back of his head.

"I'm okay, Dad, I wasn't shot. I must have just tripped on something."

"Thank God! Help me get Mark, the chopper just landed!" Randall pulled his son to his feet.

They grabbed Mark and resumed their sprint.

The Chinese regulars were nearly on them now. Tracer rounds chewed at the ground around them. They ran in a zig-zag pattern, trying to avoid the onslaught of bullets.

The Blackhawk was a dozen yards away. Its door opened, and several servicemen jumped to the ground, returning fire on the Chinese army. The sudden counterattack slowed their advance. One mountain-sized soldier ran up to the group, grabbed Mark with one arm and tossed him over his shoulder, relieving John and Randall.

Without the added weight, the two reached the open door of the chopper just as it lifted from the ground. A side-mounted fifty caliber machine gun rained rounds on the enemy, churning up the earth, causing them to take cover.

Exhausted, Randall slumped into an open seat next to John while another soldier examined Mark.

"Dr. Randall, General Flores wants to confirm that you found the information," one soldier said.

"Yes, we did, but we paid a steep price for it."

Chapter Forty-Five

August 24, 8:47 P.M.
Dulce, New Mexico

Randall rubbed his tired, red eyes. His sleep on the multiple flights back from Europe to Dulce had been fitful at best as his mind replayed the scenes of Captain Steele and his men sacrificing their lives. He now tried his best to clear the cobwebs from his mind as he waited for General Flores to return from the meeting with Dr. Chandra.

He glanced over at John, who sat slumped snoring in his chair. In an odd way, it made Randall feel good that his son, who was more than 20 years younger, was as tired as he was. Between the ordeal in Tibet and jet lag, Randall felt like he was in a dream.

More like a nightmare. He corrected himself, fighting back thoughts of what Jamie and Rob might be going through.

Despite his exhaustion, he was anxious to find the base and rescue his friends.

The sound of the office door opening brought him back to reality as Flores entered the room, placed his hat on the desk, and dropped into his seat.

"Dr. Chandra confirmed your findings. We have the location of the base. Sorry to keep you waiting so long—I was making arrangements for the next leg of the journey," Flores said as John opened his eyes, trying to focus on the conversation at hand.

"What? Where is it?" John asked, disoriented from being awoken.

"Several miles off Ross Island in Antarctica. We have a research station not far from the coordinates you provided. We'll arrange air transport to Williams Field, where my men will meet you. They'll take you the remainder of the way to the base."

"And what's the plan once we get there?" John asked.

"I have one of my best teams arriving at the base. They're being briefed on the assignment and will be responsible for obtaining the material we need. All I'll need you to do is help them get there and assist with any translation they need."

"You mean like in Tibet? With all due respect, there are variables outside of your control, so please don't try to whitewash the situation and make it seem simpler than it is. Also, what about Jamie and Rob? Is there any news about them?" Randall responded.

"No there isn't, but we can assume that your friends are safe because the Chinese didn't get the information you found in Tibet. The Dragons will undoubtedly use them as a bargaining chip if they need to. If they view them as a potential asset, I believe they'll keep them alive," Flores rubbed the stubble on his unshaven chin.

Randall turned to his son with a serious expression on his face. "John, is there any way I can convince you not to come on the next leg of this trip?"

"Not a chance. Rob and Jamie are depending on us, and besides, you need someone to keep an eye on you," John said, covering a yawn.

"After what happened in Tibet, I'd really prefer you stay here. There's no way we can guarantee your safety," Randall replied.

"What about your safety?" John asked.

"I don't really have a choice. I need to see this through to the end."

"I feel the same way. Remember, it's my serum that's causing most of this fuss."

Randall shook his head, too tired to argue. "I guess it's settled then. When do we leave, General?"

Chapter Forty-Six

August 25, 3:01 P.M.
McMurdo Station, Ross Island, Antarctica

Randall stared out the window of the Lockheed LC-130 ski-equipped United States Air Force plane as it banked high over Williams Field. A variant of the C-130 Hercules, the four-engine turboprop military transport was designed and built by Lockheed and could use unprepared runways for takeoffs and landings. This made it the logical choice for use in the unforgiving Antarctic landscape. The airport, approximately seven miles from Ross Island, and serving McMurdo Station, would be the launching point for their expedition to find the alien base.

From their vantage, Randall could see Ross Island protruding above a blanket of white and blue sea ice. As the plane approached McMurdo, Randall could make out small structures on the ground below. Large rectangular buildings intermingled with round storage tanks comprised the station, which was gearing up for the upcoming winter research season. As the station transitioned from the warmer summer months to the colder season, the entire composition of the base changed. With research more intense during the fall and winter months, the staff at the station tripled. For a moment, Randall was lost in the beauty and tranquility of the peaceful view below.

His reverie was short lived as Captain Valverde — the soldier assigned to guard Randall and his group — approached.

"Dr. Randall, once we land, we'll deploy the squad, top off our fuel tanks, and head out to the coordinates you and Dr. Chandra provided. We'll maintain a satellite link with our base for updates on potential hostile forces encroaching on our position. Do you have any questions?" Valverde asked.

"No, I understand. Thanks."

"Just stick by me, and I'll make sure you and your son are safe."

Randall nodded and resumed his post examining the wintry world outside his window. He touched the glass to confirm what his eyes were seeing. It was freezing outside.

"Better button up, you wouldn't want to catch a cold," John commented.

Randall smiled in reply.

"Is everything okay?" John asked.

"Yeah, I just don't like the idea of you being out here in these conditions. We have no idea what we'll run into and I would feel a lot better if you would have stayed in Dulce with your sister."

"And miss out on all of the fun? Look, Dad, I know you're worried about me, but we're in this together. Besides, after everything that's happened, I'm not about to leave you alone out here in the middle of nowhere."

254

"I wouldn't be alone. In case you missed it, I have an armed escort," Randall said, motioning to the soldiers from Valverde's squad.

"You know what I mean," John replied as his father smirked. "Besides, it's nice for me to be a part of your research this time. Aside from the rough patch you guys just got through, you and Sam have always shared a special bond over your love of archaeology. Now it's finally my chance to share the experience with you and I'm not going to miss it."

All Randall could do was nod in agreement.

"Do you think Sam and Dr. Chandra will discover anything else in the message before we find the base?" John asked.

"I'm not sure, but it's really amazing to think we're actually reading information written by a previously undiscovered culture. There's so much we could learn from them. Think of the possibilities!"

Now it was John's turn to smile at seeing his father's mood suddenly brighten.

"Oh, by the way, there's something we need to do before we find the base," John said, reaching into his jacket pocket and removing a small container.

"What's that?"

"It's a drug that Jacob and I synthesized to block the mind control properties of our original research compound. We've only had limited testing, but it seemed effective. I hid a sample of it in my car about a month ago when I started having a strange feeling about what was happening at work," John responded, sinking a syringe into a vial.

"Is it safe?" Randall asked, rolling up his sleeve.

"Our human trials showed no major side effects. The only thing that might happen is you might feel a bit woozy for a while and have dry mouth," John said, sinking the needle into his father's arm. "It's a neuro-blocker that fills the nerve

255

receptors, preventing a foreign substance from binding. In theory, it should help counteract the mind-control powers caused by the alien secretions if you happen to meet the substance."

Randall rolled his sleeve down and put his jacket back on. "How long will it work?"

"According to our tests, about 72 hours. That should cover us during our time here. I have one extra dose for each of us if we stay longer."

The captain's voice boomed through the intercom. "Fasten your seatbelts, we're coming in for a landing. This might get a little rough."

As John put away the serum, Gabby joined the two of them and they all strapped themselves into the wall-attached harness system. John offered the serum to her as well. Gabby accepted, each of them having one dose in their systems.

The C130 rolled to a stop on the makeshift tarmac. A cavernous door opened in the rear section and the soldiers began descending with their equipment. As the door lowered, a heavy blast of freezing Antarctic air spilled into the craft. Despite the many layers of polar-rated clothing, Randall shivered as his body registered the sudden drop in temperature.

"Folks, you'll be riding in that vehicle," Captain Valverde pointed to a camouflage painted Bv206S Tracked Armored Personnel Carrier. "We'll keep the three of you safely tucked in between the lead and trail vehicles. You'll be accompanied by a squad of men led by Staff Sergeant Howard. In the event of a firefight, I want you to stay in the carrier and get down. Sergeant Howard and his men will do the rest."

Randall eyed the APC, wondering if it was warm inside.

Valverde walked to Randall, handing him a black phone.

"What's this?" Randall asked.

"Satellite phone. If you get separated from the group, you can contact us, and we can do the same. We programmed it with my team's satellite phone number. Just hit the first preset," Valverde showed Randall how to operate the device. Randall tucked it into his coat's inner zippered pocket.

"Okay, load up and move out!" Valverde shouted.

The treaded vehicles carved their way through the ghostly white terrain in single file. Outside, a nearly seamless blanket of white snow was punctuated by the occasional craggy rock formation jutting from the ground like sentinels keeping watch over the lifeless void. Randall peered through the side window of the personnel carrier and marveled at the stark beauty of the frozen Antarctic graveyard. Since they had started their trek from McMurdo, they hadn't encountered another living creature. Randall assumed that they wouldn't for quite some time.

The weather had also deteriorated since McMurdo, and their visibility had dwindled to a few dozen yards. A storm moved across the frozen expanse and they were pushing headlong into the worst of it.

"What do you think we'll find when we get to the base?" Gabby asked.

Randall considered the question. "It's hard to say. We're speaking about a highly intelligent species, probably considerably older than our own. Their technology almost certainly puts ours to shame and we have no way of knowing what their home environment is like. That's what makes this so interesting—we'll be the first humans to experience this type of habitat."

Gabby nodded. "How much farther till we get there?"

"Less than a mile."

A monstrous explosion obliterated the personnel carrier directly in front of them. The flames licked the windshield of their own vehicle. Fragments of glass and metal rained to the ground, littering the pristine white snow with dark shards of debris. The blackened hull of the destroyed vehicle skidded onto its side, smoldering.

"Shit! Sergeant, we've lost the lead vehicle!"

Before Howard could register a reply, another explosion annihilated the carrier to the rear of them, sending flaming pieces of that vehicle cartwheeling into the wintry sky. Their own vehicle rocked wildly from the compression wave generated by the blast and the back window cracked in a spider-web fashion as large pieces of distorted metal slammed into the APC.

"Fire teams, I want a perimeter around us, now!"

The soldiers poured from the carrier, taking defensive positions in the snow. They fired wildly into the frozen landscape, hoping to repel their unseen attackers. Small arms fire crackled in the distance as a hail of bullets smashed into the exterior of the Snow Cat. From their perch inside, Randall heard the sergeant yelling orders to his men, who tried desperately to defend them.

The enemy gunfire increased, causing the hardened side windows to crack under the relentless barrage. Randall heard the shouts of Sergeant Howard's men as one by one they succumbed to the relentless assault. They fought bravely, but there was little they could do. They were trapped, and their attackers held every advantage.

Another blast detonated several feet from their vehicle, sending soldiers' bodies somersaulting into the air. The already weakened APC windows shattered. Bits of tempered glass rained down on Randall as he pressed himself against the floor for protection. The acrid smoke from the blast poured through the broken window, choking everyone inside.

The door to the carrier burst outward. Sergeant Howard struggled to pull his bloodied body into the vehicle. Grabbing him by his wrists, Randall yanked him in and John jammed the door closed. Blood oozed from the many wounds covering his battered face as Howard stumbled past the others to the communication system.

"Base, this is Eagle, we are under heavy attack by unknown opposing force! All fire teams are down, commence Operation Terminus, code delta–delta–four–niner, repeat, commence Operation Terminus immediately!"

"Eagle, this is base, code authenticated, commencing Operation Terminus."

"What in the hell just happened! What's Operation Terminus?" John blurted.

"Operation Terminus is our contingency plan in case the Red Dragons reached the base before us. One of our subs is preparing to launch a nuclear-tipped cruise missile to the coordinates your dad provided for the alien base. I'm sorry folks, but we can't allow anyone else to get to that base before us."

"You mean there's a nuclear missile heading our way right now and it's going to destroy the base?" John growled. "General Flores never said anything about this!"

"It was a need-to-know option and the General decided you didn't need to know."

"Dammit, I don't appreciate you taking license with the well-being of my son and Gabby," Randall said.

Howard looked to the floor of the carrier. "We didn't expect this to happen."

"How long before it strikes?" Randall asked.

"Seven hours to impact."

Randall spun in Howard's direction. "Seven hours?" He turned to see John and Gabby both staring at him, eyes wide.

Nothing more was said as silence descended on them like a heavy winter cloak.

Outside the carrier, the shooting subsided, replaced by the sound of soldiers shuffling through the snow. The enemy was moving into position around them.

"In the APC, we have you surrounded. Come out with your hands up," an enemy soldier ordered.

Howard cracked the door open. "I'm unarmed and coming out." The sergeant turned to Randall. "Wait here and stay low."

He pushed the door open and stumbled out of the vehicle, arms held high above his head. A single cracking sound emanated from the distance as a bullet struck him in the temple, jerking his head backward. His lifeless body slumped to the ground as a pool of crimson formed behind his head.

A soldier in white winter fatigues appeared in the doorway, his assault rifle at the ready. Randall moved in front of Gabby and John, shielding them from him. As he did, another man appeared by the soldier's side, smiling beneath his fur-lined parka.

"Dr. Randall, we really need to stop meeting like this," Dumond said, smirking.

Randall could only stare at the face looking back at him, blinking in disbelief.

"How did you find us?" Randall asked.

"With the help of your friend, Agent Gutierrez."

Gabby snarled. "What the hell are you talking about? I would never help a psychopath like you!"

"Your partner Charlie was a very clever man. He installed a tracking device in your phone for Colonel Shaw to know where you were at all times. A detail we learned after interrogating one of his men. All we needed was for you to take it with you."

"You son of a bitch! If I get a chance, I'm going to kill you!" Gabby yelled, trying to scramble past Randall. He held her back, grabbing her arm as she tried to rush Dumond.

"That's highly unlikely. However, we do need Dr. Randall's help with the location of the base. Dr. Randall, I'll need the coordinates."

"And if I don't provide them?"

"I'll have to kill your friend and your son."

"If I tell you, you'll kill us all anyway. Let them go and I'll take you to the base myself. You may need help communicating with them and I'm the only one here who can read their language."

"An interesting proposition, but I have a better idea. We'll take all three of you and this time, I promise, if you cross me, I'll kill them myself."

Chapter Forty-Seven

The massive soldier standing next to Dumond reached into the APC and yanked Randall out, tossing him into the snow. He did the same with John and Gabby, then stood towering over them.

"Lieutenant Reilly, escort our guests back to base," Dumond said. "And in case you have thoughts of escaping, my snipers would love nothing more than some target practice."

The group plodded slowly through the thick snow, their feet sinking several inches with each step. Dumond's men fared much better, wearing snow shoes for the trek back to their base. As they crested a small hill, Randall spotted a small tent city secured to the icy terrain in anticipation of the storm. Sitting directly north of the tents was a BELL 212 Twin Huey helicopter. Painted bright red, the chopper stood out against the white landscape like a hundred-watt bulb in a darkened closet.

As they approached the encampment, it became apparent that Dumond had spared no expense in assembling a small army. Dozens of armed men in white camouflaged uniforms guarded the outer perimeter of the base, armed with an assortment of small arms and heavy artillery. Of special interest to Randall were several men holding what appeared to be hand-held missile launchers. His eyes shifted to Dumond, who was in front of the group, engaged in a lively conversation with one of his direct reports.

"Anti-aircraft missiles, Dumond? Don't you think that's a bit excessive, even for you?"

"I pride myself on being prepared. After all, who knows what we might discover once we get to our destination?"

"While I appreciate your desire to overcompensate for, well, for something, don't you think these creatures would be advanced enough to survive an attack by technologically inferior weapons?"

Dumond ignored Randall's baiting and returned to his previous conversation.

While they hadn't traveled far, the difficulty of walking through the deep snow had made Randall exceptionally tired. He stood on the edge of the base, hunched over, trying to catch his breath. A ringing noise started in his ear. He tried to ignore it, but it grew louder and more prevalent taking on a whistling tone. The sound grew in intensity, causing Randall to turn and look at John.

"Do you hear that?"

"You mean the whistling sound?"

"You hear it, too! I thought I was just my imagination."

"No one told you to stop! Keep walking!" Reilly shouted.

The noise grew louder and more piercing. The group, almost in unison, looked toward the sky just in time to see a blurred streak followed by a fiery tail strike the center of the encampment, obliterating a large portion of Dumond's base and creating an enormous impact crater in the snowy ground.

"Move!" a soldier yelled, ramming the butt of his gun into Randall's back.

"To where?"

Another shriek filled the sky. The mercenaries scrambled for cover, searching for signs of their attackers. Dumond cursed as one of his men pushed him to the ground, covering him just as another missile slammed into the earth, sending an eruption of snow, dirt, men, and machinery skyward. Smoke billowed from the ground where the missile had impacted, and debris rained down from the heavens.

"They're targeting the base! Take cover behind the Snow Cats and return fire!" Reilly ordered his men.

Randall watched as Dumond and his bodyguard raced for one of the large personnel carriers on the edge of his compound.

"Who's attacking the base?" Gabby asked.

"Follow them!" the guard yelled, ignoring Gabby's question, nearly knocking Randall to the ground as he shoved him. The group surged forward with two of Dumond's men prodding them toward the APCs. Randall heard the distinct cracking sound of gunfire from behind him and turned in time to see the mercenaries behind them fall to the ground, blood running freely from numerous bullet wounds in their bodies.

They were sitting ducks.

Randall scanned the terrain and spotted an outcropping of rocks to the east of the camp.

"We need to find cover! Head for those rocks over there!"

The three sprinted to the ice-covered stones as the battle raged on. Caught by surprise, Dumond's men were taking a beating. Looking back in the direction they had come, Randall saw dozens of figures rising from the snow like ghosts, fire spewing from the barrels of their guns. They mowed down Dumond's men, who returned fire in a futile attempt to repel them.

A thunderous thudding arose from the north as two green military choppers crested the hill and descended on Dumond's base. They unleashed a fury of rockets, raining death on the contingent of remaining men. Someone on the ground managed to launch a missile at the attackers. The contrail rose from the ground, striking one of the choppers in its fuselage. The helicopter shuddered upon impact, a shower of flames emerging from its side as it spun wildly out of control and summersaulted into the snowy earth.

The remaining chopper, having seen the attack, homed in on the missile's origin point and fired round after round of rocket pods into the ground. The resulting devastation defused the attack and turned the pristine landscape into a bloody, smoldering pile of rubble. Seeing the threat neutralized, the chopper commenced its attack on the tent city, laying waste to the encampment as another helicopter joined the fray.

Dozens of soldiers and heavily armed vehicles descended on the remnants of Dumond's troops, mercilessly cutting them down with a relentless barrage of automatic gun fire. Randall watched as mercenaries tried to flee the massacre only to be shot as they ran away. Only a handful managed to escape.

The destruction was unlike anything he had ever seen. In a matter of minutes, the invading force had eradicated Dumond's troops as easily as a man squashing a bug with his thumb. The attackers patrolled the camp, searching for survivors and dispatching any living thing that still moved.

"Stay down," Randall said, crouching behind a large block of ice.

"Who the hell did this and do you think they saw us?" John asked.

"If I had to guess, I'd say it's the Red Dragons. We just need to stay put and wait for them to leave. We'll see if we can find a working Snow Cat and put as much distance between us and this place as possible before the missile hits."

"But Dad, we're so close, we can't leave now!"

"Son, there's no way I'm putting the two of you in danger any longer. Besides, the missile will destroy the base, and no one will have access to the mind control substance."

"What about Rob and Jamie?" John asked.

"You and Gabby head back to McMurdo to get help. I'll follow the Dragons and keep an eye on them until reinforcements arrive."

Randall peered from behind the frozen rock and watched the soldiers milling about the remains of the camp. They appeared to be searching for something, but what?

"What are they doing?" Gabby asked.

"They're looking for something ... or someone." Randall replied.

He looked over at John, who was craning his neck around the ice block to survey the area. Randall was certain that his son had also caught sight of the men searching the wreckage, but something else had caught his gaze. Randall turned to look at the vehicles gathered near what had previously been the outer rim of the camp and noticed something about them. Emblazoned on the doors were unmistakable bright red figures.

"Dad, look at the doors of the trucks. I think you're right and I think I know who they they're looking for."

Randall nodded his understanding. It was The Red Dragons. "They must know I found the Rosetta Stone and want the coordinates to the base. We can't let them find us."

He withdrew behind the rock. A loud ringing noise came from his parka.

"Shit, the satellite phone!" Randall said.

He struggled to remove his gloves. The phone rang again. He finally tore the glove off and opened his parka, fumbling to unzip the pocket. The phone rang a third time. Nearly ripping the zipper open, he scooped the phone from his jacket and silenced the ringing.

"Do you think they heard us?" Gabby asked.

Randall inched his way to the edge of the ice block and peered around the corner. Several armed soldiers had fanned out and were approaching their position, followed by a heavily armored vehicle.

"Stay here!" Randall ordered.

He stood from behind the rock that had concealed him and walked toward the soldiers, hands in the air.

"I'm unarmed, don't shoot," he said.

He continued walking toward the Red Dragons, clasping his hands behind his head in a show of submission. His plan worked, the soldiers surrounded him and took him captive, completely oblivious to John and Gabby's presence.

Chapter Forty-Eight

The Dragons marched Randall to a group of heavily protected armored vehicles. His hands zip-tied behind his back, there was little he could do but comply with their orders. He reviewed the carnage that had once been Dumond's base and, as much as he hated Dumond, couldn't help but feel pity for the brutal death that had befallen him and his men. They approached the rear of one of the APCs and stopped. The motor controlling the rear hatch whirred to life and the opening slowly descended in front of them. Randall was shocked to see Rob sitting in the back, his hands cuffed to a metal rail behind him.

"Rob! Thank God you're alive! Where's Jamie?"

Rob raised his head slowly. "She's gone, they took her."

"Who took her, what do you mean?"

"They did … those creatures! It was horrible. I couldn't do anything to help her, it was like I was drugged and couldn't move. They took her, Nick, and God knows what they're doing to her."

"It's okay, Rob, we'll find her. I promise we will."

The soldiers pushed Randall into the back of the APC and closed the hatch. The big armored vehicle rumbled through the snow.

"Are you okay, have they hurt you?" Randall asked.

"I'm okay. Hell, I don't really care what they do to me. I'm just worried about Jamie. Poor kid."

After a short while, the APC stopped, and the big rear door slowly opened again. Randall, Rob, and their escorts descended from the vehicle. For the second time in the same day, Randall was amazed to find himself amid a large, temporary city of tents and heavy military machinery. The juxtaposition of the green structures and heavily armored vehicles against the pure white background of the Antarctic wilderness was a shocking contrast. The fact that they had made no attempt to conceal their presence spoke to the Dragons' confidence ... or arrogance.

Accompanying the structures and large weapon transport platforms were smaller support trucks, helicopters, and nearly a hundred soldiers. The Red Dragons had transported a small military base from China to the Antarctic, and their purpose was clear: they were going to get the mind control substance, and crush anyone who got in their way.

The soldiers led their two prisoners to a rectangular metal box situated on top of a large, flatbed tracked vehicle. The structure looked like a shipping container used by stevedoring companies to move freight, except this one was painted completely green, except for the Red Dragon logo emblazoned on its side. Randall was led up a ramp where a guard stood waiting for him outside the door. The guard punched a code into a recessed keypad, unlocking the entrance. He escorted

Randall into the container while Rob was spirited away to another location.

The inside of the structure was appointed with all the creature comforts one would expect in a well-appointed office. Thick, brown carpeting lined the floor and large, overstuffed cloth chairs were neatly arranged by one wall, which was decorated with beautiful lithographs depicting the ancient Chinese countryside. The room was well lit by wall sconces and several chandeliers, draped from cream colored ceiling tiles. Tucked away in the far corner of the room was a beautifully hand-carved ebony desk with the Dragons' logo inlaid in the side facing the entrance. A polished brass lamp sat atop the desk, which was otherwise devoid of anything except a single folder. The appearance of the room gave the impression of standing in a Wall Street CEO's office instead of a military headquarters.

Seated behind the desk was a man in a perfectly tailored uniform resplendent with medals and ribbons befitting someone who had dedicated his life to serving his country. He carefully studied the contents of the folder, seemingly unaware of the intrusion into his private domain. Finally, he lifted his moon-shaped face and locked his eyes onto Randall, studying him carefully.

"The coordinates to the base, I need them now," he said.

"Sorry, I don't know what you're referring to. McMurdo is back that way," Randall replied, pointing his handcuffed hands out the window of the office.

The soldier stood up from behind his desk, his six-foot-tall athletic frame cutting an imposing figure. He walked around to the front of the desk and sat down facing Randall.

"I know you have the coordinates, we monitored you after you returned from the underwater cave. If you want to see your friend live, you will give me what I want."

"Do you really think I'm stupid enough to believe you'll let Rob and I live?"

The soldier reached back into his desk drawer and removed a cigarette and a lighter. He carefully placed the cigarette into his mouth, methodically lighting it. Taking a puff, he stared directly through Randall as if he wasn't there. After a long, smoky exhale he replied.

"I can guarantee a quick and painless death for both of you, or I can make it a slow, excruciating process. It's your choice."

"I missed your name."

"I am General Keung, the leader of the Red Dragon Brigade."

"I'm Dr. Nick Randall."

"I am familiar with you and your work, but I don't have time for small talk. I need the coordinates to fulfill my mission."

"You mean you couldn't figure out where the base was with the footage from Rob's camera?" Randall goaded.

Keung wasn't taking the bait. "An oversight on my part, which will now be remedied. The coordinates, Dr. Randall."

"You know your plan will never work."

The General took another puff of his cigarette as he continued to study Randall. A thin smile spread across his lips. "Typical American. You think you know more than everyone else and can control every situation. Your country's time as a world leader has already passed, but you are too arrogant to realize it. Now, my country stands on the threshold of controlling the greatest power known to man and you have the last piece of information we need to make it a reality. If you believe for a moment that I will hesitate to take any action needed to attain this knowledge, you are gravely mistaken. Now, I will ask you one last time. What are the coordinates to the alien base?"

Randall dropped his glance to the floor. Nodding, he glanced back up at the General. "Okay, Keung, you win. I'll give you the coordinates, but I ask for one favor in return. Before you kill us, I want you to take us to the base with you. As men of science, this is a momentous occasion in human history and we would like to be a part of it. Please allow us this small indulgence and I promise to give you the coordinates and even help you translate any messages you find."

Keung stared directly into Randall's eyes and took another puff of his cigarette. He turned, reached into his desk drawer again and retrieved a polished brass ashtray, setting it on his desk. He flicked the burning embers into it.

"I will grant your request as you may yet serve a purpose, but remember," he said, holding the cigarette in his right hand, "if you try to deceive me or escape, I will crush you and your friend."

Keung squashed the cigarette into the ashtray.

Chapter Forty-Nine

The armored personnel carrier rumbled through the snow toward the coordinates of the alien base. Randall and Rob sat in the middle of the back seat sandwiched between two enormous soldiers, looking out into the dreary gray sky. Although the snowfall had stopped, huge clouds hung in the air, blotting out the sun and casting an eerie pale over the newly fallen snow. They had been traveling for nearly an hour and were rapidly approaching the coordinates Randall had provided, but there was still no sign of the base.

Keung's contingent followed closely behind the lead vehicle. The general was growing impatient as they traversed the large flat plain. Soon, they approached an ice shelf jutting out of the white earth.

"Stop the vehicle!" Keung ordered, turning to Randall.

"Where is the base? I warned you not to trifle with me." Keung nodded, and a soldier sitting next to Rob produced a pistol and pointed it at Rob's head.

"I swear, these are the coordinates," Randall said, searching the area outside of the vehicle.

Keung nodded again to the soldier, who now cocked the hammer of the gun and pressed it into Rob's left temple. "Do you take me for a fool? If you don't tell me the location of the base by the count of three, your friend is dead," Keung said.

"It has to be here, if we just get out and…"

"One."

"It could be buried in the snow, send out your men with…"

"Two."

"Wait! Look up there!" Randall said, pointing out the window of the carrier toward the ice shelf. "It looks like there's an opening in the side of the ledge."

Everyone in the APC turned to look in the direction he was pointing. Against the bright backdrop of the low hanging sun behind the ice ledge, they could see a small dark, rounded opening in the otherwise blue-white ice cliff.

"How much farther until we reach the exact coordinates I provided?" Randall asked the driver.

"One hundred and seven yards."

"That seems about right. If we keep going in this direction, we'll be at the base of the ice ledge. Don't you see? The base might be built into the side of the cliff and not on the ground. We need to at least investigate the possibility."

"Lower your weapon." Keung instructed his soldier. "Take us directly below the opening."

The vehicle lurched forward and resumed its trek through the snow, stopping at the base of an incline leading up to the opening in the ice ledge. Everyone exited the APC and stood staring up toward the possible entrance. The ice shelf was easily two hundred feet tall and over a mile wide, the opening approximately fifty feet from the top. Standing in the howling wind, Randall felt like little more than a dark spec against the pure white background, the cold cutting through his down parka. Despite his gear, he could feel his core body temperature slowly dropping.

Rob leaned close to his friend's ear. "How much longer until the missile hits?"

Randall glanced at his watch. "Four and half hours, give or take a few minutes."

He then turned to look at the men and equipment Keung had assembled, and for the first time noticed one long-tracked vehicle carrying a missile.

"What in God's name is that?"

"A Dong Feng 21 missile carrying an electromagnetic pulse weapon. Did you think the general would enter into battle against these creatures without a way to neutralize their systems?" Randall's guard said before shoving him in the back to move forward.

Randall staggered up the icy slope trying to keep from sliding on the frozen ground. Rob walked next to him, prodded along by another soldier tasked with watching him. Keung followed close behind, trailed by his personal escorts and a platoon of Red Army regulars. The group slowly made their way up the treacherous path until they finally arrived at the opening.

Randall's initial reaction was that the opening was much larger up close than it had appeared from the bottom of the hill. The wind buffeted him as he stood in awe of the dark fissure that fed into the icy ledge. He stared into the darkness but couldn't determine how deep it went … or what awaited them inside.

"What are you waiting for?" Keung asked.

"A light would be nice. Call me crazy but it would be helpful to know what we're walking into before we go in."

The general motioned for one of the soldiers to give flashlights to Randall and Rob. The two switched on their beams and entered the opening. The wind howled down the tunnel, drowning out all other sounds as they slowly made their way into the icy chasm. The lights reflected off the blue iridescent ice forming the walls of the cavern, creating a shimmering effect.

As they moved forward, all signs of the exterior world faded away, giving way to a surreal landscape of undulating ice cut into the frozen mountainside. Icicles dangled from the ceiling like long, slender daggers ready to drop onto an unsuspecting intruder.

The tunnel was deep. Although Randall's light pierced the darkness ahead, he could only see more icy walls and ceilings. The group followed a slight left turn in the path and the opening changed dramatically.

The rectangular entrance was fifty feet wide, half as high and a hundred yards deep. The floor consisted of large, square sections ten feet on end that protruded from the ground by several inches. A grid-shaped channel measuring three inches surrounded each segment, creating a checkerboard appearance. The walls were flat, save for large rectangular compartments resembling air conditioning units lining the surface approximately twenty feet from the floor. Thick pipes — not unlike electrical conduits, only larger — were neatly arranged in a parallel fashion spanning the roof with rectangular lights spaced at irregular intervals.

The poorly lit interior was a matte black color with dull metallic surfaces interspersed throughout. Randall noted the increased humidity inside the base, which caused him to sweat the moment they entered the long corridor. The temperature was noticeably warmer than in the ice tunnel and the air smelled like Sulphur. As he checked the area, he observed a large white cylindrical object that spanned from the floor to the ceiling, located directly at the end of the entrance. It looked like a giant, glowing pillar holding up the ceiling.

"You men, take the two prisoners into the facility," Keung ordered his soldiers.

Four Red Dragons prodded Randall and Rob forward, while Keung and the rest of his men waited in the relative safety of the ice tunnel.

Randall was astonished at the size of the facility, which dwarfed any warehouse he had ever seen. They walked briskly down the hallway and arrived at the cylinder. Upon closer inspection, Randall realized that it was a lighted control panel that likely operated this section of the base. He depressed a small section of the cylinder that was outlined by a glowing blue band and a panel retracted to reveal a keypad with the same strange writing from the underwater cavern. When he began typing, a large section of the cylinder transformed into a clear, glasslike surface. Symbols appeared on the screen in response to his query. As he continued typing, a diagram of the multilevel facility appeared with notations describing each section. His translation was slow, but Randall eventually understood most of what he read.

Focused on the task at hand, he hadn't noticed that the General and two additional soldiers had joined them. Apparently, Keung had determined it was safe to enter the area.

"What does it say?" Keung asked.

"I'm searching for information on the facility to see where we are and where we should go."

Randall touched the screen and a small section of the facility map enlarged and specific details not previously visible became clear. He touched the screen again and video imaging appeared on a separate section of the cylinder next to the facility diagram. The image showed a room with a bank of six large metal containers with glass spanning from their midpoints to their tops. The glass of each container was foggy as if tinged with frost.

Keung impatiently pushed his way past Rob and appeared by Randall's side. "What are you doing and why are you focusing on this room?"

"Because he's looking for his friend," a voice said from directly behind them.

The two rear guards spun on their heels, guns at the ready, but collapsed onto the floor as gunfire ripped through them. The remaining Dragon team members raised their weapons, prepared to engage their assailants. Keung grabbed his own side arm and moved to the far side of the cylinder for protection, while Randall and Rob ducked for cover as well.

Randall seized the opportunity. "Come on!" He grabbed Rob by the arm, making his way to a hallway on the right.

"What the hell just happened?" Rob protested.

"It's Dumond! He must have followed us here!"

"I thought he was dead! That guy keeps turning up like a bad penny!"

The two dashed down the corridor as bullets tore through the air around them. Shattered glass and metal fragments showered down as they ran through the passageways. The sparks created by the gunfire resembled fireflies dancing around them as they sprinted. Randall reached an intersection of the building, paused for a moment, and resumed his mad dash to the left.

"Where are we going?" Rob asked.

"The holding area where Jamie should be. We're almost there."

The two came to a flight of stairs and Randall sped without pause down a level and emerged onto a well-lit hallway. It extended twenty feet, terminating at a polished metal door, inset into a wall that was otherwise completely devoid of almost any other noticeable features.

"What now?"

Randall approached the wall and noted a small depression outlined by a thin blue line. He placed his finger on the spot and pushed. A section of the metal wall silently opened upward, revealing a surgical room. The two slipped inside, the door closing behind them.

The room was bathed in pure white light, which emanated from the walls so brightly that it caused them to squint. His hand shielding his eyes, Randall examined the room as he approached the first of the five metal cylinders. Touching the first one, his hand registered extreme cold. Reflexes caused him to pull his hand back. He then rubbed the glass to clear the frost and peered inside. It was empty. He did the same with the three next cylinders, finding them empty as well. The last cylinder was adjacent to a series of six-foot ledges protruding from the wall. One of the ledges contained what appeared to be neatly arranged surgical instruments and a single vial with clear liquid.

Randall wiped the frost away from the glass of the fifth cylinder. This time it wasn't empty.

"She's here! Help me find the controls!"

The two searched the outside of the cylinder, found a blue outlined depression like the door switch. Randall pressed it. The top of the container separated from the bottom, opening like scissor blades, causing a hiss of cold air to spill from the chamber.

Jamie lay like a lifeless corpse on a narrow pedestal. Her eyes were closed, and her skin was cool to the touch.

"Help me get her out," Randall said.

The two men lifted her from the cylinder, gently placing her on the nearest shelf. A sticky residue remained on their fingers from touching Jamie. Randall bent down to listen for signs that she was breathing. He felt a faint breath of warm air touch his ears. Buoyed by this, he felt for a pulse. At first, he couldn't detect a heartbeat, but finally found a weak throb.

"She's alive, but barely," Randall said, removing his coat and placing it over Jamie's body, which was covered in a light, shimmery, skin-tight material.

"We need something else to warm her," Randall said, taking her hand and clasping it in his own. "Come on kiddo, wake up so we can get you out of here."

"Nick," Rob said, tugging at Randall's elbow.

Randall turned to look at his friend, whose face relayed his concern. He followed Rob's eyes and found himself face to face with two men. Dressed in the same clothing as Jamie, they simply stood there, watching them. The men were unarmed, but there was something strange about them that Randall couldn't immediately identify. Then it struck him. They were completely devoid of any hair. Bald heads, no eyebrows, no stubble. Their skin was completely smooth, almost as if made of plastic.

Randall watched as Rob dropped to the floor, his eyes wide and his mouth hanging open. Randall turned from his friend and faced the strangers. He stepped in front of Jamie, placing himself directly between her and the men.

"I'm not letting you take her," Randall said.

The faintest of smiles crossed the lips of one of the men as he stared directly at Randall. Randall felt an odd tingling sensation in his extremities, which spread up his legs, chest, and arms. His body suddenly felt heavy and his mind hazy, as if he had been drugged.

Fighting off the feeling of fatigue, Randall steadied himself, taking a step toward the man. "You're one of them, aren't you? You both are. You kidnapped Jamie and brought her back here to your base to experiment on her."

The men looked at each other, then turned to face Randall again.

Randall's eyes narrowed. "We've developed an antidote against your powers. Your ability to control us is over."

Randall detected a feeling of interest on the part of the beings. "Why are you here and what are you doing to my friend?"

No response.

"Whatever your purpose, my government knows you're here now, so your secret is out."

The beings shared a glance, then looked at Randall again. He could sense their confusion.

"My God. Someone knows what you're doing. Who's helping you and why?"

Their expressions became serious. Both beings held up their arms. Randall suddenly felt as if lead weights had been hung around his neck, arms, and legs. His balance became unsteady. Randall braced himself against the table, struggling to resist them. John's compound was clearly helping him but wasn't entirely effective.

The room suddenly rocked, dust particles dropping from the ceiling. Distracted, the beings dropped their arms.

"The Chinese are attacking you," Randall said.

Randall sensed great annoyance from the beings, who focused their full mental energy against him. This time, he felt not only weakness, but outright pain. He sensed that they no longer wanted to subdue him. They wanted to kill him.

Randall struggled to remain upright. His body ached, and his mind burned. The beings closed in for the kill. Randall fell to the floor, writhing in pain. He gripped his head, which felt like it would explode. Screaming in agony, he closed his eyes, ready for death. He heard two distinct popping sounds and assumed he was about to die.

He didn't. The pain suddenly stopped.

Randall lay on the floor of the lab, unsure of what had happened. His body spent, he slowly opened his eyes and saw the beings lying on the ground. They weren't moving. He forced himself to focus his eyes and look around the room. Seeing the silhouette of a man standing over him, Randall's eyes started at the man's feet and worked their way to his face. His vision was still blurry, and he couldn't make out the face, but he recognized the voice immediately.

"Fortunate for me I happened along when I did. I wouldn't have wanted those things to have all of the fun of killing you."

Dumond had returned.

Chapter Fifty

Randall's mind raced as he stared into the eyes of his nemesis. He slowly rose to his feet, wobbly from his near-death encounter. While Dumond had saved him from the beings, his intentions clearly weren't noble. The crazed industrialist strode purposefully into the room, his pistol pointed directly at Randall. He moved to the far side of the room and sat on one of the ledges protruding from the wall.

Randall watched in amazement as Dumond unlaced his boots with one hand while keeping his gun trained on him with the other. The industrialist slid his boots off and set them neatly to one side. Next, he removed his jacket, one sleeve at a time, careful not to break eye contact with Randall throughout the process. He neatly stacked his jacket and gloves on the ledge and walked over to Randall in stockinged feet, gun still pointed at his chest. Dumond stopped several feet in front of Randall, directly next to Rob, who still lay unconscious on the floor.

"Turn around," Dumond said.

"And if I don't?" Randall asked.

Dumond turned his weapon to Rob. "Then I kill your friend."

Realizing he had no choice, Randall turned to face Jamie. He was rewarded with a sharp blow to the back of his head. Randall tumbled to the ground, dazed. Sprawled on the floor, he turned to face Dumond, who set his gun down on the ground.

"Get up."

Randall complied, rising to his feet.

"Not feeling so well? Let me see if I can help."

Dumond unleashed a brutal kick to Randall's abdomen, causing him to double over in intense pain. Already weakened by the blow to the back of his head, Randall struggled for a breath of air. Dumond watched in amusement for a moment, then bent over and grabbed Randall by the shirt collar and forced him upright, propping him against the wall. He slapped the Randall's face, then grasped it with his free hand, and shook.

"Wake up!"

Randall opened his eyes, his chest heaving to capture a breath. Dumond spun him away from the wall.

"Did I ever tell you about my affinity for Muay Thai? It's also known as The Art of Eight Limbs because it's characterized by the combined use of fists, elbows, knees, and shins. The punch techniques in Muay Thai originally involved landing the blow with the heel of the palm, like this."

Dumond struck Randall in the chest with his hand, driving him back several feet before he toppled to the ground. Intense pain radiated from Randall's ribs where Dumond had landed his blow. Randall rolled on the ground in pain, clutching his aching torso. Dumond slowly walked over to him and lifted him once again and placed him against the wall to continue his cruel lesson.

"But blows to the body are actually discouraged as they leave the attacker's head open to counter strikes. It's actually better to use your elbow for an attack because it can cause damage more quickly or be used to gain a tactical advantage over your opponent."

Dumond swung his elbow from the side, striking Randall above his left eye, opening a gash in his eyebrow that released a cascade of blood.

"For example, the technique I just employed causes the opponent's vision to become obscured, thereby impeding his ability to utilize effective counter measures."

Randall struggled to raise a hand to his injured eye. Dumond swatted it away with ease. He spun Randall again and released him into the center of the room. Randall swayed on his feet, like a punch-drunk boxer. He fought to stay upright, the coppery taste of blood filled his mouth.

"Personally, my favorite move is one you've probably seen in movies. Do you like martial arts films? I've loved them since I was a child. In fact, it's part of the reason I so enjoyed learning this wonderful sport. My favorite move is the roundhouse kick. The attacker gains his power from the rotation of his hips, like this."

Dumond lifted his body from the ground, spinning in a clockwise fashion and landing the kick to the side of Randall's head. The professor tumbled sideways, struck the side of the open containment unit, and fell to the ground like a rag doll. He lay motionless for some time, blood trickling from a new gash on the side of his head. Slowly and with great effort he began to move. His head throbbed with each heartbeat and his ribs felt like they were broken. Randall tried to prop himself up on his bruised elbows, his arms shaking against the strain of holding up his injured body. He collapsed to the floor.

Dumond smiled as he watched Randall groan in pain. He was impressed with how well the professor had absorbed the punishment but was ready to finish him once and for all.

"You've cost me dearly—money, power, my best mercenaries—but do you know what I really hate about you? You adore your children and place their well-being above your own. Worse still, they love you back. Do you know what my father was like? He was an abusive drunk. He beat my mother and me nearly to death, but guess what: he made me strong, and I eventually killed him. Now I'm going to do the same to you."

An evil grin spread across Dumond's face like a crooked river forming after a heavy rain. He walked over to Randall, towering over his injured body.

"Goodbye, Dr. Randall."

"Hey asshole, you forgot something."

Startled, Dumond spun to face the voice behind him.

It was Rob. Catching Dumond off guard, he plowed into him like a free safety laying into a receiver who had foolishly ventured into his territory. He drove Dumond backward and into the containment pod, then hit the blue button on the side of the unit, causing the container to close. Dumond pounded on the glass as it began to frost over.

Rob walked over to his friend and knelt beside him.

"Nick, are you okay? Talk to me, buddy."

Randall lay face down on the floor, his body aching in a thousand places. The throbbing pain in his head was tremendous. He was unable to do much more than roll over on his side.

"You saved my life. Thank you."

"Thank God you're all right. Can I help you up?"

"Give me a few minutes. Go check on Jamie."

Rob arrived by Jamie's side. Some color had returned to her cheeks, but her eyes were still closed. Rob gently lifted her hand in his and then placed his other hand on her shoulder.

"Jamie, can you hear me? It's Rob and Nick, we're here with you."

Jamie's eyes fluttered open. She tilted her head in the direction of Rob's voice and looked at him groggily.

"I never thought I'd see you again," she said, offering a weak smile.

Rob smiled back down at her.

Randall managed to get to his feet and stumbled over by his friend. "Hey kiddo, it's great to see you awake again."

A tear rolled down Jamie's cheek as she looked at the two men.

"I thought I was going to die. When they put me into that tube, I knew they weren't going to let me go. I could have..."

"We never would have let that happen. If we're around, you're safe. Do you think you can walk? We need to get out of here, fast," Randall replied, brushing away her tear.

As he did so, the room rocked violently. Rob looked up toward the ceiling as the lights swayed back and forth.

"You're hurt," Jamie said, lifting a hand to Randall's face. "What happened to you?"

"I ran into Dumond. He roughed me up a bit, but Rob took care of him."

The room rocked again, this time causing bits of dust to fall from the ceiling.

"What's going on?" Jamie asked.

"The Red Dragons know something happened to the general and his men. They're attacking the base," Randall replied. "Can you stand?"

"I think so."

Jamie swung her legs over the side of the table and gingerly touched the floor while Randall and Rob braced her from the side. The added weight of holding Jamie caused Randall to wince in pain.

"Are you okay?" Jamie asked.

"Yeah, just a bit sore," Randall lied. The pain in his head was only upstaged by the intense jabbing feeling coming from his ribs, which he was certain were either broken or severely bruised.

Jamie regained her balance, clutching at the jacket Randall had placed around her for warmth.

"What about shoes?" Rob asked, looking down at Jamie's feet, which were covered with something that resembled an enclosed slipper.

Randall walked over to Dumond's clothes and brought them to Jamie.

"Here, you can use these. They're a bit big, but they'll work," he said, handing her his shoes and pants. Randall donned Dumond's jacket.

"We need to take this," she said, picking up the vial sitting on the table. "The creatures used it to keep me under control. I think it's made of whatever substance they secrete for their mind-control powers."

Randall took the vial and shoved it into his zippered pocket. He then led the three out of the lab, back up the stairs, and into the ice tunnel. As they approached the entrance, they could hear a raging battle as the Chinese continued to attack the base. They skulked to the entrance, peering out for a look.

Chapter Fifty-One

The Red Dragons were launching an attack using their heavy weapons. Randall saw several tanks maneuvering into position and firing shells into the mountainside while helicopters zigzagged through the sky firing rocket pods into the icy cliffs. Infantrymen had taken defensive positions behind rocky outcrops and were launching rocket propelled grenades and mortar fire at the base. The focus of the attack seemed to be on the top of the plateau, which would have served as the top of the facility.

Spent munition casings and metal fragments littered the once pristine white and blue landscape. Upturned ice and rocks were scattered about, appearing as dark splotches staining the icy field. Despite the bedlam, the battle seemed to be one-sided. Only the Red Dragons were engaged.

Randall also noticed that soldiers were guarding the base of the long incline they had used to access the tunnel. By his count, there were eight positioned at the bottom of the icy ramp. He surmised that they were the remnants of the platoon that had entered the ship with the general. He also realized that getting by them would be next to impossible. Randall withdrew into the ice tunnel.

"What's going on out there?" Rob asked.

Randall slumped against a rocky ledge for support, pressing the sleeve of his jacket against the cut above his eye to stem the bleeding. "It's mayhem. The Red Dragons are attacking with everything they have and making a big mess. It doesn't seem like there's any response from the other side. At least not yet. I'm not sure how we're going to get past them."

"We need a distraction," Rob said.

"I agree, but what?"

A new sound joined the chorus of anarchy outside the chamber. Randall peeked out to find the source and spotted a lone missile launcher slowly churning through the snow, far from the rest of the main Chinese force. It was at the far end of the ice field, well away from the alien base.

"They're getting ready to launch the missile carrying the electromagnetic pulse weapon!" Randall shouted.

Jamie and Rob appeared by his side, anxious to see for themselves. The large tracked vehicle carrying the missile moved into position for a launch. The missile carrier stopped, then its launcher tilted upward, the tip of the projectile lifting high into the gray sky.

A bright flame ignited from the base of the weapon as it rocketed into the heavens, leaving a smoky trail in its wake. Before long, the missile was little more than a dark pinprick in the sky and then it disappeared entirely.

"Are they insane? How are they going to direct the EMP blast, so it just takes out the base and not their own equipment?" Rob asked.

"I guess they know the yield of the weapon and the range affected by the blast. What I don't understand is why there hasn't been a response against them," Randall replied.

The Chinese troops began pulling back, their vehicles turning in unison as they increased the distance between themselves and the base. As they did so, the troop stationed at the base of the cliff entrance entered an armored vehicle, retreating as well.

"Look, they pulled back. Maybe we can get out of here!" Jamie said.

"Maybe so, but they'll probably come back after the EMP blast to guard the entrance. If they do, we'll be sitting ducks," Rob replied.

The thought of being trapped between Chinese Special Forces and a hostile force of unknown origin from the facility they had just escaped was chilling. Randall struggled to devise a better plan to escape. "I think Jamie's right. Our best chance is to head down the ramp before the missile impacts and the Chinese move back in to cover the entrance again."

"What about the missile? When it blows, we'll be roasted if we're sitting out in the open," Rob said.

Randall smiled at the thought. "That's true, but what's one more bomb to contend with?"

"What do you mean, one more bomb?" Jamie asked.

Realizing that Jamie was unaware of Flores' backup plan, Randall explained the details.

"How long do we have before it strikes?"

Randall checked his watch. "A little more than two hours, by my calculation."

"That doesn't leave us much time," Jamie said. "Like Rob said, what do we do when we make it to the bottom?"

"We'll have to hope that the Red Dragons are too busy with them to care that we're trying to escape," Randal said, tossing his thumb back to the base they had just exited.

The three waited until the APC carrying the guards was well clear of the ramp before beginning their trek back down the ice shelf. The bitterly cold wind howled, gnawing at them as they worked their way to the midpoint of the slope. Winded from the run, the three stopped for a moment, huddling against the side for some relief from the gale. Jamie and Rob arrived first, with Randall struggling to keep up. His body ached from Dumond's beating.

A loud cracking sound appeared overhead. Then another and another. The sound was unlike anything they had ever heard and repeated every several seconds. The three looked back toward the entrance to the ice tunnel. Spaced at even intervals within the icy cliff face, were approximately a dozen new openings matching the size and shape of the tunnel they had used to enter the alien base.

"This isn't good," Rob said.

Jamie nodded. "I get a feeling someone's not happy with the Red Dragons."

The three resumed their trip down the icy slope, this time running as hard as possible in anticipation of the encroaching battle. As they approached the lower quarter of the ramp, a single Red Dragon APC lurched forward from the ranks of the other vehicles, bearing down on them.

"So much for the Chinese not taking an interest in us," Rob observed.

They continued their run down to the base of the hill as the APC raced toward them. Randall searched the landscape, hoping to find a natural feature for cover when the battle began. He spied an orange fleck in the distance moving quickly across the white terrain. It was moving in a path that would take it directly to the base of the ramp and on a collision course with the APC. The dot grew larger and larger and began to take shape.

The base of the vehicle was a long, low, black stripe and Randall judged its speed to be 60 to 70 miles per hour. It grew larger as it approached, its form becoming clearer. The craft was long and wide, with a low hump in the back and another at its midsection. Randall finally realized that it was a hovercraft traveling much more quickly than the APC. Although it was farther away, it would easily beat the Chinese attack vehicle.

"I think we have our way out!" Randall yelled, pointing at the quickly approaching hovercraft.

The APC bore down on the base of the ramp, but additional movement began in the Chinese ranks as a tank pivoted and pointed its giant muzzle in the direction of the hovercraft. A tongue of orange and yellow fire spewed from the barrel as it lobbed a large projectile in the direction of the craft, which began zigzagging in anticipation of the attack.

A large plume of black snow and rocks churned up from the ground directly in front of the hovercraft, just as it jogged to the right. The blast struck harmlessly to its left, spraying the side with snow. The orange vehicle zipped forward, picking up speed, looking like an orange and black streak staining the pure white snow. The next shell fell just behind the charging craft, which was now cutting back to its left.

While the hovercraft danced around the tank rounds, another loud boom thundered from the sky. The ballistic missile had broken the sound barrier on its return arc toward the earth, announcing its impending arrival.

Randall, Rob, and Jamie chugged their way down the remainder of the ice ramp, as the Chinese APC closed on their position. The armored vehicle was no more than three hundred yards away. The hovercraft was slightly closer, but its forward progression had been greatly slowed as it was forced to dodge the artillery fire. It was going to be close.

A solitary figure popped its head from the main cabin of the craft holding something long. It took several minutes for the vehicle to cover enough distance for Randall to see it was a rifle. For their part, the Red Dragon soldiers seemed unfazed by the prospect of a single gunman firing on them. They ignored Randall's would-be rescuers and focused their shots on the three figures running down the slope.

A loud buzzing noise emanated from deep within the mountain, joining the chorus of chaos. The sound fed through the large tunnel openings, amplified as it bounced through the icy inner surface.

Fearing that all hell was about to break loose, Randall turned to Jamie and Rob. "Run for the hovercraft and don't stop!"

The three sprinted through the deep snow, struggling to make progress as their rescue vehicle closed within fifty yards. The slower APC was twice the distance but continued firing in Randall's direction. Bullets buzzed by his head like angry hornets seeking revenge on someone for disturbing their nest. Small bursts of snow sprang up where the large caliber gunfire impacted the earth.

The gunman in the hovercraft fired small bursts back at the APC, trying to distract the gunner from the three exposed figures running through the snow. As before, the Chinese gunner wasn't biting. A stream of shots pecked at the ground in a straight line directly behind Jaime, Rob and Randall as they zigzagged to avoid being hit.

The hovercraft finally skidded to a stop a mere twenty feet from Jamie, who reached the vehicle first. Rob was next, turning to look for Randall, who lagged badly, holding his midsection as he struggled forward. When he finally reached the vehicle, the door kicked open to reveal John in the driver's seat.

"Get in!"

With everyone inside, John wheeled the craft around one hundred and eighty degrees and pushed the throttles to their stops while the APC closed to twenty-five yards, unleashing a punishing volley of large caliber gunfire. The rear window of the hovercraft disintegrated under the barrage as bits of orange-painted fiberglass and metal splintered everywhere.

Not to be left out, the Red Dragon tank fired another volley, which struck perilously close to the right side of the craft, showering it with snow. John kept the vessel on a heading straight in the direction they had come.

"Where did you find this?" Randall asked.

"Dumond's base. After the Red Dragons captured you, Gabby and I combed through the wreckage and found this tucked under a white tent. At first we didn't see it because the tent blended in so well with the snow."

"Thank God you got here when you did!"

"Incoming!" Rob yelled.

John swerved the hovercraft just in time to avoid a round fired from the tank. It landed harmlessly to his left. Randall gazed out the broken rear window as the distance grew between them and the base.

"Nick, you've gotta see this!" Rob called out.

Randall climbed over the seat and made his way to Rob's side. The sight that befell his eyes was extraordinary. The rumbling sound from the tunnels in the ice cliff grew louder and louder. Just as it seemed the mountain would crumble, dozens of craft appeared from each tunnel, momentarily blotting out the gray skies. The craft were unlike anything they had ever seen, their angular features and reverse swept wings cutting a fearsome silhouette against the bright gray sky. The craft descended upon the Chinese force, unleashing a brutal assault on the Red Dragons.

The Chinese were slow to respond, the enemy catching them unprepared. Dark green attack choppers attempted to engage the attacking aircraft, but they were simply too slow. Pulses of light emanating from the craft annihilated the Chinese choppers, leaving burning metal hulls floating briefly in mid-air before smashing into the ground.

Like passing black ghosts, the sleek craft swooped in and out of the main battlefield, stinging the Chinese forces and herding them back toward the alien base. The Dragons struggled to defend themselves, unable to get radar lock on the advanced craft, which operated with impunity. As quickly as they had arrived, the stealthy craft banked hard, flying over the ice shelf, leaving the Red Dragons to lick their wounds.

The reprieve was short-lived. The Chinese missile carrying the electromagnetic pulse weapon streaked back toward the earth. The ballistic device whistled through the air, detonating above the Red Dragons' force, which had been forced back toward the base by the marauding aircraft. The electromagnetic pulse sent a shockwave through the air that disabled all the Chinese vehicles.

The ensuing scene resembled ants escaping from an ant hill. Dozens of soldiers scrambled from their vehicles, trying to determine what they should do next. Some attempted to repair their damaged craft. Others rushed to take defensive positions around their vehicles, seeking shelter from another anticipated attack. A final group simply dropped their weapons and ran in sheer terror.

The rumbling sound from above the ice cliff grew louder again. The black craft reappeared, heading back toward the defenseless Dragons. However bad the first attack had been, this one was far worse. From a distance, the battle played out like a slow-motion scene from a war movie as the advanced craft descended on the incapacitated Chinese force. Some of the soldiers tried in vain to fend off the attackers with nothing more than small arms fire. They fared poorly. The battle was decidedly one-sided.

The single Chinese APC that had broken ranks and attacked the hovercraft tried making a mad dash from the base to the safety of the icy fringes. It was unsuccessful as well. A single craft left the main battle and tracked the vehicle down. Like a hawk circling its prey, the black vessel closed on the carrier, swooping in for an attack. It was over quickly as a single strike instantly reduced the APC and its inhabitants to smoldering wreckage.

John had opened a large gap between the battle and the hovercraft. Randall judged they were more than a mile away, the terrifying scene fading into the distance. The stealth craft, having finished off the Red Dragons, were returning to the ice tunnels from where they had come. All except for the one that had destroyed the APC.

To Randall's horror, it took a path directly after them.

"John, step on it. Looks like we have company," Randall said, gripping his son's shoulder.

"It's already at full throttle," John replied.

"How much further to Dumond's base?"

"About ten to fifteen minutes."

Randall scrambled over to Gabby. "What weapons do we have?"

"Small arms. We picked up a couple of hand guns and assault rifles, that's all we could find. Why?"

Randall pointed out the window to the attack craft. It was getting closer.

"I don't think we have anything that can damage that thing, never mind take it out completely."

"We'll just have to work with what we have. What's the effective range for these rifles?"

"Under these conditions, a couple hundred meters at best … if we're lucky."

"Okay, we'll have to hold our fire until that ship is within range. Rob, take the right, Gabby take the left."

"What about you?" Gabby asked.

"I'm going out there," Randall said, pointing to a small flat area on the back of the hovercraft.

"Be careful, it'd be easy to fall off, and at this speed you'll be nothing but a dark streak on the ice if you do!" Gabby warned.

The hovercraft sped forward over the flat snowy surface as John piloted the vehicle in a nearly straight line for Dumond's former camp. The fan motor protested loudly as John pushed the vehicle to its limits.

Despite their high speed, their pursuer easily closed the gap, aided by the fact that it didn't have to contend with terrestrial obstacles.

Randall climbed through the broken window and flopped down onto the rear of the speeding ship. He struggled to find his footing and was nearly knocked over the side as the vehicle sped over a rough patch of ice. Randall tumbled, grasping the side rail before nearly toppling over. He moaned as he struggled to regain his balance, his injured ribs burning like fire from the strain of staying upright. He finally made his way back to the small flat opening in the rear of the ship. Finding an old tarp used to protect cargo, he slipped beneath the plastic sheet.

Their pursuer closed within a couple hundred yards, prompting Gabby to fire her gun in short bursts. Seeing her do so, Rob followed suit. Gabby's training paid off as she landed several rounds on the slowing aircraft, which momentarily broke pursuit, shaken by the hits to its exterior.

The victory was short-lived as the vessel resumed its pursuit. Rob and Gabby continued to fire on the ship, but despite landing hits, the pilot was unfazed by the small arms fire.

"This isn't working!" Gabby yelled.

"We have to keep trying!" Rob replied.

The hovercraft cleared a small rise and Dumond's former base came into view. They were within several hundred yards of the camp when the otherworldly vessel moved in for the kill. It weaved back and forth, avoiding Gabby and Rob's shots, closing in on the hovercraft. Her assault rifle spent, Gabby tossed it aside and resumed firing with a handgun. Several rounds pinged harmlessly off the aircraft. Rob did the same, and soon they were both out of ammunition.

No longer receiving cover fire, the craft simply followed them in a straight line, continuing to draw closer. A section of each wing began to rotate outward from the main body as the craft slowed. A loud whining noise arose from its bottom as a single pulse of light emanated from its belly.

The electronic gauges in the hovercraft spiked momentarily and then went out. The fan motor fell silent and the craft skidded to a halt.

The vessel slowed and began circling the hovercraft. It finally stopped in mid-air floating directly behind the stalled vehicle as a soft humming noise emerged again from its belly. A single panel opened on the craft, revealing a long circular weapon.

Randall popped up from his hiding place and fired on the vessel, striking its nose repeatedly. He unloaded his weapon into the craft, which began to dart wildly, the pilot shaken by the surprise attack at such close range.

His weapon empty, Randall watched as the vessel nearly crashed to the earth. It came within a few feet of the snowy terrain but recovered and slowly ascended back into the sky and resumed its position directly behind the stalled hovercraft.

"What do we do now?" John asked.

"I think we're out of options," Gabby replied.

They steadied themselves for the final attack, having fought valiantly but ultimately coming up short.

The craft aimed its weapon at them as a loud thudding sound came from its rear flank. It exploded in mid-air, sending sparks and flames darting into the gray sky. The craft fell to the earth in a great fireball that illuminated the darkening afternoon.

Dumbfounded, Randall watched as it tumbled to the ground and lay in a smoldering heap. It was then that he saw the reason: a large, black helicopter hovered in the sky directly behind where the alien craft had been only moments earlier, smoke rising from its rocket pod.

The chopper hung in the air like a menacing bird of prey ready to pounce on its victim, and Randall feared the worst. But instead of attacking, it hovered to the side and landed softly on the snow beside the stricken hovercraft. A solitary figure exited the helicopter, making his way to Randall.

He was huge, and his black thermal suit only added to his bulk. As he drew closer, he removed his face mask and goggles, revealing a familiar visage, one Randall hadn't seen since his encounter with the shooters in the alley in D.C.

"Michael! It looks like I owe you again," Randall said, scrambling from the hovercraft and walking over to his rescuer.

Instead of extending his hand, Michael Thompson drew a gun from his jacket.

"Sorry, Randall, but I'll be taking Ms. Edmunds from you."

"What? Why?" Randall asked.

"Orders. Ms. Edmunds's blood contains all sorts of goodies that my employers want, and they need to extract them as soon as possible. The more time we waste the more the chemicals will dissipate. We believe we only have a few hours to extract the mind control compound."

Having seen the exchange, the others had exited the hovercraft and stood watching from the distance. John, Rob, and Gabby formed a human shield around Jamie, their body language implying that they wouldn't relinquish her without a fight.

"You can't have her," Randall replied.

"I don't think you have much of a choice. Even if I wanted to, the blokes back there wouldn't let me come back empty-handed. Sorry, Randall, but we need the young lady."

"What if I give you something better?"

"Such as?"

Randall produced the small vial of clear fluid he had taken from the base.

"This is the substance that was pumped into Jamie to keep her drugged while she was held captive. I'm sure your employers would be happy with this," he said, passing the vial to Michael.

Michael studied the container and then looked at Randall.

"You wouldn't be trying to pull a fast one on your old friend, would you?" Michael cocked his head to the side and smiled.

"No, I'm not, and I think that's more than fair. The mind-control substance in pure form for Jamie's life," Randall said. He could see the wheels in Michael's head turning as he mulled the offer.

"It's a deal. But remember, if it's not what you say it is, I know where you live," Michael said, his smile broadening as he tucked the vial into his coat.

Randall sighed in relief.

"You know, under different circumstances, we would have been mates," Michael said, lowering his weapon.

Randall nodded, turning to walk away.

"You're a good man, Randall, just like she said you were."

Randall stopped in his tracks and turned to the side, not facing Michael. "Who said I was a good man?"

"Someone who knows you better than anyone else. In fact, probably knows you better than you know yourself."

Randall's blood ran cold and he spun to face Michael. "Who are you talking about?"

"I think you know."

"Ann? Is she still alive? Randall took a step toward Michael.

Michael simply smiled. "Remember, things aren't always as they appear." He turned and walked back to the waiting chopper.

"I don't understand! What happens next?" Randall called out to Michael, who stopped before climbing into the open door.

"I'm sure we'll see each other again."

The door closed, and the black helicopter lifted, banked, and slowly disappeared, leaving Randall to consider the puzzle that had just been presented to him.

Chapter Fifty-Two

Randall stood motionless, his breath forming a cloudy vapor each time he exhaled. He stared at the earth, eyes blinking as he tried to decipher the riddle he had just received.

John walked up to his father, unaware of the exchange. "You traded the substance from the base for Jamie's life, didn't you?"

Randall didn't respond.

"We better get going, Dad, we have a little over an hour before the missile hits and we need to put some distance between us and the detonation."

Randall remained in a catatonic state.

"Dad, we have to go!" John shook his father's shoulder.

Randall blinked his eyes. "Do you think we can get the hovercraft working again?"

"I doubt it, but I'll try," John said, walking over to the stricken vehicle. He hit the ignition switch but failed to get the motor running.

"Great, what do we do now?" Rob asked.

303

John smiled. "Well, it looks like we're walking ... to the helicopter."

"What helicopter? I don't think Michael is coming back," Randall replied.

"When we scouted Dumond's camp, we didn't just find a hovercraft," John quipped.

Randall smiled, placing a hand on John's shoulder. "Judging by the circumstances, I guess he wouldn't mind if we borrowed it."

The group jogged the remaining distance back to the camp, following John and Gabby who led them to a large white tent, which blended into the snowy backdrop. John drew back one side of the cover, revealing the helicopter.

"Well, I'll be," Rob commented. "Can you fly this thing?"

John nodded. "I was about to take my final flight test before we left." Having removed the remaining sides and top of the tent, John conducted a pre-flight check and loaded everyone into the chopper. He tried starting the engine. It wouldn't catch.

"Is there a problem?" Jamie asked.

"I'm not sure," John replied, walking through the startup process again. He tried to start the engine two additional times but was still unsuccessful.

"Probably a frozen fuel line. Even with these jet engines, water gets into the line and forms ice crystals that cause the fuel to gel," Rob said.

They exited the chopper and John checked the fuel. Rob was right, it had gelled.

"This isn't good. If I kill the battery trying to start it, we're stuck. Any ideas?" John asked.

"Can you unfreeze the line?" Gabby asked.

"We would need a heat source to do that, like a space heater. We'd also need an enclosed space to trap the heat. Unfortunately, we don't have either." John replied.

"With all the gear Dumond brought here, he must have had spare parts to make repairs. Maybe we can find something that can help us fix the hovercraft," Rob answered.

"I guess it's worth a try. Let's see if we can find anything."

The team split up and slogged through the camp, searching for anything that might help. A short time later, they reconvened.

"Any luck?" Randall asked.

"Nope. If there was a motor pool, the Dragons thoroughly wiped it out. Unless there's a parts store and a good mechanic around here, we're not going to get that hovercraft running again. Did you guys find anything else that would help?" Rob replied.

John shook his head. "We rechecked the area thoroughly and the only operational items we could find were this helicopter and the orange flash over there. That leaves us with one option. We need to build a fire to unfreeze the line, and we need to do it now. We're running out of time."

Gabby frowned. "Do you really think starting a fire around jet fuel is a good idea?"

"I know what you mean, but I don't think we have a choice," John replied.

Gabby nodded. "I guess you're right, but how do we start it and trap the heat?"

"What I wouldn't give for my old Webber grill right now," Rob said, scratching his head.

John snapped his fingers. "I have an idea. We need to get the tent set up again. Gabby, Rob, and Jamie, get the sides and top put up to make a windscreen. Dad, you and I need to find something to start a fire. Someone out there must have matches or a lighter."

Gabby and her crew struggled against the wind to assemble the tent, but twenty minutes later, they had created an enclosed space to trap heat. All they needed now was a fire.

Randall and John returned carrying paper scavenged from the various vehicles, along with bits of wood from smashed crates. They used the scraps to create the base for the fire. John produced a lighter retrieved from the body of one of Dumond's men.

"Thank God he was a smoker," Rob joked.

Using the lighter, John lit the fire. The cover produced the desired effect, shielding the would-be fire from the wind. He checked his watch.

"We have thirty-eight minutes until the missile hits ... if the captain's timeframe was accurate," John said.

No one responded. Their silence implied an understanding that the cruise missile could strike at any moment and they were too close to survive the blast. They could only wait now and hope that the captain's estimate wasn't overly generous.

The minutes dragged by. Each noise from outside the tent resulted in panicked stares as everyone's imagination ran wild. The sound of the slightest breeze was interpreted as the arrival of their impending destruction.

John checked his watch again, then touched the fuel tank. The warmth was noticeable. Under normal circumstances, lighting a fire near a fuel tank would be madness. Today, it was the lesser of two evils.

"Do you think we should try now?" Gabby asked, looking at her watch.

"A couple more minutes," John replied, feigning indifference. Inside he was screaming, each heartbeat amplified. Finally, with eighteen minutes remaining, John decided it was time to try. He extinguished the fire.

"Once I get the motor started, I'll need you all to pull the tent away quickly, so it doesn't get wrapped up in the rotors."

The group nodded in unison, each person getting into position. The top of the tent coming off first.

John climbed into the helicopter, flipped the requisite switches, and said a quiet prayer. He hit the ignition. The motor coughed but didn't catch. He tried again with the same results. He looked through the windshield at the faces watching him; a mixture of anticipation and fear stared back at him.

John took a deep breath. He looked down at his watch. Fifteen minutes until impact.

He hit the ignition switch again. The starter whined but didn't catch.

John jumped down from the cockpit and slammed the door. He lifted the panel covering the fuel line and followed the line to the fuel control valve.

"I need something heavy!"

Gabby handed him her service revolver.

John tapped the control valve repeatedly. Next, he followed the fuel line to the fuel filter and tapped it as well. "Get ready!" he shouted, climbing back into the chopper.

John hit the ignition and the engine roared to life.

"Get the rest of the tent down!" he screamed over the din.

The crew tore down the structure, then climbed aboard the craft.

John checked his watch. Eleven minutes. He jammed the throttles to full and lifted the Bell helicopter off the snow. He banked it hard, following the same flight path that Michael had taken earlier. He climbed slowly, more concerned with putting distance between them and the base than gaining altitude.

It was now a race against time. Randall glanced back at the camp as it fell away into the distance. He checked his watch. Eight minutes to impact. He looked around at the others in the chopper. There was complete silence, everyone staring vacantly into space.

Randall walked to John's side and knelt by him.

"Do you think we'll clear the blast zone?" he asked quietly.

"I'm not sure."

"Regardless of what happens, I want you to know I'm proud of you," Randall said, squeezing John's shoulder. He walked back to his seat and sat down next to Jamie.

"How much longer until the missile hits?" Jamie asked.

Randall checked his watch. "Five minutes if Sergeant Howard's estimate was right, but it could be any time."

"I want you to know how much I appreciate what you've all done for me. I felt completely alone until I met all of you," Jamie said.

Dumond's camp was nothing more than a dirty speck on an otherwise pristine blanket of snow and ice as the helicopter surged forward. Jamie reached for Randall's hand and gripped it, squeezing hard. Randall reached out and hugged her for assurance.

Three additional minutes dragged by. Still no detonation. Under ideal conditions, the helicopter's top speed was 120 knots. These weren't ideal conditions. Unsure of the size of the nuclear warhead, Randall had no way of knowing if they would survive the intense heat waves that would follow the detonation.

One minute remained. Randall watched the second hand sweep across the dial of his watch as Jamie tightened her grip on his hand. His heart raced.

"Ten seconds."

A quiet countdown began in everyone's mind. The time for detonation came but no explosion occurred.

Everyone turned to look at each other.

"What happened?" Rob asked.

"It was only an estimate. I don't think we're out of the woods yet," Randall replied.

An additional minute and a half passed. A brilliant flash of light streaked across the sky followed by a thunderous noise from the direction of the base. An enormous cloud erupted above the horizon, its tail trailing down to the surface of the white earth. The helicopter shook as the concussive sound wave passed through the air, rattling the windows and tossing the helicopter about.

For a moment, it seemed that the chopper would be shaken apart by the rumbling, but John deftly managed the controls and eased the craft back into a normal cruise pattern. Flying safely again, the danger having passed, Randall unbuckled his safety restraint and walked to the back of the helicopter. He stared out the rear window and one thought crossed his mind:

Francis Dumond will never threaten my family again.

Chapter Fifty-Three

August 26, 4:51 P.M.
McMurdo Station, Ross Island, Antarctica

John brought the helicopter down for a soft landing just outside McMurdo. Having radioed ahead for permission to land, the group wasn't surprised to find a cadre of soldiers dressed in military fatigues along with several armored vehicles waiting for them at the landing pad.

"Looks like we have company," John said.

Randall exited the helicopter first, followed by the others. As he did so, a young sergeant walked over to speak with him.

"Dr. Randall, the general sent me to bring you back to Dulce. Please grab your equipment and come with us. We have a plane waiting for all of you on the runway," the sergeant said, gesturing to the C-130 transport plane already stationed on the tarmac, its engines running.

"We don't have any equipment, just people," Randall replied wearily. "Before we take off, we'd like to use the restroom and get something to eat."

"We have restrooms and food on the plane. General Flores was very specific. He wants you all back at the base ASAP."

The sergeant held out his arm directing them to the plane. Tired, Randall and the group complied.

The trip from McMurdo to New Mexico was uneventful, if not exceedingly long. Exhausted, most of the group slept for a good portion of the ride on cots provided by the military. Randall, although exhausted, found it exceptionally difficult to sleep. Michael's comments haunted him as he tried to decipher the cryptic message repeatedly in his fitful dreams.

As the plane touched down, Randall saw that they had a military escort waiting for them once again. The troops whisked them away as they debarked from the transport in the blazing mid-day sun. A short time later, they arrived at the base. Rob and Gabby grabbed a bite to eat while Randall and John found themselves in General Flores's office waiting for him to arrive.

"Dr. Randall, good to see you all again. When Captain Valverde radioed about the Chinese attack, I was concerned you might not make it," Flores said, extending his hand to Randall.

"Why, because the Red Dragons had taken us captive or because you launched a nuclear missile at us?" Randall replied, ignoring the general's gesture.

Flores lowered his hand.

"You have to understand the gravity of this situation. I needed to ensure that the Red Dragons didn't achieve their goal … even if that meant losing a few good people. The safety of many outweighs the survival of a few," Flores said, walking over to his desk.

"A convenient response when the 'few good people' aren't your own. Where's my daughter?"

"She went home once we found out you'd survived."

"And Jacob, my son's research partner. What have you done with him?"

"Dr. Taylor has been returned home as well. We offered him a considerable payment as gratitude for his work."

"You mean you paid him off to keep him quiet."

"Were you able to retrieve the mind-control substance?"

"Yes."

"That's wonderful," Flores said, genuinely surprised. "Do you have it with you?"

"No. I gave it to someone else."

Flores blinked at the response, turning to John, then back to Randall. His mouth hung open, a series of unintelligible sounds all he could manage. "What do you mean? Do you realize what you've done? You've placed the entire free world in danger with your irresponsible act!" Flores came out of his seat, his palms pressed against the desk as he glared at Randall.

"Do you know a man named Michael Thompson?" Randall asked.

Flores flinched at the name, but quickly recovered. "I have no idea who that is. Why?"

"He said that the people he worked for wanted Jamie, so they could take her blood to withdraw the mind-control compound. He didn't say exactly how much blood they would need to take, but I suspect they were going to have to kill her to get it and I wasn't about to let that happen. I traded the vial for Jamie's life and I would do it again in a heartbeat."

Flores face contorted into a frown. He dropped into his chair. His gaze no longer on Randall, he stared blankly at the wall.

"I get the feeling there's much more going on here than you've let on. Is there something you'd like to tell me?" Randall asked.

Flores rubbed his palms into his eyes, sighing deeply. He didn't look up at Randall. "I don't know what you're talking about and I certainly don't know this Thompson character. All I know is that you've put me in a very difficult situation."

"We're finished here." Randall stood.

"One of my men will take you where you want to go."

"Take us to the airport."

Chapter Fifty-Four

August 27, 10:08 A.M.
Hamilton, Bermuda

Randall sat in the passenger seat of the rented Jeep Grand Cherokee as John conversed with Jamie at her front door. He had already said goodbye to Gabby, who'd returned to Nassau on a flight earlier that day. Rob had also returned to his facility, leaving only Jamie, John, and Randall to say their farewells.

It was a great relief to know that Jamie's troubles were finally over, and Randall was grateful he had played a part in helping her through her difficult times. Now she could focus on the things common to most young adults: her job and potential relationships. The latter of which might involve John.

Randall watched as the two sat on the front steps of Jamie's apartment building talking. His son was in rare form, talking a mile a minute while Jamie smiled profusely, covering her mouth at certain points in the conversation to hide a giggle. At times her eyes went wide as John shared information she must have found exceptionally amazing. The two had clearly formed a connection and Randall sensed he could be seeing more of Jamie in the future. As a father, he was happy for his son, who had been so wrapped-up in his research that he really hadn't pursued a relationship for quite some time. Maybe things were changing.

John and Jamie finally stood and exchanged a long hug, followed by a kiss. Randall watched his son walk down the stairs, looking back at Jamie as he did, almost tripping and falling in the process. This elicited yet another laugh from her as she smiled and shook her head. John recovered and flashed a sheepish grin at Jamie who waved back, a warm smile on her face. She watched him all the way back to the car and waited for him to get in.

"It looks like the two of you hit it off."

"I really like her, Dad, she's so down to earth, and funny, too," John said, putting on his seat belt.

"I see what you mean, son. She reminds me of your mother."

John pulled the rental car away from the curb, turning one last time to wave to Jamie. She waved back, smiling until the car turned from her street, leaving father and son alone for the first time in days. The two sat quietly in the car as they made their way to the airport to catch a flight home.

"What are you going to do when you get back home?" Randall asked.

"I hadn't really thought about it. I guess the first thing I'm going to do is see how Jacob is doing. After that, I'm not sure. Maybe I'll apply for a teaching position. After all, it seems to be the family vocation."

Randall smiled.

"How about you, Dad?"

"I have classes starting soon and need to get things ready for the fall term, but first I'm going to take a long nap." He sighed, rubbing his eyes, the fatigue finally catching up with him. His body sank into the car seat.

The two men sat in silence for several minutes.

"You know, I wouldn't want to repeat what we just went through, but I'm glad we did it together. I understand what you and Sam went through and, to be honest, I feel like I'm more a part of your life now," John said, staring at the road ahead.

"Me too, son. You and your sister are the two most important people in my life and I'd never trade a moment spent with either of you for all of the money or accolades in the world."

Now it was John's turn to smile.

Sitting in the car, warmed by the glowing tropical sun, Randall realized, for the first time in many years, that he felt content.

The late afternoon sun was drooping low on the horizon, casting a long streak on the aquamarine sea as a trade wind lazily plied its way through the palm trees. The scene was as different from the harsh beauty of Antarctica as night is to day.

Randall and John dropped off their rental car and caught the shuttle to the airport. The terminal was busy with travelers arriving to start their adventure and others catching flights back to wherever they called home. For his part, Nick Randall was happy knowing that John was safe and that this chapter of their life was closed. He had had his fill of adventure and looked forward to returning to the quiet life of academia.

About the Author

Robert Rapoza is the award-winning author of THE RUINS, a 2015 Clive Cussler Adventure Writers Competition Semi-Finalist, and THE BERMUDA CONNECTION, a 2017 Pinnacle Award winner. His action-packed thrillers have been described as a cross between Dan Brown and Indiana Jones, keeping readers riveted from beginning to end. Tommy Howell from Readers Favorite calls protagonist Nick Randall "A statesman and action hero worthy of Pierce Brosnan or Liam Neeson." A member of the Southern California Writers Association he was selected to the 2015-16 International Thriller Writers Association Debut Authors program and was among several new authors featured at the Debut Author session at ThrillerFest in New York City.

Learn more about his books at www.robertrapoza.com.

9 781732 391246

Printed by Libri Plureos GmbH in Hamburg,
Germany